"Who are you?"

Zach heard her question, but raised his hammer and bent one of the nails anchoring the rope closer to the beam.

Addy was a reporter.

Anything he said could end up on the internet, in print and on television.

He looked into her face. The angle of her head, the lines of her mouth, even the slant of her eyebrows said she was asking because she wanted to know, not that she wanted to broadcast the information to the world.

No one had ever asked him that question, not his classmates, his coworkers, the women he dated. No one wanted the answer to that question.

She stepped in close, too close to ignore her.

The wind flapped the tarp and the rain smashed into it like the sound of distant gunfire.

He leaned in toward her and her lips parted as if she were about to ask a question, but she did not. He pressed his lips to hers and captured her gasp.

Dear Reader,

Readers, thank you so much! I hope you like Addy and Zach's story.

Practically the only people who will talk to reporter Adriana Bonacorda are her blood relatives. Everyone else thinks she's a liar, a con artist or both. Disgraced, broke and on the scent of a big story, Addy races from Boston to Maine—in a hurricane. Her quarry? Big-time swindler Zachary Hale. Exposing the deepest secrets of this billionaire schemer will put her right back on top of the journalist heap. But when she ends up at his mercy, she finds there is so much more to this man...and she finds her heart and her livelihood are in so much jeopardy.

And wait! Will they find *All That Glitters*—inside a pirate's treasure chest?

I'd love to hear from you. Visit my website at www.marybrady.net or write to me at mary@marybrady.net.

Enjoy the Harlequin Superromance authors' blog at www.superauthors.com.

Warmest regards and bright blessings to all,

Mary Brady

MARY BRADY

—

All That Glitters

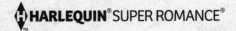
HARLEQUIN® SUPER ROMANCE®

Recycling programs
for this product may
not exist in your area.

ISBN-13: 978-0-373-60884-3

All That Glitters

Printed in U.S.A.

ABOUT THE AUTHOR

Mary Brady lives in the Midwest and considers road trips into the rest of the continent to be a necessary part of life. When she's not out exploring, she helps run a manufacturing company and has a great time living with her handsome husband, her super son and one cheeky little bird.

Books by Mary Brady

HARLEQUIN SUPERROMANCE

1561—HE CALLS HER DOC
1691—PROMISE TO A BOY
1730—WINNING OVER THE RANCHER
1888—BETTER THAN GOLD*
1924—SILVER LININGS*

*The Legend of Bailey's Cove

Other titles by this author available in ebook format.

Don't miss any of our special offers. Write to us at the following address for information on our newest releases.

Harlequin Reader Service
U.S.: 3010 Walden Ave., P.O. Box 1325, Buffalo, NY 14269
Canadian: P.O. Box 609, Fort Erie, Ont. L2A 5X3

A large *thank-you* to my clever and intellectual friends Pamela Ford, Victoria Hinshaw, Olivia Rae, Laura Scott and Donna Smith.

CHAPTER ONE

ADRIANA BONACORDA gripped the steering wheel of her rental car until her aching knuckles blanched white. Rain made it nearly impossible to see more than a few car lengths in front of her and the wind rocked the tiny compact. Addy prayed she could stave off the dark threats coming at her from all angles long enough to get to Bailey's Cove, Maine, in one piece.

"Stay away from the coast, folks" had been the last bit of coherence she had gotten from the car's radio. All she heard now was squawks and dead air.

Her phone still worked because it started ringing the raucous tones she'd assigned to her younger sister, Savanna.

"Hello, Savanna, sorry, warning, the signal may break up."

"Where are you?"

"I'm in Maine after Zachary Hale." Addy peered through the wind-driven rain searching for her turnoff.

"That's what I called about. Hey, what's he doing in Maine?"

"He's headed to ground and I hope to get to him before he's in hiding."

"Why isn't he in jail?"

Addy harrumphed. "It doesn't work that way in the world of high finance."

"I end up with nothing and some fat cats get rich. And he gets off without any punishment?" Savanna almost squealed the last few words in indignation.

"Calm down. During the huge Ponzi scandal, it was early December when the FBI got involved and early March, fifteen months later, before any jail time began to be served, and that scandal involved over fifty billion dollars."

"Not fair. Just not fair."

"Savanna you must have called for something besides a rant about Hale and Blankenstock."

"I guess you just answered my question. I wanted to know how you were doing at getting Hale to fess up." Savanna sounded sad. Her life was a wreck and she was newly unemployed.

"And you need more money."

"I do. I hate to ask but can you lend me another hundred? I want to—"

A sign, big and green, loomed off to the side

of the road heralding her exit and then vanished into the downpour.

She could barely see the road she was driving on and her sister was a distraction on a good day. "Savanna, I gotta go. I'll have some funds transferred as soon as I can."

As soon as I see if I have enough, she thought.

"I need to take the girls shopping. They didn't get any new clothes for school and now they're on sale cheap and they really need them."

"I get it. Yes, I'll do it when I can. Bye."

Addy thumbed off the phone and tossed it onto the seat beside her. She squeezed her already hunched shoulders tighter and concentrated hard on seeing through the rain.

The exit ramp popped into view and she braked hard, rocked in the wind and dove off the nearly deserted interstate onto a narrow two-lane road. She had known this drive wasn't going to be easy in the remnants of a hurricane, but some things had to be done.

Moving closer to the coast, deeper into the fringes of a storm whipping up the Atlantic Ocean, made for bad driving, but maybe not a bad day. There was a pot of gold at the end of this rainstorm, maybe even a Pulitzer Prize.

At the very least she'd get a stab at retrieving her pride.

A sudden blast of wind sliced down hard across the road trying to take her small car with it. Addy answered with a fierce jerk of the wheel.

"Please, let me get there." The sound of her voice eerily muted in the din coming from the outside. "That guy needs to pay."

As she moved slowly down the road, the windshield wipers beat wildly at the sheets of rain, giving her occasional glimpses of the wreck and ruin going on outside. A branch skittered across the road and a river ran where the shoulder of the road should have been.

This storm, a has-been hurricane, was to brush the coast as it headed north toward the good folk of Nova Scotia.

Well, it was "brushing" hard, Addy thought.

There had been a point when the weather forecasters wondered if Hurricane Harold would break records and head directly for the central coast of Maine. Luckily for the citizens of the rugged state, that was not going to happen.

Braving the storm, Addy felt a touch of the old Adriana Bonacorda. She had been tough and smart. She had needed to be in order to survive. Not every reporter would be daring enough to chase a story into the middle of Afghanistan, a rebel monk to his hideout in Nepal or a billionaire criminal into the fringes of a storm.

She jerked hard again on the wheel to avoid hitting a piece of siding or a door or whatever it was and then hissed out a breath as she brought the car back into her lane.

In addition to the radio warnings, a State Trooper had sternly advised her to stay away from the coast. She had the distinct feeling they would have arrested her for reckless something or other if she'd tried to drive in this weather in Massachusetts, but not here in Maine.

Desperation could make one nuts.

After her big disgrace, she had tried to get worthy stories under more sane circumstances. Instead of a scoop or a better angle, she had gotten scorn, and worse, derisive snickers from the other reporters at every news scene. When she had tried to defend herself online, the whole world was then alerted that she had put her heart and soul into one giant piece of fiction she had unwittingly called news.

She had been duped, an apt word for eager and stupid. Today she battled to recover *eager,* but *stupid* she'd left buried in the humiliation.

When the sign marking the turn off toward Bailey's Cove flashed at her through a break in the rain she popped the wheel with the palm of her hand. "Yes." She was going to make it. Maybe there were still lucky cards in her pile.

Just then a piece of debris plastered itself to her windshield and, for a terrifying moment of blindness, stuck to the wipers and refused to move away. When it finally flew off, she hunkered down with passion, renewed by luck, and after fifteen more minutes of concentration reached the town.

Bailey's Cove, Maine, population fourteen-something-thousand, the wildly undulating sign read as she slowed the car to a crawl.

The low-slung buildings of small-town urban sprawl blinked in and out of view as she crept into the small fishing village in the late afternoon storm-filtered light. Some of the buildings had boarded-up windows. A few had sandbags. There were no lights anywhere.

A service station called O'Reilly's had its large glass windows boarded up, but huge letters scrawled on the boards, OPEN and CALL. She supposed there was a phone number somewhere to be found, but she couldn't see it for the rain.

These people had been preparing for a direct hit by the hurricane called Harold. Even though the storm was passing them by, they had not known until two days ago they were to be spared the brunt of it.

Addy peered out at the sealed-up buildings, wondering which ones had people inside. There had to be someone here who would refuse to leave and who could tell her where Zachary Hale would hide out. Nothing on the internet had narrowed it down to anything less than "somewhere near Bailey's Cove, Maine." In fact, Bailey's Cove got no direct hits on the internet.

With this storm raging, Hale would think he was safe, sheltered from prying eyes.

Ha!

When a puddle nearly swallowed the compact car, Addy pulled onto the higher ground straddling the lanes. She stretched her beleaguered fingers and retrieved her mobile phone that had flown off the seat during one of her dodges.

She had a signal, but with the exception of her sister who needed money for school clothes, or makeup for herself if she found nothing she wanted to buy for the girls, she had no one to call.

Sad.

Silly.

Stupid.

Shut up, she thought. None of those things

mattered. They were the past. Intrepid. Hard-hitting. Totally inquisitive, she said back to the nagging voice inside her head.

After today, Adriana Bonacorda would be headed for the top again. And the frosting…her sister and all the others Hale had robbed would get a chance at recovering some of their losses.

The road continued to descend into town. Buildings appeared and disappeared through the windswept downpour. On the ocean side of the road, she spotted a small wooden church. Soaked and dark, the siding seemed to shudder, but that might have just been the strobe effects of the rain.

After a moment, Addy realized a woman stood in the arched doorway of the church. Her mop of hair swung wildly as she waved. A crazy woman, a comrade, a sister against the storm.

Addy checked for traffic. Nothing but rain. She intended to make a U-turn to question the woman, but when she looked across the street again, the doorway was empty.

Okay. Now she was imagining people. Maybe she was seeing herself in forty years. They both might be crazy and the woman had the same out-of-control mop, but the woman's had been gray.

Keep driving, she told herself, and she did. She had little alternative.

Scuffling with the wind, she eventually reached what seemed, by the age of the buildings, to be the center of the old town. More boarded-up and shuttered windows greeted her, their darkness almost a grimace.

At the corner, in front of a restaurant called Pirate's Roost, a sign pointed to the harbor. A sliver of hope gleamed. Maybe that's where the people were, trying to save their boats or piers or whatever seamen did in a storm.

As she crept several blocks down toward the harbor on what had become a torrent instead of a street, Addy could see she was right. Luck again or savvy? She hoped the latter. Two crews in rain slickers wrestled with boats as one crew tried to secure a boat they had already rescued from the water, the other struggled to pull one out onto the dock. Each small craft dithered dangerously in the wind as they worked.

All one of these people had to do was point her in the right direction and then she'd leave them to their task.

She let the car roll slowly toward the pier.

Once she found him in his hideaway, she'd get a reaction from the scum, swindler Zachary Hale, and if her luck still held, an interview.

The whole interaction would likely be a series of bald-faced lies on his part, but it would give her starting points from which to tear this guy to the ground, kick him into the hole he'd dug with the pension funds and life savings of old ladies, blue-collar workers—and her widowed sister. Then Addy would cover him with the truth until he begged to return every dime he had left of his ill-gotten booty.

The trickle down from this story was the gravy. People were going to recoup some of their hard earned money. Retirees, pensioners, kids trying to pay off college loans might actually get a break. Nuns. And Savanna, her sister, who had thought she was on her way to a secure future.

This story would turn the tide for Addy and all the cheated.

Darn, but she was good, and people were going to realize the lies about her for what they were.

As if tired of her fanciful boasting, the bitsy car rolled to a stop on its own as it faced off against the wind.

The closest four-man crew of yellow rain-suited workers had managed to raise the pleasure craft from the ferocious water and pull it onto a boat rack with ropes. But they struggled to rescue it from the wild wind and secure it on the stand.

Addy left her fashionable fedora on the passenger seat, flipped up the hood of her lime-green Ilse Jacobsen rain jacket and snugged the zipper up under her chin. The car undulated in a scary shimmy as she leaped out and hurried toward a man holding a rope for all he was worth.

Halfway there, the wind whipped off the hood of her jacket, slapped her long, hyper-curly blond hair against her cheek and stole away her breath. Her steps faltered and she stopped.

Wet and chilled, she hauled her hood back on, but not before cold rain poured down the back of her neck and, as she leaned into the wind and managed to take another step—into her shoes.

These people were crazier than she was to be out here. These were just boats, pleasure boats, and not someone's livelihood. And since the remains of Hurricane Harold were passing right by this little-known corner of the world, their efforts were probably unnecessary.

Forcing one foot and then the other, she struggled closer to the workers.

Several boats had already been hauled out and sat tethered in place with taught ropes. Still out in the harbor, hardy lobster boats strained and rocked at anchor, and one particularly large yacht looked as if it were ready to break free and crash everything into flotsam on its way inland. Some poor rich guy was about to be short one boat.

Zachary Hale, she hoped.

As she got within a few feet of the boat, the closest man clinging to the rope hollered above the rushing wind, "Lady, get out of here."

"I need to ask you a question," she shouted, and wasn't sure her voice even got past the end of her nose until he wrapped the rope around one arm and pointed at the flapping overhead. Two identical red flags with black centers curled and snapped above them.

Hurricane! Even a landlubber like her knew the meaning of those flags. Marine warning flags for a hurricane.

Harold had beaten the odds and headed inland. The wind hammered at her as she stood immobile, wavering between the insanity of the storm and the lunacy her life had turned into.

She suddenly saw herself once again standing on a stage facing a jeering crowd at the university. When the booing started, she had thought it was a joke, and then as it continued, she expected rotten eggs, but it had been a more intellectual crowd, and all she got were death threats and promises of a lifelong ban from journalism.

The wind took another shot at her and she tensed her whole body. When she didn't leave, the man waved her away with a jerk of his head, but it was another shout from him to "go away" that revved up her reporter mode.

She swiped at the rain running down her face and, when he turned in her direction, stepped forward.

"I just need to find Zachary Hale." She screamed into the wind and it screamed right back at her.

"'Et…. 'Ell. 'Way." The rising wind carried much of his shout off, but she got the gist.

She inched closer to him. "Tell me where to find Zachary Hale."

Just then the wind ripped at the boat and one man on the other side lost his grip. With horror, Addy realized the craft, lifted by the wind, now tipped. Then, in slow motion, the boat began to fall in her direction.

She stumbled back, but not quickly enough. The man grabbed her by the shoulder of her jacket and hauled her aside like a net full of cod as the boat crashed into the spot where she had stood a second before.

The white-and-red boat rocked and settled half on one side.

When the wind couldn't blow her over, she realized the man had not released her. She looked up into his dark, angry eyes. How sweet. A savior. A tough guy with a heart of gold.

A cliché.

Oh, God, she was *not* always this cynical. Once upon a time, she had actually been nice, she thought, as her feet nearly left the ground. Her savior propelled her toward her car, where he opened the door and pitched her in.

"Go," he shouted against the wind and then slammed the door turning away as if he had fixed that problem.

"Ah-yuh" and "ahm tellin' you" she was in Maine.

Addy stayed in the rental car, watched the men and dripped all over the seat and floor mats. Rental car—it was okay. These boat rescuers were going to have to leave sooner or later. They might even need a ride. A grateful man, out of the wind and rain, might be willing to chat about Zachary Hale.

After several more minutes of struggling, the workers finished their task and then raced toward a nearby shed. A short moment later, a black SUV burst out and defied the wind as it made a quick arc and sped near where she parked.

The SUV stopped suddenly and the driver side window lowered. Glowering out at her was her rescuer, his face covered with soft golden whiskers, his hair both plastered to his head and sticking out at endearing angles. Hero type. Handsome and good-hearted. Maybe he'd tell her where the manicured billionaire was hiding.

"Unless you have a death wish, get out of here," he said as the wind buffeted both vehicles.

"I just—"

The window closed and the SUV took off up the hill leaving her with no answers, a scant few feet above sea level, in a rising storm.

She looked to the second crew who were securing their boat and decided her best chance for an answer was fleeing up the hill. "You are not getting away so easily, buddy."

Addy slammed the car in gear and hurried after the SUV's taillights. A year ago, she would have felt the gut clench of paralyzing fear. Today, she almost savored the chase. There was a kind of freedom when one's tail was dragging along the bottom of the barrel as hers was.

She had nothing to lose.

Water rushed down the street, high enough to make her add a prayer to her bravado as she rode a gusty tail wind steadily up the hill. At the top, the SUV turned the corner and disappeared from sight.

Addy gave the car more gas than was probably prudent, but a hot scoop waited for no one.

When she reached the stop sign at the intersection, the SUV sat parked at the curb around the corner in front of a place called Braven's Tavern. Addy realized they must be waiting to see if she could climb the hill. Good. She might yet get a chance to speak with someone.

Just then, three of the SUV's doors popped open and all but the driver leaped out, splashing in their rubber boots. The yellow-suited passengers hurried toward the boarded-up tavern. As Addy inched her car around the corner, the SUV made a U-turn and headed back down toward the harbor. Maybe the driver was crazier than she was.

The yellow suits hurried into the tavern, the big, solid oak door slamming shut behind them.

She let the madman driver go and parked the worthy compact rental in a high spot just past the tavern in front of Pardee Jordan's Best Ever Donuts where water swirled but didn't collect.

The donut shop gave her some shelter from the wind, but there was no shelter from the rain. By the time she got to the tavern's old-fashioned oak door, rain poured down her shoulders, wicked up the pant legs of her jeans and threatened to dampen her underwear.

She grabbed the long brass door handle, tugged hard, and when the door swung open, dashed inside. These Mainers might be rough around the edges, but they would not toss her back out into the storm.

She hoped.

The short, dark hallway of the entry led to an open area where, on the right, hooks lined the wall and the SUV's three passengers were shedding their rain gear and hanging it up to drip.

To the left, the bar stools stood empty at the square-cornered, U-shaped bar and no bartender leaned over the bar in greeting. Shelves of liquor and a couple unlit beer signs decorated the back wall of the bar lit by flickering candles.

The three workers stopped and turned as a unit to gape at her. One man was tall and lean with a lot of red hair plastered to his head and around his face. One was stocky and white-whiskered and the third man who was somewhere in the middle of height and girth had graying dark brown, unruly curls around his thin face.

Not one of them said a word.

Addy pushed her hood back from her wet hair and gave each of them an even look. Well, what she hoped was an even look because when one's underwear was starting to take on water it was hard.

They stared back for a moment and then turned away to continue removing their rain suits. She had the feeling they would have stripped down to their underwear if she hadn't been there—maybe they still would.

"Eh, Michael, sorry about Francine," the stocky, white-whiskered member of the trio said to the red headed man.

Addy remembered the word *FRANCINE* as it had headed directly for her upturned face. Francine was the boat's name.

The shoulders of the tall thin man with what now seemed like a bushel of wet red hair slumped. "Ah-yuh. Wish we'd'a known sooner."

"...that the storm wasn't going to pass us by." In her head Addy filled in the missing words.

She stepped up behind the group. "Excuse me. I'm looking for Zachary Hale."

A choking kind of cough made her she realize the four of them were not the only people in the bar. She looked over her shoulder to see scattered tables in a room off to the left of where she stood. People, men and women, sat in clumps of two, three or four at timeworn tables with mismatched chairs. All of them stared at her.

She peered first into the faces of the people at the tables to make sure the billionaire hadn't shed his fancy business suit to hide amid this crowd.

When she didn't see anyone resembling the slick, manicured tycoon in disguise she turned halfway back to the three men so she could address everyone. "Can anyone tell me where to find Zachary Hale?"

A few of the people continued to stare at her, but most turned back to their beers and bowls of snacks.

"Pardon me, miss." The red-haired man spoke to her in a friendly voice as he pointed toward the door. "You don't want to be going anywhere in that, so come sit at the bar and I'll pour you a beer."

Before she could even respond, he walked around the bar, and pulled a glass from under the counter.

Addy held her ground and pulled her hood back on. "That's very nice of you, but I really need to get going. If someone could just tell me where Mr. Hale lives or where he might be right now."

"You'll get blown off the road trying to get up Sea Crest Hill in this weather." A woman's voice came from the crowd at the tables.

A few heads turned in the middle-aged woman's direction and she hushed quickly. Her ruddy face got redder and she turned her chair away.

At least these people knew the man. In this small town the hill called Sea Crest couldn't be too hard to find.

She decided to try a less direct question. She might get another nibble. "Does anyone know if he's here in town?"

Silence.

Hale was a thief, but she doubted he'd physically harm anyone. He wasn't that kind of bad guy, so these folks were mum because Hale grew up in this town and not because they were afraid of him. He was one of them and they weren't going to give her much information.

She rubbed her back where a bead of water trickled down her spine between her shoulder blades. She could lie to them. Make up something about being Hale's worried fiancé or secretary with important business.

She looked around the room. Every one of them except the woman who had given away Sea Crest Hill was staring at her with varying degrees of resolute.

And she was such a bad liar. Even the slowest of this crowd would call her on it.

Until a year ago, anyone in the news field would have said if there was one thing Adriana Bonacorda could be relied on for, it was the truth.

"Listen, miss." The red-haired man, evidently the bartender as he had tied an apron around his thin waist. "You can stay here if you want. There isn't much in the way of amenities, but we're far enough up hill from the harbor to be safe and dry in this sturdy old building."

"Thank you. I'll be all right, but I need to find Mr. Hale."

"There is no place else for you to go in town or for twenty miles. Sit down. Relax. Have a beer or—" He reached under the bar and pulled out a bottle of red wine and held it up.

Wine for the city girl. This guy already had that much figured out about her. By the look he gave her, he knew enough about her to know she was not here to heap rewards or praise on one of theirs.

She shook her head slowly. She could almost feel the tread of sneaks and stilettos on her back as the other reporters trampled her to get the story. If they convinced Hale to talk while she sipped Pinot Noir, she might as well start fabricating a résumé, because no one was ever going to hire her with her real one.

She pushed damp hair from her forehead.

Wile might be in order.

Or maybe something brash, near the truth.

What were they going to do? Toss her out into the storm?

Addy leaned over the bar and gave the thin, redheaded bartender an earnest smile. She didn't need to make enemies out of these people.

"Look. I'm a reporter. Zachary Hale has a story to tell and I want to get his side out to the public before there are any more accusations." She took a breath hoping her message of benevolence would get through. "Or worse yet, charges are filed against him."

"Aw, just let her go out there 'n' look, Michael," a burly, dark-bearded man said to the bartender as he nodded toward the old oak door.

Michael folded his arms over his chest but remained silent.

"I know that he's from around here," Addy brushed at her sodden hair, tipped her head to the side and continued. "And I get that he doesn't want to be hounded by reporters, but that's going to happen, anyway. It'll just be more civilized if he has a chance to lay his side out before the lies get too vicious."

Before the real truth gets out, she thought. Was her nose growing?

"You can't go out in this." The bartender tried again, his arms not budging from their determined pose across his chest.

"But if the storm—"

"Hurricane, miss. Hurricane."

The wind took that moment to snap the boards covering the windows as if to reinforce the bartender's statement.

"All right. If the hurricane is already here—"

"This is merely the build-up." He interrupted her with a warning glance that made her insides slightly queasy. "They expect winds of up to a hundred miles an hour to hit us in a few hours."

She sighed. Did they think she was going to stand on a street corner and wait for a hurricane to blow her away? She had work to do. At least two other reporters already knew where Hale might go to ground.

"If you just give me directions to Sea Crest Hill, I'll be out of here."

"Hale's not there," the dark-bearded guy said, looking as dark as the storm clouds outside.

He had to be in Bailey's Cove. Her lead

had been sound, as reliable as one could get these days.

If not at his home, where in this town could he be? Bailey's Cove was his comfort zone. This is where he'd go, said Savanna, her sister who had worked in the off-site records department of Hale and Blankenstock Investments, LLC, for over two years.

Peering into their faces, she examined the crowd once again to reassure herself Hale wasn't cowering there in the disguise of a local. That would be just like a scoundrel. She got a lot of petulant, stoic looks and plain blank stares, but Hale's slick good looks weren't there.

Saying Hale wasn't at his home on Sea Crest Hill was most likely a misdirection. She'd find Sea Crest Hill and have a look for herself. She'd know his home once she got there. It would be the biggest and the fanciest.

"Thank you so much for your offer of shelter," she said to the bartender and started to leave.

The door to the tavern burst open and six people entered—two women and four men—sodden, weary and breathing hard except the man who had pulled her away from the falling *FRANCINE*. He stood tall, brooding and soaked, taking inventory of the people in the tavern as if he were somehow responsible for each one of them—and ignoring her.

CHAPTER TWO

ADDY'S SAVIOR FROM the docks signaled a farewell to the bartender and turned to leave.

"Where's ah— Where's he going?" The stout white-whiskered man asked from his bar stool at the near corner of the bar's U shape.

One of the newcomers stepped forward. "Said he had to get back to—"

The bartender shot a hand into the air and he, too, seemed to make a point of not looking at Addy.

Addy studied the red-haired man and the retreating newcomer for a moment. The retreating man was her quarry.

He had to be Zachary Hale.

As impossible as it seemed, tall, rough looking and seething was Zachary Hale. Stripped of his business suit and the affable expression, the whiskered man with his wet hair plastered to his head seemed like a Maine fisherman instead of a criminal tycoon. She was such an idiot for not seeing it in the first place.

She started after him.

"Leave him alone, miss." She had taken only a step when the sharp demand stopped her.

When she turned, the short white-whiskered man was no longer on his bar stool but standing inches behind her.

"He's not who you think he is," the man finished in a deadly calm voice.

Facing him squarely she looked directly into the faded blue eyes and told a lie that at least might fool him for a moment while she fled. "It's a family thing." If anyone would understand this, it would be a man from Maine.

The man's look did not change.

She fled the tavern in time to see the SUV pull away from the curb.

Uncaring any more about the drenching rain, she flew to her car and jumped inside. Gripping the steering wheel as tight as she could, she headed out after the beckoning taillights.

The road was still deserted except for her car and the SUV.

No other reporters. Wally Harriman and Jacko Wilson would be sitting snug in their dry Boston condos waiting for the storm to pass, sure no one would be gutsy enough to travel in such weather.

"He's not who you think he is"? This man was Zachary Hale and he was hers.

She followed, pushing the rental car as much

as she dared as water ran down the back of her neck, down her body and into her bra. She wiggled her shoulders. This, too, would pass.

The street was worse than when she arrived in town. A slick of water covered most of the surface spraying out from the tires of the SUV and then filling back in.

When she passed it, she could barely see the old church through the blowing rainfall, so she spared the historic building a nod.

The hammering of the wind had escalated in the short while she had been in the town and every time the car took a broadside shot of the gusty stuff, she was sure the bitsy rental was going to tip over and tumble her like towels in a clothes dryer. But each time, the hatchback car held on to the ground and kept up the insane pace she asked of it.

Doggedly, she followed the SUV's taillights off the town's main street onto a side road leading away from the ocean and climbing gently up a hill. The rain slashed and the wind ripped at the trees surrounding the bungalows lined up along the road. The press of houses eventually thinned out and the road began to climb and curve through pine trees that seemed to close in behind her as she drove.

When a large tree branch plopped down onto the almost absent shoulder of the road, it brushed Addy back toward the center and she stayed there.

If she hadn't been so fired up about clinging to the sight of Mr. Bad Guy's taillights, she knew she would have been scared boneless. Now she held on to determination as a way of survival both mental and physical.

The SUV ahead of her turned once again, this time onto an impossibly narrow road or a driveway she would not have seen if he hadn't turned there.

She slowed and followed with growing trepidation. He for sure knew she was tailing him, but he might also know she was a reporter. If his cell service worked, surely someone at the bar would have called him.

A thought occurred to her that tried to be amusing, but wasn't. He could be trying to lead her to some remote place where he could get rid of her and hide this minuscule car and no one would ever be the wiser.

The folks of the town would be convinced she had gone away. Or because they would think she was trying to bring down one of their own, especially one who was so obviously a part of the community, they might help him cover up her disappearance.

Was the story worth dying for?

Was she crazy for thinking such things?

Heck, yeah.

But if she could wipe away the memory of the hopeless look on her sister's face when she first told her story to Addy, it was worth every slick road, every gust of wind and even facing down a fleeing tycoon.

But, she wasn't going to die. He didn't frighten her. The FBI agent she had interviewed had said scam artists rarely seriously hurt anyone. They were usually cowards, often helpless if they were forced into a face-to-face confrontation.

After what she had seen of this guy, she had to admit he wouldn't be terrified of her. Maybe he'd want to come clean, bare his soul to cleanse himself.

Keep dreaming, she told herself.

She squeezed the wheel and followed the lights. After a quarter mile or so of the steeper, rocky grade, and one particularly deep water-filled rut, she patted the steering wheel. "It's okay, rental car, you can do this."

The road turned suddenly and a stand of trees gave her a small respite from the wind. Wherever they were going they had to be arriving any time. She breathed a long sigh. The sun would be setting soon and she wasn't relishing the darkness.

Where Hale was going and what she would

do when they arrived hadn't been very well planned in her head. Somehow, she had always seen herself confronting him in an office, a bar or a coffee shop, or even on the front steps outside his condo building in downtown Boston.

"You're leapin', but you're not lookin'," her granddad always told her when she did thoughtless things as a child.

Well, she was nothing if not adaptable. When she found out he had left town, she ran toward the place few people knew about. She would chase him into his mansion and follow him into his man cave, whatever it took. She didn't care as long as he talked.

She hit a jarring bump.

"Whoa, baby." She patted the dashboard with one hand.

In the past year and a half, she had changed a lot. Zooming to the top and crashing and burning six months later did that to a person. Climbing out of the crater she had made on landing had been the most difficult part and she was not sure she had found the rim yet.

Zachary Hale was going to help her regain her footing. Her old boss at the Boston Times was going to have to give her back her job when she brought this story to him.

Once clear of the sheltering trees, the wind rocked the SUV's taillights and then a few seconds later slammed into her car. The wheels fought for traction as the car shifted sideways. When she tried to correct, the wind lifted the rear end.

The world seemed to shift as the car slid backward toward the edge of the road. Water coursed around both sides as terror grabbed hold of her and squeezed hard until she couldn't breathe.

With a snap, the rear end of the car dropped and she screamed. Braking and steering did nothing except perhaps hasten her descent.

The nose of the car shifted suddenly upward toward the angry sky and the sound of her renewed screams bounced off the cheap vinyl and plastic around her.

With a sudden jolt the car stopped, the headlamps pointing upward at a forty-five-degree slant and lighting up the torrent of raindrops. She had no idea how far she had gone. Ten feet? Twenty?

Or how much farther she would drop.

Gingerly she sat up in the seat trying to see outside the confines of the car. There was nothing but rain in the headlights. Darkness was falling.

She tried for a calming breath.

Was this all?

Was she about to plunge off the edge of some bluff?

She turned slowly in the seat to recon the area behind her. Just then, the wind rocked the car, shifting the tires, loosening their hold and the vehicle shifted downward even farther.

Fear of having made yet another stupid mistake moved in for a tick, until she reminded herself there was a prize to be had if she could just buck up and get through this.

The car shook again, but held fast.

Okay.

Now. Stay in the car or get out and run after the story of her the life? For her pride and her sister, she popped open the door.

When she leaped out, the wind hit her like a hand grabbing her, hauling her upward.

The strong hand hefted her up the few feet to the edge of the road and Zachary Hale tossed her onto solid ground. Through the sheets of driving rain she saw the black SUV.

"Get in," Hale yelled and she eagerly grabbed the door and did so.

A couple minutes later the driver's-side door popped open. Hale led with her duffel bag and backpack with her electronics as he jumped in and continued up the road.

She closed her eyes for a moment of thanks for being alive and then she glanced at the driver.

Brooding was kind of an understatement, as she observed him in the shed of he dashboard lights. The wind shook even the big SUV and the driver concentrated on the road.

After a few minutes more of driving, he stopped and backed into a short driveway and up to a three-car garage. One garage door raised and he parked the vehicle safely inside.

Addy hadn't gotten but a glance of the mansion through the downpour. Large and brooding, old, not what she had expected.

Once inside the garage, she did not give herself a second to sag in relief. She grabbed her bags and scrambled out of the vehicle. For a reporter it was probably more apt than for most people to ask for forgiveness for trespassing rather than ask for permission. If she was out of the vehicle, he could see she planned to stay.

As she stood next to the SUV and dripped, the garage door lowered. In the dimness of the light, she could see that a very early model car and a buggy of some sort filled the other two garage spaces. He must be a collector of some kind.

Then a disgusting thought occurred to her. Maybe he bought these with OPM...other people's money.

Move, she told herself. The moment would

never get better than this, and if she invited herself to stay...

She let herself into a breezeway between the house and the garage. The enclosed space ran the length of the garage and was undoubtedly a twentieth-century addition designed as shelter only. Stark and serviceable, the room had hooks on the far wall holding coats for all seasons with men's boots and shoes lined up on mats below the coats.

Off to the left there was a large box of wood and a set of flip-up doors to a cellar. The doors would have been outside before the breezeway had been built. Outside and close to the entry to the kitchen so the food stored down there could be easily accessed. It was a very old house.

When Hale didn't follow her, she moved to where she could see him through the window in the door to the garage. If he picked up an ax or a chain saw, she could run out a door on either end of the breezeway.

She put a hand to her wet hair and shoved a large clump out of her eyes. Maybe if she could see more clearly, she wouldn't think such dire thoughts.

He rounded the SUV making a beeline for where she stood in the doorway. Coming to murder her? "Con men don't usually turn to murder, unless it's a last resort" were the FBI agent's exact words. The woman had seemed confident in herself, but Addy wondered if she was pushing this guy toward said last resort. She had once thought of herself as a good judge of character, but now she'd just have to rely on being extra careful.

She stepped away as he swung open the door. Inside the breezeway, Hale seemed to be racing to remove the rain suit, hanging each piece on hooks on the wall. Then he ripped off his overshirt and damp baggy work pants, tossing each item onto the top of a nearby washing machine. When he turned in her direction, a sweep of raw appreciation for the masculine body made her face flush. She had no idea what had been living under those business suits.

With his dark T-shirt and dark athletic shorts clinging to his body, there was little she could not intimately imagine about this rat. Too bad.

He took a step toward where she had made a large water spot on the floor, and she stood up taller. Getting timid would not get her the scoop every journalist wanted and only she was brave or crazy enough to go after.

"Zachary Hale, I'm Adriana Bonacorda. I'd like to get your side of the story."

He looked at her for a long moment. Drops

of rain fell from his water-darkened hair still tipped with summer's blond, and splatted onto the smooth, clean concrete garage floor.

"I'd like to throw you out in the rain." There was only candor, not malice, in his deep voice, a voice to fit the body.

He turned and strode away. When he went through the door to the house and didn't close it behind him, she tore off her coat and hung it on the hook beside his. Ripped off her wet clothing and hung it there also.

Then, in her girl shorts and tank top, she grabbed her bags and scrambled inside after him.

When she flipped a light switch, she found herself alone in a large old-fashioned kitchen with a cold wood-burning stove and a wooden icebox with shining brass hardware. Antique pots and bowls hung from hooks and the fireplace with a stone mantel had to have been built with the house, perhaps two hundred years ago.

She put her bags down on the old-style braided rug, and shivering, dug in her duffel for the fleece pants and hoodie she brought because she knew Maine was colder than Massachusetts. Darn cold, she thought as she shoved a leg into the pants.

"Close and latch the shutters in there. Cross-tape every window without a shutter." Hale had disappeared into the interior of the house but his barked commands filtered back to her through the sound of the pounding rain. A roll of wide masking tape sat on the wooden counter next to the icebox.

The first window, long and tall, was flanked by sheer curtains with tulips fancifully stitched across the bottom.

She surveyed for a moment.

Open the window, reach out in the pounding rain and pull the shutter closed.

Easy peasy.

She struggled to push up the first heavy window and when it wouldn't stay by itself, propped it open with her shoulder while she reached out and pulled the shutters closed. The shutter's latch fell easily into place, but she struggled to lower the heavy wood and glass window without letting it drop and shatter into a million shards.

After she was finished, a large puddle of rainwater stood on the linoleum around her feet and she was wet again.

When she heard shutters slam in the next room, she closed the next two sets, grabbed the tape and a flashlight from the old wooden kitchen table, just in case, and hurried past Hale into the parlor to do the same in there.

The light she had turned on blinked out, as
did the ones in the rooms she had left behind.
She flipped on her flashlight.

In the beam of light she could see furniture and fixtures she might have seen in her
grandmother's home or at one of her old aunts'
houses when she was a kid. Her flashlight
paused on a round table with three tiers that
would serve no purpose in today's world and
then a pair of bulldogs that might be banks.
Hale was trying to protect the place as if it was
a museum. Wait. It was a museum, of sorts.

When Hale strode past her, she got busy
and finished the parlor. A library across the
hall and then a maid's quarters at the back of
the house needed her attention next. When
she heard Hale run up the stairs, she finished
two more rooms and followed. The first bedroom she worked on had a dark four-poster
bed complete with a wooden canopy—if that's
what they called the wood ones—and velvet
curtains. On a stand sat a pitcher and bowl
that had once been used for washing up in
the morning. A small primitive bathroom sat
tucked between this and the next bedroom and
she closed the shutters on all of them and taped
a window in the hallway.

She could hear Hale on the third floor or

attic or whatever was up there slamming shutters and then his footsteps hurrying.

By the time she finished a fourth bedroom and third sitting room, Hale stood, a shadow in the doorway. She resisted the urge to shine the beam in his direction and the ambient light was too dim to see the expression on his face. A spark of fear sent a prickle of pain along the nerves just under her skin, but there would be no "flight" today.

"Thank you," he said and vanished. This time, he didn't call back to her.

The lights flickered on and she wandered out of the bedroom to look in the other rooms down the hallway. Every bedroom had an antique bed or two, some older than others. One was even a rope bed used by the early settlers in lieu of a mattress. The house seemed to be a collection of antiquities spanning the ages.

Addy was not an expert, but she had seen enough around Boston to know colonial American through early-twentieth-century furnishings when she saw them. None of the rooms looked as if they had been lived in for a very long time, with the exception of the four-poster bedroom. It had a space heater sitting near the fireplace. He could entrench himself in this room and make her sleep on the stiff and formal settee in the parlor.

She loped down the stairs doubting Zachary Hale was going out into the storm again, but he wasn't in the kitchen or the rest of the house. When she heard sounds in the garage again she went out to see him unloading groceries and water from the SUV.

He now wore a navy pull-on shirt with a button V and jeans, and she assumed dry underwear. She'd give a few bucks herself for some of those right now. She had some in her duffel bag, but since she might be tossed out into the storm at any moment...

Throwing her out was exactly what she expected a guy like Zachary Hale to do. He wouldn't steal from old ladies and then open his home to a reporter, unless he had other plans for the reporter.

She swallowed against the tightness in her throat, let herself out into the garage and grabbed four of the gallon bottles of water from the SUV and followed Hale up a set of stairs at the back wall of the garage. Wherever he was going, there must be a place to make food.

If anyone understood why people went into an ax murderer's dark basement without back up, it was an investigative journalist, especially one with no options in the outside world short of minimum-wage jobs—if she could even get one of those.

Only her sister would miss her, and that was a maybe, because her sister was busy with two children, living in a tiny apartment and had only called her because she was in dire straights.

Addy shook her head. Their lives were such a mess.

She shouldered open the door at the top of the stairs at the rear of the garage and stopped short. The door opened into a large loft where vaulted ceilings spread out over a comfy living space. This explained where in the unused house he stayed. He didn't.

A kitchen sat to the left, small, open with a freestanding work island. Two bar stools sat tucked under the lip of its butcher-block counter. To the right of the kitchen area was a more formal dining space with a table—all wood and with six chairs. In the middle of the back wall sat a fireplace flanked by a couch and cushioned chairs.

On the right of the room was a large bed covered with a duvet of large burgundy and forest-green squares. The whole place looked woodsy, spare and masculine with the exception of a few touches that said a woman had been here on more than one occasion.

She put the water on the counter and started to go down for more.

"I'll get the rest."

She began to protest, but he held up a hand and continued. "In the bedroom with the four-poster bed, there are dry towels and a space heater."

She took the dismissal for what it was. He had no idea what to do with the enemy, but apparently even a rat couldn't throw an intruder, no matter how unwanted, out into a hurricane to fend for herself.

Not getting any dryer, she hurried down the stairs, through the garage and breezeway and to the kitchen. She plucked her duffel and backpack from the braided rug and headed for the bedroom with the four-poster bed...and a space heater.

What she was going to do when the electricity went out, and it surely would, she had no idea.

Worse than the cold, sitting in the cold dark she wasn't going to get the story from Hale. She needed a plan to put herself in his space where she could glean knowledge from his reactions.

As she carried her bags up the stairs, she wondered if somewhere in the clattering din of the storm would eventually be the hum of a generator to keep the space heater functioning.

In the four-poster bedroom, she flipped a

light switch. When the dim bulb came on, it was barely better than nothing.

Part of her wanted to sit down in the semi-dark and write up what she had already learned about Zachary Hale and the other part, the overachiever survival part of her wanted to rush back over to the loft. She would demand Hale tell her all there was to know about his company, Hale and Blankenstock Investments, LLC, and about the partner on which his attorney tried to blame the scandal.

So close. She was so close to all the answers. If she could get Hale to trust her, to open up…

When she shivered almost violently, she remembered she was cold, her fleece suit was damp and her underwear wet.

She put her bag on the old carpeting and flipped on the space heater that stood on the slate floor in front of the old fireplace. Standing in the glow she let it warm her. Well, her ankles. The heat didn't rise much farther than her kneecaps.

She didn't have to lie to Hale. She had already told him she was a reporter. Maybe she had fudged just a bit by telling him she wanted his side of the story. She already knew his side of the story and she wasn't going to be fooled by the face-of-innocence thing. What she wanted was to build her story, her series of stories, on what made such a man tick. How did small-town Maine's smiling baby boy get to be a billionaire swindler in Boston in thirty-three short years?

Still shivering in spite of warming ankles she pulled her bag closer and shed her wet clothing.

All right, so Hale had only been charged and convicted by her fellow reporters and not a court of law. But as far as that man was concerned, every good reporter knew the percentages on *where there's smoke there's fire*. Where there was the suspicion of huge amounts of misappropriated money, there was some kind of malfeasance committed by someone.

Dancing in the cold she pulled dry underwear from the bag...

But no one had interviewed him. The person closest to him, his partner, had been interviewed and she was freely, if meekly speaking out, though only after his attorney had thrown her under the bus.

How deeply into Hale's personality did the creepiness penetrate? When one swindled men and women who had worked at hard-labor jobs all their lives, did it take more of a deeply rooted problem than if one swindled fellow white collars?

...and soon the primal relief of dry underwear loosened a knot in her stomach. When that happened some of the old courage and determination, each threaded with a touch of recklessness, had her quickly sliding on her last change of clothes.

She was going to go kick some swindler butt.

Slow down, she thought as she snapped her jeans. Take some time to think this out. She looked around at her surroundings. The fireplace where the heater sat was in the wall to the left of the door and had been capped, either because it didn't work well or to keep out the winter cold and errant wildlife. The heavy four-poster bed with its dark blue curtains had been placed against the inner wall to the right of the door and beyond it were matching chests of drawers.

On either side of the bed was a large braided rug and portraits of, she supposed, family members hung on most of the walls.

Several feet beyond the end of the bed were two tall windows. Between the windows was a washstand, a commode, with an ewer and bowl sitting on top. Unreasonably she hoped there was no chamber pot in the small cupboard of the stand; she had seen a flush toilet here, after all. The washstand had a granite top and above the towel bar was the picture of a woman.

She walked away from the heater to read the legend.

The nightstand, it seemed, was made for Millie Mauston when she first came to the mansion on Sea Crest Hill in 1889 as Mrs. Colm McClure. The Maine granite top of the stand weighed about eighty pounds and the chest was made of black walnut at her request. Millie, a bright young woman with a head of thick dark hair was pictured beside the legend. The birth and death date said she was twenty-four when she died.

Young. Too young to even get to experience her nightstand for long. Addy turned toward the bed and wondered if Millie had slept there.

"Well, Millie, I hope I get a chance."

Right now it was time to find out some dark and sturdy info about Zachary Hale. Dark because readers and therefore editors liked the juicy stuff and sturdy because the tale of intrigue surrounding her last conquest in Afghanistan turned out to be diaphanous at best.

The lights flickered out.

Dark. Why had she used the word *dark*?

Didn't matter.

If Hale had not locked the door to the loft, she'd take that as a signal she was welcome for a nice fireside chat.

He would not, after all, expect her to sit up

here with only the glow of her computer screen and when that went dead, to sit in the rural Maine blackness.

She groped around.

And where was the damned flashlight?

She stopped for a moment in the pitch black.

She used to be nice. She had friends once. She held the door for old men. She used to carry her elderly neighbor's trash to the chute. Though for a while a year and a half ago, the best she could muster was to find a neighbor kid to carry it for her. She had been too busy pursuing a story, too busy trying to gain the status few reporters ever touched. And she had done it, been on the top of the heap, the star news reporter everyone envied, in orbit with those who might be up for a Pulitzer Prize, everyone said.

Crash and burn would have been a good outcome compared to the embarrassing punishment she had gotten from the press she used to hold so dear.

She searched again for the flashlight.

Aha! On the edge of the bed. The room brightened as she flicked on the beam.

She shrugged into a second tank top and cropped cardigan. When she clutched the sweater around her chest, she cringed at how *not* warm these clothes were. It was still seventy-five degrees in late September in Boston this year and maybe when the storm passed and the sun came back out, it would be sixty in Maine before the snow started.

With another shiver, she grabbed her laptop and headed down the stairs. *Zachary Hale, here I come,* she thought.

If her last dry underwear got wet in the storm because he threw her out, so be it.

CHAPTER THREE

Zach held his cell phone to his ear and listened as his attorney warned him that there was a reporter in town asking about him.

"She's here," he said as he took a loaf of bread and a package of cookies from the grocery bag and placed them on the kitchen's island countertop.

"At the mansion? That's not a good idea." His attorney, Hunter Morrison, sounded worried and he probably had reason to be.

"She ran her car off the road following me up here."

Hunter snorted. "I guess leaving her in the ditch to sit out a hurricane might have been a bit much. I don't suppose she did it on purpose."

Zach thought of how far her car had left the road, how frightened she had been when he had hauled her out and wondered if anyone was that desperate for a story. "I doubt it."

"You don't have her in the loft with you."

It was a nonquestion that begged a negative

response. "I put her in the house. We've got power now. If Owen did his job, the generator is functioning and there's plenty of gas."

"Well, the old guy's intentions will have been good."

Zach snorted this time. He didn't trust Owen Calloway to be a perfect groundskeeper, but he trusted the old guy and his wife not to meddle and not to gossip. Those two qualities made his only close neighbors gems.

"At any rate I've got plenty of wood. As long as the fireplace works, and according to the contractor there should be barely a puff of smoke even in a hurricane. We've got food and hot water."

"You might find Delainey and I squatting up there one of these days."

Hunter had a new fiancé who enriched his life in every way and Zach was glad that kind of thing worked for the two of them.

"Anytime. Anytime," Zach said putting a bag of apples and one of oranges on the counter beside the bread. "And I'll keep the reporter at arm's length."

"A little farther away might be better."

"Maybe she'll stay tucked in the house."

"They predict the storm could stall."

"I'll feed her once in a while."

"Be careful of what you feed her. She has

a lot of good journalism to her credit, but her last story has been labeled as a desperate grab at a Pulitzer. She's been down and out since, so she's most likely very hungry."

"I'll slip food under her door."

Hunter laughed. "Yeah. Be careful and good luck, Zach."

"Thanks, and I meant it about you and Delainey."

He signed off with another promise to be wary.

Zachary McClure Hale in loyal and patriotic fashion had been named after his grandfather Zachary Hale and an ancestor by the name of McClure who had brought his wife and infant to the very young United States of America in the early 1800s.

By time and attrition the McClures of New England had either died out, or a few, but not many, had left Maine and lost interest in the family heritage. Virginia McClure, his grandmother, had drilled into him that a Mainer knew where he came from and he protected that legacy. For most of Zach's adult life, it had been up to him to maintain the ancestral home and the antiques within.

The old McClure mansion was his to look after, but caring for the heritage home had not been a burden. Money to keep the house in good repair was also not a problem. At issue, he had little time for the place and there was scant interest outside himself for keeping it in the best historically accurate repair.

He didn't begrudge the time he gave. The loft above the garage had become a place to retreat, where he didn't usually allow people to follow him. Since the time when control had been bequeathed to him, there had never been a reporter and never a woman here other than Cammy Logan, who cleaned the house and the loft and kept a keen eye on any repairs or issues that occurred with either.

Reporters he usually met at a café or his office. Women he wished to entertain in private, he met at restaurants or posh hotels. His penthouse condominium in Boston was also private territory.

The mansion on Sea Crest Hill he kept to himself, until today.

He'd deal with this reporter exactly how he'd dealt with those in Boston. She'd get referred to his attorney for a blanket statement neither confirming nor denying any wrongdoing at Hale and Blankenstock. He gave the loft a quick inspection. The windows were specially installed to withstand a strong nor'easter and even an occasional branch or bit of debris. He was hopeful they would hold out in a hurricane.

The interior with its old blond wood of the 1950's had withstood time and even come back into fashion a few times. The light-colored paneled walls gave the place a feeling that it was larger on the inside than out. And it was a welcome and necessary refuge he needed in his life.

He had updated the appliances last year and made sure the bed was large and comfortable. Cammy had added a pillow here and there, a few fabric wall hangings and a handmade quilt on the back of the couch to soften the man-effect, but he had to admit they added more comfort.

Zach had barely finished the conversation when the lights flicked out again. He'd have to check the generator.

He grabbed the flashlight and a baseball cap from the ones on the wall pegs and headed down the stairs where he donned a dry jacket from a hook in the garage. Then he sprinted toward the generator shed.

The wind slapped him and the rain did its best to blow him off course as he approached the shed, where behind the lawn mower, weed whacker and other tools to maintain the exterior of the old home, would sit the rarely used generator that powered the essentials of the house whenever necessary. Right now all he needed were two rooms.

When he got inside, out of the storm, the shed smelled of old wood, fuel and age. Built sometime in the middle of the last century the wooden frame could withstand a direct hit from a hurricane if it had to.

The bright beam of his flashlight spread out, illuminating the shed as he closed the door behind him. The fuel cans sat lined up behind the lawn mower next to the generator. Zach moved the mower and grabbed a can of fuel. The can lifted easily. Empty. The second can, same as the first.

Owen did outside maintenance and kept the gasoline rotated and stocked in the shed for emergencies, or he was supposed to keep the fuel stocked. Today two cans stood full and all the spare cans were dry as "bones guarding a pirate's treasure," Owen would say. That meant there was enough fuel to fill the generator with a bit to spare. Apparently Owen had mowed and weed-whacked all summer and he was always "Ah-yuh, goin' ta get more gas tomorra."

If the reporter used the space heater, the lights, her computer and who knew what else the woman would plug in, the gas would last less than a day. This storm was not going to pass for at least thirty-six hours.

He rubbed the back of his neck as he considered the fix Owen had left him in. A day. Maybe a day.

He dropped his hand to his side. By himself, he could make the generator last several days.

He should have left that woman in the ravine. Other than claiming to be a reporter, he had no idea who she was and didn't want to find out. Grandmother might frown on his spare hospitality, but he hoped the woman would sit huddled in front of the space heater, burn up the gas with a hair dryer and use her laptop as long as the power lasted and then sit in the dark under a quilt and wait out the storm.

He poured gas in the generator, and when he pushed the start button, it snapped from silent to loud in an instant.

That was luck.

With his hands over his ears, he stood waiting to make sure the old thing continued to run, that nothing had clogged during the year or so of only being started as a test from time to time.

Two things were "at leasts" today. At least he had gotten back from Boston in time to get the house closed up and at least the woodpile out under the tall white pines behind the house had been stacked high and straight.

He'd have a heat and light source when the gas burned up.

What he wouldn't have for the day or two it took for the storm to pass was peace from a sensation seeker. Now all he had to figure out was how to keep Ms. Bonacorda in the dark, literally, when the lights went out.

These days most reporters he came into contact with were gossip seekers who could take a corn-flake-sized bit of banal and build it into a sensational story. Worse, when a story was written with enough adjectives or read with enough enthusiasm it would be considered by the masses to be gospel. He wondered how many adjectives this woman had in her cache.

He let his hands fall to his sides disgusted with himself. Whatever and whoever this woman was, he had gotten into the mess with Hale and Blankenstock, and he knew the world was going to demand answers from him.

Answers were going to be tough to come by.

Convinced the generator would continue to run, he turned to leave and spotted the note tagged to the door.

Me and Margaret Louise are hunkered down and well taken care of. Don't you worry about us. You come over if you want to. It was signed *Owen and Margaret Louise.*

He had no choice but to smile. "Well taken

care of" meant the two of them were holed up with enough food for a small regiment and plenty of scotch for the whole army. Owen knew creature comfort and he deserved them, and Margaret Louise knew how to cook, therefore the food in Zach's freezer...

He tugged the hood of the jacket back on over his baseball cap and stood in the doorway of the shed. He was fascinated, watching the show presented by nature. Lightning flickered in various degrees of strength for almost a minute before it abated to small flashes.

In the near dark, he saw no light coming from the room where he'd sent the reporter. He could have gotten lucky—maybe she'd gone to sleep already.

He doubted it as soon as he thought it.

When he sent her away, she had looked shocked and might have left in a disappointed huff. She might even have been foolish enough to go back out in the storm to see if she could rescue her car. He could have told her that car was going nowhere until O'Reilly's tow truck hauled it out of the ravine. She was lucky she hadn't gone in a few yards farther up the road, as that part of the ravine ran down the steep side of the hill.

She must have thought he was story-worthy

to risk her neck and she helped shore up the old mansion without question.

Did those things make her someone he'd be interested in knowing or someone he should lock out of the loft and hope she went away without actually damaging the old home and contents? His grandmother had loved the mansion on Sea Crest Hill and his own mother had rejected it as the shabbier side of life.

He turned and gave the generator a last visual once-over. Satisfied, he shifted the cap so the storm had less of a chance to blast rain into his eyes and headed out.

The wind whipped the pine trees relentlessly over his head and the rain pelted down as he fled sure-footed along the stone path to his refuge. In five minutes he'd have a fire going and a glass of finely aged red wine in his hand.

Hopefully that reporter was tucked away in the four-poster bed, her computer in her lap, capitalizing on someone else's misfortune.

WHEN ADDY HEARD the sound of boots tread on the steps to the loft above the garage, she drew herself up to her full five foot five inches and whispered encouragement to herself. There was a time when no man could make her back down, but this man had already shown signs of ignoring her and had all but thrown her over his shoulder and carried her off to his cave.

One of his many talents, no doubt, along with the ability to talk, bully and cajole people out of their money, was to carry women off. Already he had shown her that murdering her to keep her out of his business was not plan number one. If he wanted to kill her to shut her up, he could have just left her in her car. She might have been silenced by a flying tree limb or been washed off down the hill into the ocean if he had left her to fend for herself.

Most likely he just planned to stick her up in beguiling Millie McClure's room full of antiques and ignore her.

She smiled and a shot of courage buzzed inside her.

The door swung open and the man who appeared in the dim light was not the slick swindler she had seen in Boston, nor the Maine backwoodsman. Nor was he the man who would show up briefly, a glittering beacon of humility according to her sister, Savanna, at the holiday parties for Hale and Blankenstock where her sister had met him exactly twice. He would stay for a few minutes, greet each employee and then leave, according to Savanna.

Everyone now knew the glittering beacon was part of a lie.

Hat in hand, the shadows made the furrow of his brows deeper and his unguarded expression more dramatic. He was handsome in his rough and outdoorsy look, and in this moment he appeared to be a man who had many troubles to deal with, many concerns for which he had to be responsible.

Under other circumstances, she might want to walk up to him, put her hands flat on his chest and brush his damp hair back off where it had fallen on his forehead. She would sweep her hand across the furrows of his brows, draw his head down and put her lips against his full and slightly drawn ones. And...

What was she thinking?

This was the enemy of the people.

Hale slowly swung his gaze in her direction as if he had expected her to be there. His features relaxed to neutral, he became a hybrid between woodsman, because of the four- or five-day growth of sandy whiskers, and slick swindler, because of years of practice.

Addy drew in a breath to sort out her thoughts.

"I wanted to speak with you," she said into the silence. They were in his territory, and short of death by storm or felony theft of his SUV, she was stuck here. She wanted to sound non-confrontational, perhaps professorish, someone who was just looking for facts, not trying to crucify him.

If his guard went down to anywhere near what it had been when he had opened the door, she'd get something related to the truth, or at least as much of the truth as a person like him could find in his life.

He didn't answer, but hung his hat on a peg, turned and walked out.

Degenerate…

Running away. Or maybe it was a ploy to have her follow him and then he'd get her out of the loft and out of his hair if he ran back inside and locked the door with her on the outside.

A kid's game, like musical chairs. She'd be left out. Too bad, so sad. But that was not going to happen.

Make herself useful. That's what she should do.

What did men like? Couldn't resist?

She looked at the bags of groceries on the island counter.

Food. Even swindlers had to eat.

She couldn't cook at all—not even boil a decent pot of water, but maybe she could manage something. She grabbed the nearest bag and started poking around.

Fusilli? Other than being pasta—she knew because she could see its curly shape through the window in the box—she hadn't known anything about it, hadn't needed to know what it was named to eat it. Nope. Just stick a fork in it.

Cans of plain tomato sauce. What the heck was she supposed to do with that?

The door across the room popped open and Hale entered with his arms bulging with firewood. He turned his back to her as he unloaded and stacked wood in the bin near the fireplace.

Then he walked out again.

A fire, of course. She was probably much better at fire-starting than cooking. Actually, she once tried to combine the two. Unfortunately, the smell of burned pizza stuck around her condo, and to be fair, the hall of her building, for a week.

She hustled over to the fireplace and searched for fire-starter logs or those cute pinecones stuffed with candle wax or something to make fires start easier.

There wasn't so much as a fireplace match, just a book of matches with the name of the bar in town. Braven's. She could have, should have stayed there in the bar. Too late.

She poked around for fire-starting aids and gave up.

She wasn't any better at fire-starting than she was at cooking, so when she heard the footsteps on the stairs, she fled back to the kitchen area where she could keep the center island between them, duck behind it if she had to.

He unloaded the wood and knelt on the floor in front of the fireplace. Then he reached inside and opened the flue. Oh, she would not have remembered that. With wood chips and bits of flimsy bark, he started a small fire, feeding it twigs and shards of wood, and of course, he had used the stubby matches.

Just like now, she always managed to have someone around to start her fires and usually to cook. She wondered if he expected her to do it, to cook. *Good luck with that one, buddy.*

The fire grew tall and she was a bit envious. She'd have to research fire-starting when she had time.

When the fire blazed, he stood and headed in her direction.

His sandy blond brows drew together in fierce concentration. There was clearly a side of this man she knew nothing about, possibly a deeply dark and sinister side. She should be running away. She should go back to the house, push the four-poster bed up against the door and tie the sheets together to let herself out the window in case she needed to flee into the storm.

He paused and dropped his keys into a dish on the long table behind the couch.

His expression did not challenge nor welcome as he continued toward the kitchen.

Nonreactive. Ego-sheltered.

Serial killer? Chain-saw murderer? At least the two of them weren't in a basement alone. A basement? Did the place have a basement? Yes, the lift up doors in the breezeway would lead to a cellar of some kind. Maybe that's where she'd be buried.

She was crazy, the chatter in her head crazier.

Maybe it was he who should be afraid.

As he drew closer, he seemed to grow in size and his expression in intensity. She stiffened, searching for the best exit if she had to run.

And then she relaxed.

Yeah.

She could run away, go back to a world where she would cover stories for microfame and a couple of dollars.

Then she could go live under a bridge in a refrigerator box and wear newspapers on her feet and stuffed into the sleeves of her lightweight coat as she had done when she investigated and had written the series *Life Without a Cause* to critical acclaim only four short years ago.

Hale came around the counter and stopped

a mere two feet from her. He placed one hand, deliberately it seemed, on the counter beside her, and she inhaled.

By being here in his living space, she had made her move, set out her pawn. The next move was his.

A second later he stepped around her to the freezer, from which he took two glass bowls filled with something green. He took off the lids, popped them into the microwave and covered them with a sheet of crinkly sounding paper he'd taken from a box in the drawer under the microwave.

Eat? His move was to feed her. Or maybe he was hungry and planned to eat both...in front of her...while she salivated.

Addy watched the bowls spin on the microwave's carousel and then realized he was heating pea soup.

Food was a good move on his part. She hadn't eaten since early this morning. If she accepted food from him, she would be in his debt.

Yeah, as if she wasn't already—deeply.

He pulled two plates from the cupboard.

He was dreadful at portraying himself as a bad guy, or he was as "diabolically clever" as the tabloids had called him when they alluded to his making off with a few billion dollars.

If she didn't have an absolutely reliable source, she would begin to doubt the veracity of her facts. The SEC, Securities and Exchange Commission, a U.S. government agency set up to prevent investment fraud, had come down hard on Hale and Blankenstock.

More importantly, according to her younger sister, Savanna, this guy was worse than a robber or a thief who stole once and disappeared into the night, Hale was heartless. He had repeatedly taken from Savanna—trusting, single mother Savanna—and many others.

He went back to the fire, hunkered down and carefully placed a pair of logs on the flaming pile. He stayed squatted, silhouetted in the soft light until the fire roared.

He looked handsome. And fit. She wondered how fit—she couldn't help it, picturing him naked and… It was easy to see, this man lifted heavy things, not just fountain pens and martini glasses.

She shook her head at the silliness of her thoughts.

He had set out a pea soup pawn. Now she was going to have to sit down and eat with him or give up the game without trying and walk back to town beaten down by the storm and failure.

Lunch it was, and so be it.

She pulled open a drawer in the butcher-block island and found place mats and napkins that most likely had never been used. Carefully she set them on the table in strategic places. At right angles so she could better watch him when she wanted and ignore him if it seemed necessary.

She took the plates he had placed on the counter, where they would have sat side by side on the bar stools, and moved them to the table.

If she was to get a story, if she was going to find out what made this guy tick, she'd have to make nice. Pea soup with a swindler. She had done scary things before to get to the truth.

She'd do worse to get his real story if need be.

She opened another drawer where she supposed spoons would be and bingo, there was a tray of flatware. She took a soupspoon for him and a teaspoon for her. Soupspoons were too large and made her slurp soup. She preferred a teaspoon where the contents cooled faster and the spoon fit her mouth. Her former boyfriend had called her a delicate flower for demanding such things. He never did understand her.

Her former boyfriend had also deserted her when the fiction she had unwittingly written had hit the fan.

Former. Back in the part of her life when she

soared, Wesley had stuck himself to her side whenever she was home in Boston. He hadn't liked the falling-flat part, however, so he split quickly, taking with him everything from her condo she had thought was theirs.

So long and good luck.

When Hale left the fire, he came over to where she stood waiting for the microwave to finish. Reaching into the cupboard beside her head, he grabbed a bag of oyster crackers.

He smelled of wood smoke and she could feel the heat of the fire radiating from him. She inhaled and when she shivered, the quaking in her knees wasn't just because the place was one degree warmer than freezing. She wanted to…move in on the story, grab it and not let go until she had everything she could ever want.

But she held her ground. Letting him know how eager she was would not help her bond with his deepest soul.

When he took the oyster crackers and turned away toward the table she asked, "Why are you doing this? Why are you treating me as if you don't hate me? You must hate me."

"You give yourself too much credit," he responded calmly without turning around.

Good one, she thought. Attack her and keep her on edge. Maybe he didn't want to play nice after all.

"All right." She moved around so she could see his face. "You don't hate me, but you know why I'm here. Is there anything you want to tell me?"

His shoulders stiffened and he drew in a breath. "You have all your facts and you're looking for that personal touch to make your story more sensational." Again his words were not angry.

Under his assessing gaze, she suddenly felt as if he knew exactly who and what she was. As if he had been there that day when her source in Afghanistan had been exposed as a liar.

She felt the humiliation try to submerge her again, as if he was qualified to judge her.

She gathered her wits. "You did what you did and I came here to try to make some sense of it. To try to understand."

In Afghanistan she had been stupid and too eager. She had almost caused others to lose their lives, and that might make her as morally corrupt as he was.

Disgust and repugnance aimed at herself suddenly seemed much worse than it had ever been. It made her sick to her stomach, made her head flood with the images floating around on the internet that portrayed her to be the lowest kind of life-form.

She looked up and he was standing almost toe-to-toe with her.

"What do you think you will be trying to understand?"

His question brought her back into reality, the loft, the hurricane, the many people this man had cheated. His words had been soft as if trying to assess her again, not to challenge her.

"How—how things started. I thought you might tell me how things started."

He stepped away but watched her warily.

With both palms pressed to the counter she continued. "Did it start out as a swindle?"

She expected him to smile at this, to pull out his charm to deflect her. Perhaps put on enough of a show to make her believe he had been wronged, to make her go sit in the four-poster room and use what she already had about him, type up a tidy article that looked just like everyone else's.

Not to dig around inside his head for deeper motives. Maybe his mother withheld love. Maybe his father exiled him to the military academy he attended for four years and supposedly hated.

He didn't smile at all. He looked tired. He had a right to be exhausted. She'd give him that. He had been out saving boats and rescuing women who wanted to tear his life apart.

And that was exactly what she wanted to do, to tear his life apart as he had torn apart her sister's.

She wanted to disassemble him.

Limb by limb, she thought and then asked, "At what point did you realize things were spinning out of control? That you were going to have to distance yourself from the fray so as to look innocent?"

CHAPTER FOUR

AS IF ADDY hadn't spoken, Hale walked away and brought one bowl of soup from the microwave and placed it on a plate she had set on the table. Then he returned to the microwave for the other. She was sure he was going to put the second bowl back in the refrigerator or even pour it down the drain or, better, over her head.

He did none of the above.

He placed the second bowl on the other plate and looked over at her with a look that said, "Sit."

She scrambled to do so—for the story, of course, and because she was really, truly, so very desperately hungry.

He sat after she did. Either there were old-school manners in this man, or perhaps, this was her last supper and he wanted to be in a position to run her down if she tried to escape. At least she wouldn't die hungry, she thought as she instinctively slid back on the heavy wood-and-leather chair.

Hands in her lap, 'cause she had some manners, too, she sat and waited for his lead. "Behave like them and they may treat you as one of them" had been the advice of one of her instructors in college and—sometimes the magic worked. It had when she donned the clothing and the persona of an Afghani peasant woman—or it had worked for a while.

He put his napkin on his lap. She did the same.

After he took his first taste of the soup, she sipped a bit of hers. It was delicious and soon she had to slow herself down, so she floated a few small oyster crackers on top of her soup. As she savored the next mouthful it occurred to her that she was concentrating too much on the food, the conversation being nonexistent.

She snapped her gaze to Hale's face.

He seemed to be ignoring her or if she left her ego out, he was thinking about something that troubled him. So should he be. He should be thinking about all the people's lives that he'd ruined, all the heartache he'd caused, all the money he had gained and was going to lose.

Then why did he look so damned mouthwatering? She swiped her lips with her napkin. His sun-highlighted hair, thick, short on the sides and not too long on the top, almost always perfectly styled and trimmed often. Today it had been finger-combed, in an endearingly youthful way. He looked vulnerable without his facade.

If he wasn't so morally corrupt and she wasn't so desperate to get at the truth, he might even look…enticing.

She yanked her brain away from that vein of perilous thinking and scrambled for a question to ask.

She needed something affable. Be his friend. Be someone he wanted to talk to, a houseguest with whom he'd at least speak politely. If swindlers spoke politely when they didn't have to speak at all.

"The home." She nodded in the direction where the big old house sat connected to the garage via the breezeway. "The antiques in the home are lovely. Tell me about some of the history over there. If you wouldn't mind." She added the last part with a warm smile.

The narrow-eyed look he gave her said he knew exactly what she was doing and why, but he cleared his throat and after a moment of silence said, "The home was built in the early 1800s by the man who originally established the town."

"The Bailey of Bailey's Cove."

"Liam Bailey. He built the house for the woman he loved." Hale's words sounded as if he read them from a brochure, but at least he wasn't declining to speak with her.

"How many generations ago did this ancestor of yours live?"

"The builder lived in the early 1800s, about eight generations back, but he isn't my ancestor."

She tipped her head and raised an eyebrow. "You live in his ancestral home and are the keeper of the family history. What do his descendents say?"

"No one knew until recently that he had descendents."

"Missing descendents sounds interesting." Juicy, better than gold in most people's lives. She almost added, "Tell me about it," but one could only use that phrase twice at best before an interviewee started feeling strip-mined.

He didn't reply and Addy feared she might have worn out her welcome already.

The wind blew outside and a branch or something clattered against the roof. The raging storm had kept every other journalist away from this story and she had no intention of blowing it now.

She started to speak, but so did he.

"Go on. I'd love to hear all about it," she said first and then she sat up straight and rested her spoon on the plate beside her soup bowl.

"In the early 1800s Patrick McClure came to the newly formed United States to avoid the English taxes. Immigration didn't help his wife, Fanny McClure, as she died in childbirth, leaving McClure with two children under a year old and the need for a new wife. My direct ascendant was Fanny's firstborn son."

He continued to speak in the staccato voice of a museum docent or tour guide, someone who had delivered the information over and over, but he was speaking so she kept quiet.

"McClure had four children with his second wife, one a dark-haired stepson now proven to be the child of Liam Bailey for which the town was named. The three others were most likely McClures. They all had flaming red hair as he did. The dark-haired son has two descendants in the town. Daniel MacCarey, an anthropologist from the university and married to the owner of a restaurant here. The other, Heather Loch, who runs the town's museum in the original church."

"The church is a museum?"

He nodded as she lifted her spoon for more soup.

"What does Heather Loch look like?"

"Sixties, a mass of gray hair. You can't miss her." His lips curved gently, and the emotion she read into the smile said, fondly.

He glanced at her still smiling and she almost coughed up pea soup. Wow. Nice smile when he wasn't being all businesslike. Electric. As quickly as her mind fired up with thoughts of Zachary Hale the real man, not monster, the smile changed to a frown. Had he seen the flicker of interest on her face?

Had she really felt it? What were they talking about? Oh, yeah, the church and the gray-haired woman. "I saw her when I drove into town. I thought she was an apparition standing in the doorway of the old church."

"She's guarding the museum from the storm."

"Against a hurricane. How could they let her stay there? It's too close to water."

"Without a doubt, more than one person tried to talk her into leaving. Police Chief Montcalm most likely sent a squad car for her."

"And she told them the church has stood two hundred years and it would stand another two hundred." Addy might interview that woman, for color if nothing else.

"Something like that."

He looked directly at her when he spoke. Almost as if seeing her for the first time. His eyes gleamed a soft golden brown, matching his hair. Oh, he was a package.

This was not the evil billionaire she'd expected. Could it be the beard?

She dismissed the notion. Zachary Hale was sly, slick and treacherously dangerous. He had created false accounting records and a trail of phony investment reports, then he put his name on them and sent them off to the SEC, Securities and Exchange Commission, as proof of his extraordinary ability to make fortunes for people.

She cleared her throat. "About the McClures. Do you know much about them?"

"Patrick McClure seemed to be in the right place at the right time and in the right circumstances."

"The woman needed a husband."

"And McClure, Irish immigrant or not, needed a wife. The situation was urgent or the second richest man in town would not have chosen such a bridegroom for his daughter."

"So the first Mr. McClure came by his fortune in the new world through this woman in need?"

"Colleen Fletcher McClure insisted her father set the two of them up in the home her lover had built. And when her father died, insisted the town's name be changed from South Harbor to Bailey's Cove."

The more he spoke, the more his voice became animated. Addy found herself leaning in, captivated.

She pushed away from the table, took the dishes to wash them in the sink.

"Has your family always lived in Bailey's Cove?" If she sneaked in a question close to his personal life, he might not notice. If this one worked, she'd sneak one in about his life in Boston.

When he came to stand beside where she busied herself drying the lid to her bowl, she became a picture of innocence.

He turned and with one hand on the edge of the sink, he leaned in toward her almost as if he'd kiss her. His light brown eyes with golden flecks stared clearly into hers.

He leaned in closer and Addy sucked in a breath.

"I know what you're doing and I'm going to ask you nicely to stop. Once."

Then he straightened and strode away to the fire and sat on the sofa near where his phone and computer rested on the wooden coffee table.

He's not who you think he is? The voice in her head insisted.

ZACH'S GRANDFATHER HAD told him his good nature would get him into trouble one day. And that day had come, in spades, four weeks ago, and now it just seemed to keep coming in the form of a reporter he wanted to toss out on her ear. He would, too, when it was safe, or at least he'd drop her off at the dry-goods store that doubled for a bus station.

His phone no longer had a signal, so he opened his tablet to check for communication from Morrison and Morrison.

The Wi-Fi wouldn't connect either.

When he left Boston, he had planned on hunkering down to think. Hadn't planned on Adriana Bonacorda. Admirable in her willingness to persist.

A flicker in the shadows told him the uninvited guest was loitering nearby.

He powered down his computer and slid it into his briefcase.

"I'm sorry to intrude," she said as she tried to push her bushel of blond curls behind her ear. "I wanted to see if you were willing to sit down and speak with me some more."

He pressed back against the cushion and studied her. She wore slim black jeans that were showing their age and a pale pink tank top under a faded black one. The tail of her sweater didn't bother to come to her waist, but the rolled collar hugged the back of her neck in a sensuous manner and dropped to her midriff, accentuating her full breasts. She wore a sloppy old pair of wool socks on her feet as her once red moccasins now sat in the breezeway most likely curling up toe to heel as the leather dried and contracted.

The way her hair frizzed out around her head in a halo of blond almost made him smile. With her wide-set deep blue eyes and her generous mouth she carried the look off well. Her small chin jutted perfectly at the end of sharp jawbones and the color on her high pink cheekbones evened out the proportions of her features. Gave them a kind of perfection.

She looked to be in her late twenties, about a hundred and twenty pounds, and she might be a natural blonde, rare, but not unheard of.

"I won't talk about anything south of the Maine border."

The lines of her mouth tightened, but she dipped her chin once and invited herself to sit on the sofa with him but nearer the fire.

"What kinds of things do you do when you're here in Bailey's Cove?" she said, asking, he thought, as open a question as possible.

He could list a few, but nothing she could use to build a story against him. He wondered when this reporter had last been interested in the truth.

The wind whistled and roared as he sat and tried to decide what to tell her, how best to lead her away from anything involving Hale and Blankenstock.

"This is a quiet town, struggling," he said softly.

"I'm afraid I didn't get to see much of Bailey's Cove."

He imagined her clinging to the wheel of her car, trying not to panic beyond the ability to function. Blue eyes glued to the centerline. Butt nearly lifted from the seat in anticipation. He wondered just how crazy she was.

Locking her in a closet might be best for both of them.

She lifted one eyebrow at him. "I was too busy chasing you."

He relaxed into press mode. She wanted to play casual, to get inside his armor with lightness and charm. Good for her. She wouldn't be any good at her job if she didn't pull out all her weapons.

She would find his armor had hardened recently. He was ready for whatever she had.

Liam Bailey. He'd throw her the pirate. Nothing she couldn't get at the local museum, hell she'd get a well-embellished version at the local bar.

"Over two hundred years ago, a privateer landed out there in the harbor. Ol' Liam liked what he saw and returned several times to seek shelter from the storms and from those who would hang him for his deeds, or so the story goes."

"He was a scoundrel?"

Did the lift of both her eyebrows mean "like you"?

"Many sea captains were." He gave her deadpan in answer. "Bailey established a settlement here with men from his ship and a few women they had enticed north from the Boston area."

"That must have been interesting." The overly friendly smile on her face softened to something less predatory.

"He called the settlement South Harbor."

The new softness in her expression made her eyes glow, her face beautiful.

Another branch clattered against the side of the garage.

"Oh," Addy cried and her hand flew to her throat as the wind howled and shrieked. "Sorry, South Harbor? Wait, if Bailey was a privateer, he was a pirate. I suppose people come here all the time looking for buried loot."

Everyone went to pirate eventually. She went quicker than most. "They did in the early, middle and late 1800s, several times in the 1900s, and even in this century, but no one was ever sure there was any looted treasure to be found. He never flaunted his take. Explained that his money for building the settlement came from personal wealth and spending long years on the high seas collecting a captain's salary."

"He called the town South Harbor?"

"Most likely after the village where he grew up. He fled Ireland to get away from what he considered English tyranny. The speculation is, he dropped the *u* from *Harbour* as a sign he was finished with the empire."

"Is the story about his illegitimate son fact or fabrication?"

"Fact, based on DNA. Are you questioning the heritage of the child or asking if he kept the treasure hidden from his lover?" He knew she was asking the questions because she was a reporter, but he admired the interest with which she asked them. This conversation had content that didn't have to do with business of some sort. Something he rarely got these days.

"The latter, I guess. What do you believe?"

He believed that under different circumstances the two of them might have friendly conversations and that he might like them— a lot. "I believe there is treasure buried right here, beneath our feet."

For a moment of incredulity she looked down, as if perhaps she could see the gold or feel it beneath her toes. Then she gazed sharply up to where he sat. "Liar." Her chin flicked up without apology.

He smiled. He'd forgotten how much fun it was to be entertained by meaningful conversation— conversation that wasn't designed to secure an investment or to divert unwanted attention. "Most of the town has been dug up at one time or another by treasure hunters."

"You are a master of diversion."

And she could read him. He had to give her that one, though. Diverting was his specialty. Channeling the river of investors toward Hale and Blankenstock was the magic he performed on a daily basis. He never suspected, and that might make him a half-wit, that Carla Blankenstock was doing her own diverting.

Adriana Bonacorda hurried on to offer. "Um, so do you think we should get a pair of jackhammers and start digging up the garage floor? Or should we go over to the house and dig there?"

"Please leave the house alone, but you're welcome to dig up the garage as long as you don't harm the three centuries of transportation used by myself and my ancestors."

"That old car made it up the hill to this house? How?"

"Backwards."

She sat forward in excited anticipation, her interest real. "Expound, please."

He couldn't help but smile again. "The car is a Model T. The gasoline tank is under the front seat of this model and feeds by gravity to the engine."

"So to keep the gas flowing you have to turn it around and back it up hills?"

"To keep the gas going to the engine, and in reverse the car is more powerful."

"Sounds like a design flaw." Her lips pursed. They looked soft and inviting.

"Innovative and cheap. That made it possible for the cars to be commercially manufactured and available to the working class across the nation."

Consternation crossed her features for a moment. "What was it like not to have the infrastructure—"

A distant crack and then a bang reverberated through the space of the loft.

He knew in an instant what the sickening sound was.

CHAPTER FIVE

"STAY HERE." HALE'S sharp command and the adamant flip of his hand pressed Addy into the couch's firm cushions as he raced toward the door. He paused long enough to slip on a pair of ratty deck shoes and soon the door slammed and he was gone.

He did not leave silence behind.

The storm gnashed and gnarled as though it might be bringing the end of the world. The flickering flames of the fire seemed to grow dimmer and the raging outside louder.

Addy leaped to her feet to chase after Hale, but stopped so short she had to catch herself to keep from pitching forward onto her nose. She returned to the coffee table and stared down at the abandoned tablet peeking out of the briefcase and mobile phone. Were they password protected? Could she guess the password?

She shoved her hands in her pockets.

How low had she slipped? She dropped to the couch and reached for the tablet and stopped. She felt like pond scum.

Whatever Hale was facing out there, maybe he needed help and like it or not, she was all he had right now.

Wherever he'd raced off to, perhaps there was a story there.

"Hurricane Harries Hale" or "Harold Blasts Billionaire."

She huffed out a breath. Pond scum was way too good for her. Maybe this man had a high slime factor, but she hadn't seen it here in Bailey's Cove. What if her sister was wrong? What if she needed to reserve judgment until she knew for sure? She had failed to pick up on the signs, failed to recognize that smart, instinctive voice inside her head last time. She had to know for sure. But she also needed to keep her opinions out of the facts and her dirty-rat detector on high.

She raced after him. In the breezeway she stopped and pressed her face against the cross-taped windowpane. A lightbulb high on a pole outside flickered wildly in the wind. The strobe effect gave off enough light to see some of the front yard and Hale wasn't there.

The window in the opposite direction showed an outbuilding with a light in front and no Hale in sight.

She called his name into the house and got

no response, only the incessant screaming of the wind.

If he had gone outside he was, above all else, crazy. For a moment she considered her squishy red mocs and then slipped off her bulky wool socks and slid on the wet shoes.

From the line of hooks across the wall of the breezeway, she nabbed a jacket that, though several sizes too large, looked waterproof. Then leaning with all her weight, she struggled to open the door to the outside. The wind caught hold of the door though and slammed it shut on her as if she wasn't there at all.

Relenting, she backed away. She had to find him and not because her story about him would be enhanced, but because she had already grown fond of the old place with all its history. She might not be a Mainer, but she had grown up in a town steeped in the importance of remembering from whence one came. And like the man or not, this house represented the history of early Maine and should not be abandoned to a storm.

Shedding her dripping coat, she rushed into the house. In the empty kitchen, she grabbed flashlights from the basket on the table and ran. The parlor was deserted and the dampened sound of the storm didn't help her figure out where he had gone.

"Zach," she hollered. "Zach."

Was he upstairs?

Addy rushed up the steps, following the harshness of the wind until she came to the room with the four-poster bed.

A pile of things sat outside the door. A blue tarp, some short pieces of lumber and a small ladder, the kind that formed an A when opened up. Zach must have put them there.

As she stepped in, she stood paralyzed by the horror of what she saw in the flashlights' beams. A hole in the wall extended nearly to the floor and reached up the ten feet or so through the ceiling into the attic above. Plaster, shingles and splintered wood were scattered across the room.

The force of the tree crashing into the room had shattered a beam. One end had dropped, pinning the braided rug on the other side of the bed to the floor.

The pretty flowered ewer and bowl lay in pieces on the rug on this side of the bed. The walnut washstand with the granite top upon which the pitcher and bowl had sat had been knocked over and was getting drenched. The photograph of Millie must be somewhere in the mess.

And she was alone in the room, alone with a storm.

After another moment, her feet became un-glued and she hurried to place the flashlights where their beams would shine best on what she needed to see, and then she flew to the four-poster bed being splattered with damaging rain. She tugged and shoved for only a couple moments before she had to give up. She'd never be able to move the heavy bed out of the direct path of the storm.

She grabbed her stuff and tossed it in a pile in the dry, undamaged hallway. Then she did the same with the bedding that included an antique quilt and feather pillows. She tugged the cotton mattress and had to settle for folding it in half and dragging it away from the rain as well as she could.

The paintings that had lined the walls had been flung about the room. One of the frames had been shattered, but she added the portraits to the collection in the relative safety of the hallway. Next she rolled up one of the braided rugs. With her back to the wind, her back-side faced the opening in the wall and the gale obligingly drenched it.

She sat back on her heels. *Where could Hale be?* Maybe he wasn't out there going through anything. Maybe he had abandoned the idea of saving the house and had dived into a "safe room" where he was all snug and secure.

Maybe he hefted the garage door open and fled in his big SUV without her. Would he? Could he? No. He was still here somewhere.

Rain ran down her neck and back, drenching her. Whatever Hale was doing, it didn't make these pieces of history any less valuable.

She finished rolling the rug and tugged it into the hallway.

On her knees she had seen Millie's photograph under the bed, so she dropped down where she could reach it, pulled it out and smiled. The graceful woman's face was unharmed. She put the black-and-white portrait safely aside with the rest.

When she finished with the smaller pieces of history, she turned to the beautiful old walnut washstand. The granite top, from what she could see, had somehow survived the fall and would not be harmed by the rain, but the walnut, if left in the onslaught, would absorb enough water to warp and ruin it.

She struggled to lift the stand. Her mocs slipped on the wet floor and after a few feet, she started to lose her grip on the slippery granite top. Stopping, she reset her hold and strained to keep the commode's historic top from ending up on the floor once again. If the gorgeous gray granite fractured it might never be able to be repaired.

Soon the rain in her face and the ache in her back made it seem as if an eternity had passed—and the piece began to slip again. She was losing the battle.

A hand appeared beside hers and then another.

"It weighs about ninety pounds," Zach said, close to her ear. An unbidden shiver of another kind raced over her and she concentrated on the task at hand.

"Thanks for helping," he continued.

The sound of his voice warmed her and a few moments later, Millie's washstand stood in the hallway, dripping and safe.

"Seriously." He softly encircled her arm with his hand. "Thank you for your help."

He let go of her and lugged a chain saw and a battery powered lamp into the room.

She followed Zachary Hale, the man she had thought she knew so much about, but had known almost nothing. There was no story here today unless it was about a man saving some of Maine's history.

"I need to unload some of the weight and some of the control the wind has on the tree," he shouted.

She nodded, grabbed the battery-powered lantern from him, and he pulled the cord on the chain saw.

As he cut away the branches, the saw hardly made noise above the storm, and when the limbs fell, Addy hauled them away so he wouldn't trip and fall. When he finally turned the saw off, he hadn't finished. The tree still lay against the house.

Addy pitched more branches out through the hole. "Are you going to cut through the trunk?" she shouted to be heard.

"If I do that…"

The rest was swept away by the wind.

"What?"

He put his mouth close to her ear. "If I do that the heaviest part of the tree might crash into the side of the house, causing more damage." His lips brushed her ear ever so slightly and an urge rushed through her to turn so his lips could brush against hers.

She nodded instead. She had no idea if what she was nodding to made sense or not. That part of her brain didn't work right now.

Pressing her head to the side of his so he could hear her she asked, "What do we do now?" His wet face warmed her cheek and she moved away instantly.

In the light of the lantern there was only the earnestness of sentiment on his face. This was not a rat. There was humility in the look

Hale the swindler would never have been able to conjure.

"I have to do what I can," he said and pointed upward. "I have to go into the attic to remove branches and then put the tarp in place."

She nodded again instead of moving in to answer. Whatever he needed to do, she was going to help him.

In the pile of things with the large blue tarp and the short pieces of lumber was a box of nails and a pair of hammers. He must have hoped she'd give him a hand.

She grabbed the lantern and an armload of supplies, happy she had risen above pond scum, and followed him to the attic stairway.

"How are we going to do this? Won't the wind just blow the tarp away?" she asked as she held up the lantern so he could see up the steps.

"I'm going to fasten the tarp inside the attic and the second floor with these short pieces of lumber. The lumber will help keep the tarp from tearing. I'll—"

"We will." She interrupted him.

He glanced down at her, the harsh light illuminating something inside herself she had not thought was possible, the thought that Zachary Hale was someone she might like to get to know on a personal level.

He continued upward, breaking the spell or whatever it was. "We'll put the tarp over the tree trunk for strength and reinforce it with ropes. I have no idea how well this will work, but I have to stop as much of the rain as possible from coming into the house."

When they reached the top of the steps, the light Addy carried showed them that Zach had more chain-saw work to do, as the top of the tree was not visible. The hole in the roof was many feet in diameter and rose five to six feet from the level of the attic floor.

There was less water up here, but a hole in the floor gaped several feet wide. She took the nails from him and they put the supplies they carried in a dry area.

If she got what he was going to do, he would have to lean across the gape in the floor and onto the tree to reach the branches that had to be cut away. The tarp, attached to the inside of the attic, would fan out and collect rainwater and send it to the ground.

Zach started out but she took hold of his sleeve. "Shouldn't we reinforce the floor before you go out there?" she nearly screamed to be heard above the noise.

"It'll take too much time," he shouted.

"Be careful." She looked into his eyes and

saw the same worry that was making her head hurt in places it never hurt before.

He nodded.

Chain saw in hand, he approached the tree, testing the two-hundred-year-old floor as he went. The wind whipped at his clothing and the rain drenched him. When he was still several feet away, the floor with its damaged supports dropped several inches and creaked loudly over the storm.

Addy clenched her fist as if she could keep him safe by holding on hard.

He backed slowly away and approached from the side closer to the roof, but farther from the branches he had to cut away. As he drew nearer the old boards dipped a bit but held him.

Addy found herself biting her lip when he tested the tree for stability.

She cared what happened, not just to his ancestral home but to him. She cared what happened to Zachary Hale.

Alarms should be blaring. Emotional attachment was what got her into deep trouble in the past. She'd better nip this one. She was only reacting to the man she wanted Hale to be, she reasoned. She knew what he was. She knew he could seduce the money out of hundreds of people, maybe thousands.

He could seduce her into walking away without a story.

The chain saw buzzed. A branch dropped and she caught it. He motioned her away, but she gestured back that she was all right and they repeated the process until the branches were stripped.

He pushed back from the tree, pulled her away from the hole and stopped, standing close enough for her to hear him when he shouted against the wind, "I'm going to attach the tarp to the roof, bring it across the tree and secure it to the roof on the other side."

She listened carefully visualizing the process.

"I'm going to need your help to get the tarp across the tree trunk or it will most likely get away and there will be no saving this part of the house."

She nodded and he continued. "It could be dangerous. I don't want you hurt."

She nodded again and he took her arm and pulled her closer to the warmth of his body and she leaned in, seeking more.

"If you feel you are in any danger at all, I want you to let go of the tarp. No matter what else happens, let go of the tarp." He shifted to try to see her face.

"No matter what. Like if you fall?" She turned her face up to his.

He stared into her eyes. Moisture dropping from his hair into his whiskers. The wind buffeting the two of them. "No matter what happens to me."

"I'll do what I need to do."

He must have accepted that because he picked up the heavy tarp.

"When I reach out—" He gestured with one hand. "I need you to hand me one of those boards and a handful of nails."

"Board and nails," she shouted. "Okay."

He fastened one side of the tarp, keeping it furled and away from the hole so the wind wouldn't catch it. Each time he held out a hand she filled it with a small piece of lumber and three nails.

Each time he got too close to the gaping hole in the floor, each time his foot slipped and he could have plunged a dozen feet to the floor below, Addy's stomach knotted tighter.

When he had the tarp attached across the hole and to the tree, he tossed the edge of the tarp to her. She caught it without falling into the hole or sailing outside. Easy. Though the tarp fought violently against them, they finished the upper end, anchoring ropes to keep the wind from just blowing the whole thing inward.

He smiled his thanks and she wanted to touch him. His shoulders would be hard and his arms firm. If she put her hands on his back and smoothed them around to his belly she was sure all would ripple under her fingertips. Ridge by ridge, she'd like to explore.

Truly, she hoped he didn't read minds.

When they got down to the second floor, the tarp had blown outside and beat against the tree and the house.

"Are you ready for this?"

She almost laughed. "I am so ready." And she wondered if she had any idea what she was ready for.

Zach leaned out the hole in the wall and reached for the tarp. After five minutes of struggling and almost losing his balance, she wanted to tell him this was not worth it. He was worth more than a house, no matter how old it was.

She had a good hold on his jacket when he got control and gathered the tarp inside. He turned and when the struggling tarp nearly tossed her to the side, he gathered her close to him so he held both the struggling tarp and her.

"I'm going to put the tarp over the tree and hand it to you. I need you to just hold on."

She put her hands on his chest and steadied herself.

"It sounds so easy." What they had done upstairs was not easy. Having him press her body to his was definitely not. This was Zachary Hale, the big-shot billionaire and he was holding her intimately.

He was also holding the tarp intimately, she reminded herself. As if listening to her thoughts, the tarp thrashed more.

"I don't need you to do anything else. Just catch it and hold on. If it gets away from you, leave it." He squeezed her closer, asking if she understood.

She agreed.

He reached a handful of tarp over the tree; she grabbed and smiled. Easy again.

When the rest of the tarp flipped over the tree and she grabbed for it.

She didn't even realize her feet had left the floor until suddenly, she was being thrown toward the hole and before she could do anything more than scream, she was dangling a good thirty feet from the ground. Scared out of her mind, she hung on.

The meager light from the lantern coming out the hole and the edge of the wet tarp she was clinging to were all she had to cling to.

All right, you helpless thing, she thought.

Move your butt. She struggled to lift her feet to climb toward the hole. Pressure on the tarp from above made Addy realize Zach had a grip from above. He pulled the tarp upward, dangling woman and all. When she was close enough, she whipped her feet through the hole and reached out a hand. He hauled her inside.

"Go back to the loft," he shouted at her.

She laughed at the idea and that only seemed to make him angry. "I just got the hang of it, pun intended, of clinging to a tarp and you want me to go sit somewhere safe," she shouted back at him. "I don't think so."

She seized one edge of the tarp, held it firmly, slipped the grommet over the nail head and bent the nail for security. Then she hammered the board into place over the edge of the tarp.

Soon they were both securing the tarp in place. After wrestling and hammering for another half hour, they added rope to give support to the tarp or the hurricane winds would have ripped it to shreds. It still might happen.

When they were finished, she came over to where he was examining their handiwork.

"WHO ARE YOU?"

Zach heard her question, but raised his hammer and bent one of the nails, anchoring the rope to the wooden beam.

She was a reporter.

Anything he said could end up on the internet, in print and on television.

He looked into her face. The angle of her head, the lines of her mouth, even the slant of her eyebrows said she was asking because she wanted to know, not that she wanted to broadcast the information to the world.

No one had ever asked him that question, not his classmates, his coworkers, the women he dated. No one wanted the answer to that question.

She stepped in close, too close to ignore her. She was not the woman he assumed she was. Not just the reporter. Not selfish. Giving. Fearless. Someone he might want to get to know. Her eyes wide, she watched him close the distance between them. When she turned her face upward, he lowered his mouth to hers and fire erupted inside him. Her lips were soft and her mouth eager as she returned his kiss. Bringing her body against his, their wet clothing warmed instantly with their heat making it feel as if they were naked.

She pressed her mouth harder to his and when her tongue met his...

With both palms against his chest, she pushed away from him. Sweeping her hand over her mouth.

CHAPTER SIX

ALONE IN THE LOFT, Adriana dropped the third load of wood into the bin, which now sat filled and brimming over. The fire crackled smartly and her whole body ached from the exertion of the last few hours.

The tarp had been as snug as possible, and reinforced, but there had been much more to do. Everything that could be removed by two exhausted people was taken from the four-poster bedroom. They had carefully draped the antique quilt over the kitchen chairs.

They had then cleared the other rooms on the windward side of the house. Polite, helpful to each other, speaking when necessary. Ignoring the kiss and what it might mean.

Firewood debris clung to the front of the work shirt she had borrowed, desperate to keep her last tank top dry. She brushed the debris into the glowing ash bed of the fireplace and watched as the bits of wood made tiny flames that died quickly away.

Addy wasn't sure what to make of Zachary

Hale or even what to make of herself. The kiss they had shared had been incendiary and she knew if she didn't stop it, there would have been more between them.

She had been in that situation more than once. A harrowing event occurred. A man and a woman high on adrenaline do what came naturally in such a moment. The sex would be great and the letdown equally as great. There would then be no story to tell because the act would stand between them. Out the window would go her credibility and objectivity.

After another moment, she nabbed her computer from the coffee table and lowered herself into the stuffed chair nearest the fire, resisting putting her feet on the puffy rectangular ottoman. She didn't want to seem too familiar or get too comfortable.

Zachary Hale clearly cared about something other than himself. He cared for his family's history and the history of Bailey's Cove. The items in the house and the house itself were only priceless because they were heirlooms handed down by his ancestors and not because they would bring a tidy profit. Their value would, of course, create a substantial boon to her meager budget but wouldn't make a ripple in his.

When he had pulled her back inside the hole

in the bedroom wall, she had wanted to take him right there on the floor. He had saved her. He could have had anything he wanted and she would have gladly given it, even—she cringed—the story. If everyone had a price, it seemed being saved from death was hers.

She rubbed her face in her hands. She was getting soft. She was glad she had pushed him away—sort of.

Staring into the blazing fire and tapping her fingertips on the top of her closed computer, she tried not to think that a smart reporter would be putting some of her thoughts into recorded notes.

She blinked. Smart would be a good thing.

After several attempts at typing and retyping, she closed the computer. Smart or not, this reporter needed to remind herself of how much she hated Zachary Hale.

Hate was never an emotion she was comfortable with, but when Savanna had spoken of what Hale had done to her, Addy couldn't control that particular dark monster.

Now she was not so sure how she felt.

Hale had been real, honest, even admirable since she tracked him down in Bailey's Cove.

And then there was the warm, firm feel of his lips against hers, the way her body responded instantly. That didn't seem particularly hateful.

She threw her head back against the cushion. She had been kissing the man she had known as her enemy, an enemy of the people at large, of her sister.

The rising tide she almost hadn't been able to control in her body when he kissed her flooded back into her mind and the feelings rushed through her.

She wanted the Zachary Hale she had met in Maine.

Think of pink elephants, she told herself harshly.

Think of how cute Savanna's girls are.

Think of what else might need to be done in the old mansion...

With Zachary Hale...

And when they kissed, she wanted him to put his hands on her to fan the flame he had ignited.

No. No. No.

In the beginning, when Savanna had first come to her, she had kept an open mind about Zachary Hale, at least about his being solely responsible for the wrongdoing at Hale and Blankenstock. Her sister had been both horrified and embarrassed that she had invested so much in one place and that she had trusted so blindly. Addy knew she had to do something.

Her sister's woe had been her own incentive to stop dithering at the bottom of the reporting food chain. She had marched into her old editor's office at the *Times* and told him what she planned to do.

He was less than enthusiastic, especially since she had refused to disclose her source, but since she was writing the story on spec and paying her own way, he had nothing to lose by promising her a big payoff if she tried and succeeded. Try she had, even before the scandal sheets broke the speculation nationwide a couple weeks ago.

She realized her fingertips were hammering on the top of her computer again and stopped and pressed them to her lips.

Who had been seducing whom was a mystery never to be solved. The emotion she felt at the time had been real, as real as any kiss could be, but there was no way the rational part of her would have kissed him and wanted more.

She pushed her palms down the front of her jeans and put her feet up on the ottoman. Zach had rebuffed her offer to help wash the dirt from some of the items they had rescued and she had no real option but to retreat with her things to the loft as there was nowhere else to stay.

The rooms on the sheltered side of the old home were clearly not equipped to accommodate guests, but maintained in meticulous detailed historic splendor or sparseness, depending on the era the room represented.

Her sister's money.

Savanna's story had made Addy sit up and recognize the time for self-pity and indignation was over. It didn't matter that she had been lied to. All she had lost was a great job and her great lifestyle—the point being "her lifestyle." Savanna had lost her home, her retirement money and her children's college funds as well as her once great job.

And Addy had kissed the man responsible, for heaven's sake, and would have given and taken anything in the moment. She got up and paced the length of the loft until she came to the king-size bed on the far side. The bed was covered with a dark duvet and had matching throw pillows that had been lined up against the headboard. It looked more like a show room than a bachelor's bed.

Of course, there was a woman involved. Sexist, but she thought he might not make up a bed so fussily. A cleaning woman perhaps.

Or another woman...

Standing at a side window watching the rain run in sheets down the glass, she felt her body begin to hum. His arms had tightened around her, and she had responded immediately. Need flooded through her. Zachary Hale had awoken something in her she did not know existed.

A storm of another kind.

How had she gotten so needy all of a sudden? Losing Wesley hadn't been a great loss because the two of them never truly clicked. There hadn't been a man in her life whose loss had been more than a casual disruption. Not even her father, wherever on Earth he was.

Grumpy and hungry, she found a tiny bathroom and then a bag of apples. She ate two and her stomach stopped howling.

Exhaustion suddenly tugged at her and she sagged down on the couch, put her head on the soft arm and closed her eyes.

WHEN SHE AWOKE there was an eerie light coming in the windows. Addy tossed back the quilt covering her, sat up and looked around. Sometime while she slept Zach had covered her and then, hours later, morning had broken in a dull gray. The storm raged on, but it seemed less than it had in the darkness.

A coffeepot hung on a swing arm in front of flames in the fireplace. The duvet had been flung aside and the sheet and blanket the bed lay crumpled. The loft was empty except for her.

She carried a cup of coffee into the tiny bathroom. The shower stall looked sparse but inviting. Zach had told her there was an emergency water supply for the bathroom but only cold unless someone heated water and refilled the shower's reservoir, whatever that entailed. She settled for washing her face and brushing her teeth with water from the plastic jug he had placed on the sink, she supposed for just such a thing.

Her fleece warm-up suit was dry so she put it back on. When she was finished, she poured herself another cup of coffee and retrieved the bed linens from the breezeway. She folded the sheets and pillowcases, smoothing them as flat as she could on the dining-room table, the only surface big enough to press the old-fashioned cotton into submission. Then she poured herself another cup of the surprisingly good coffee and retired to the couch with her notebook. She tried going online, but even before her laptop powered up, she'd known the internet would be useless.

She was truly cut off from the world with only Zachary Hale as a companion and she wasn't sure whether that was good or bad. Whether it was a story or a disaster.

To warm up, she sketched in words, the sounds, smells and sights.

Then she began to describe the man.

Zachary Hale is a surprise and a mystery. The smooth operator, the socially adept, the impeccably kempt man who interacted with the world, who swindled (she scratched that out) *who allegedly swindled several billion dollars, had another face. Where in Boston he ruled any room he entered with his beautiful presence and authoritative stance, in Maine he ruled because people trusted and liked him.*

She stretched her legs out and rested her feet on the puffy ottoman. For a moment she struggled with the feeling she had last night about being too familiar in Zachary Hale's hideout. Today she barely tussled with calm acceptance.

Relaxing, she settled back.

An occasional wisp of smoke filtered into the shadowy room as the unrelenting wind outside wailed.

She was Adriana Bonacorda and she could handle anything tossed, hurled or blown in her direction. She smiled smugly. She was even beginning to handle the consequences of the Afghanistan affair.

It had taken her long enough. The humiliation had paralyzed her and the disappointment had her doubting she was ever any good.

Her fingers flew across the keyboard producing line after line of shame and regret that had accumulated in her brain around the incident. How physically sick she was when the world called her a liar. How she would have preferred them to think she was just a fool, an honest, stupid fool.

That's what she was. Honest and maybe a fool, if wanting to help people made one a fool. But not stupid. She was not stupid.

The door to the loft opened and Zach entered carrying yet another armload of wood and a bundle of something. He looked so good in his blue jeans and flannel, she almost forgot business suits were his norm.

His gaze swept the room and stopped on her, lingering, assessing.

A flush of heat stained her cheeks and made her recoil at the feeling of desire as it washed through her.

His face, she could see as he approached, was as stormy as the hurricane going on outside. He dropped the wood onto the flagstone floor beside the bin, put two logs on the fire and then walked over to where she sat and stood at the foot of the ottoman. His storminess had abated. Replaced by a calm she knew to be practiced and slightly dishonest. She almost smiled at the knowledge. She was getting to know him.

Feeling no fear, she looked up at him. The smooth, clean planes of his face contrasted with messy hair and the plaid flannel of his shirt. No one had a right to be that good-looking without an airbrush.

Wait! Smooth planes. He had shaved.

Zach took the handful of clothing he had brought in with him and dropped it on the broad arm of the chair and tossed a length of rope on top of the pile.

"I could use your help repairing the tarp and rescuing a few of the heavy things."

She looked at the clothes and then at him. The family mansion and its treasures came first. "Of course. I'll just be a minute."

She grabbed the clothing and stood. He didn't back away as she thought he would. Across the short thirty inches of the ottoman, she was close enough to see the hue of his light brown eyes, the small golden lashes tucked among the long, dark ones, the fine crinkles of chronic concern at the corners of his mouth.

Instead of leaning across and kissing away the lines, as was her first impulse, she spun and headed for the small bathroom to change into the work clothing.

The kissing stuff could not happen again. She put the warm flannel shirt on and it hung to the middle of her thighs. She knotted it at the waist and when she slid the jeans on, she laughed. There was no doubt what the rope was for. The jeans were several sizes larger than her waist. She tied the rope around the baggy jeans, slid on a pair of just-right-sized old sneaks and headed back out.

The mirror in the bathroom had shown her how dreadful she looked and all she could feel was relief. It did not matter what she looked like to Zachary Hale. It did not matter at all.

He led the way and she grabbed one of the baseball caps from the wooden pegs beside the door as they exited. Tucking her hair behind her ears, she tugged the cap down and hoped it didn't spring off from the force of her hair.

Baseball cap was without a doubt her worst look. That should discourage any desire he might have to kiss her again.

As they passed through the kitchen, she flipped the quilt still draped over the old red-and-white enameled tabletop and one on the chairs to allow it to dry faster.

Hurrying after his fading footsteps, she joined him in the attic.

"Oh, no." She rushed over to the edge that had ripped lose and that he had tried to repair by himself. The wind made the tarp edge flap dangerously.

"I'm afraid if I pull too hard, I'll rip the side grommet out. I need you to push against the tarp while I try to string the ropes for a better network to hold the whole thing in place."

"Got it." She stepped in and prepared to brace the tarp.

"Be careful." He hunkered down at the corner of the hole in the wall.

"Yeah, I'm not falling again. I didn't care much for it the first time."

He looked up at her and gave her a bit of a smile and turned away. How, she wondered, on Earth was this man Zachary Hale? There was no humility in that man with the business suit. There was no conceit in this man with the lumberjack shirt. He was willing to do what had to be done.

Zach had almost won the battle when a blast ripped at the edge of the tarp and he lost hold of the rope. The loose tarp slapped against her and the end of the rope struck her on the cheek. Surprised, she stepped back and her foot dropped as the edge of the damaged floorboard sank under her weight.

"Addy." Zach leaped to his feet and grabbed for her, but she scrambled to safety on her own and snatched the flapping tarp from the air.

When she held out the rope end to him, he paused for a moment and touched her face where the knotted loop had smacked her, then he let his fingers trail downward to her jaw line.

She blinked as if struck again, but this time by the flash of wild desire that spun through her and he stepped away.

Taking the rope he hunkered down to settle it around the new anchor he had screwed into place. This time everything worked as planned and they moved on to the four-poster bedroom to finish anchoring the lower end of the tarp.

"Wait a minute." He gently took hold of her arm. She spun slowly and looked up into his face. Concern spread out across his features and puzzled her.

When he produced a flashlight from his pocket and shined it on her cheek she realized what he wanted.

"I'm fine." Her cheek stung, but there was nothing to be done for it right now.

"There will still be ice in the freezer. You should go get some."

He held her arm and she could read the burn inside him.

She froze, lest she throw herself into the arms of the enemy. Maybe he was a fine citizen of Bailey's Cove. Maybe he was a fine keeper of the family trust, but he was the enemy of the people rich and poor who had been swindled by him.

The swindler and the man were so at opposite ends of the spectrum in her mind by now, she had trouble convincing herself of anything with regard to him. What did she know was that in Afghanistan she had fallen for the tearful face of a young mother, and she had been "swindled" out of the truth and out of her life as a respected news reporter.

She was a sucker then and she might be one now. She pulled away, but she wasn't selfish. "You said there was more to do over here. I'll help. There'll be plenty of time for ice later."

"If you could help me with the bed." He nodded toward the four-poster bed, which had gotten wet again in spite of being on the other side of the room. "I need to take it apart to get it out of this room but the mattress should go first."

If a raging bull of a man was all that was necessary to get these things moved, Hale would have done the work alone. He was big enough and strong enough but the antiques needed finesse and some of the things required two people.

The soggy mattress, for instance.

As they struggled down the steps, she watched him for signs of a cracking facade.

Perhaps if she watched closely enough the Zachary Hale she thought she knew in the bigger world would get tired of being hidden behind the wall of humble and begin to show himself. Perhaps in impatience, he might even give up and retreat to the relative luxury of the warm fire. The insurance company would no doubt remediate all of this and put it back to as normal as possible.

All she saw was a guy working hard to save what his family had collected over the centuries. A man whose every move was beginning to fascinate her and make her uneasy at the same time. When they returned to the four-poster room, they surveyed the bed for the best angle of attack.

Dark wood, square legs and thick, spiraled posts.

"Um, this bed is, um…ugly."

"It's pirate's booty." His eyes seemed lit by more than the light of the dull day and the sparkle of the lantern.

"Pirates stole beds?"

"This one did. The bed was reportedly part of a shipment being sent to the new world that was lost at sea."

"How does anyone know?"

"The bed was handcrafted in the late 1800s. Right up at the edge of the wooden canopy, where there is not supposed to be a mark, is the symbol of one of the workers. He apparently left his mark whenever he could get away with it." When she craned to see, he put a hand on her shoulder and leaned in to point out the mark.

He should not touch her. He didn't know what he was doing could cause her to make a fool of herself.

She nodded mutely and he continued. "A bed like this one was on the manifest of a ship that disappeared at sea. Then a bed like this showed up here in the early 1800s, less than a year after it was supposed to have disappeared forever in the briny depths."

He dropped his hand and she cleared her throat. "Romance, intrigue, pirates, but it's still…"

"The ugliest bed you've seen this side of the ocean?"

"No, it's… Well, it's…"

His laughter rumbled.

"Historical," he said as he reached around to tug down on the brim of her baseball cap.

"Yes. That's the word I was looking for. Historical."

"If you'd help me get this historical thing apart, we can put it where it won't be harmed anymore."

They removed the overhead wooden canopy first and then took apart the posters and footboard. The sideboards and headboard were next. Luckily the old bed came apart mostly in pieces she could heft.

With a bit of a struggle, they carried the last and heaviest piece, the headboard down the stairway to the now crowded dining room.

"What next?" Addy asked, knowing what she wanted and wondered if he felt at least an inkling of what she did or if she had imagined it all.

"We might be able to move that chunk of beam and get the other braided rug out from underneath." He looked over where she was arranging some of the dark velvet curtains from the four-poster bed. "So what do you think? Are you feeling strong?"

She held up her arms and flexed her biceps.

"Impressive," he said even though she knew he could not tell muscle from shirtsleeve in the overlarge work clothes she wore. "Thank you, Addy, for your help."

It seemed like the right thing to do whether she got story material from it or not.

"You're welcome. I can almost tell some of the family stories just by handling the things. The bed, for instance. There have to be many stories, big stories, involving a bed that a pirate stole." He studied her and she added, "I wasn't speaking news stories, but tales that should be told nonetheless."

"Too many secrets."

She gave a wolfish laugh. "All the better, my dear. I would guess the braided rug is made from articles of clothing collected from the family over the years."

"By a woman called Ma Kimball. Apparently nothing went to waste during her reign."

"Most lore is based on fact. So, okay. I'll buy that." She tugged up the pants and tightened the rope at her waist. "Should we go rescue Ma Kimball's handiwork?"

Since the tree had already done the structural damage, other than the weight of the beam, there would be no danger from moving it.

"I'll lift. You get the rug," she said looking earnestly in Zach's direction.

He studied the size of the beam and the size of her and laughed. "In this case, I'm going to judge you by your size and get the beam."

When he moved it up and over, she tugged the rug free.

"Heavier than it looks when it's full of water," she said as she rolled it up like a jelly roll. "Should we carry it downstairs?"

"We've used all the extra tarps." He picked

it up and hoisted it over his shoulder. "I've got it. No point in both of us getting wet."

He exited with the rug and she went over to investigate the damage the beam had caused to the floor. It didn't seem too bad. Two of the floorboards had been caved in and all the ends turned up far enough to make the nails pull free.

Early in her career when reporting didn't make her any money she had worked at a small manufacturing plant that had been a converted shoe factory. The vacuum was always clattering with heel tacks that were wedged between the boards a hundred years before when people earned their living putting shoes together.

What accumulated under a two-hundred-year-old floor...? She lifted one of the boards.

When she shined the beam of her flashlight into the hole, there was—drumroll, please—dust and a paper clip. The paper clip didn't even look very old.

Oh, well, she thought. What had she expected? Pirate's treasure?

After a few hours, the four-poster's ex-bedroom had been cleared. All the rooms facing windward had cleared, and everything that needed to be dried had been wiped down or hung up.

The storm continued as though it was never

going to stop, as if it had stalled over Sea Crest Hill. As if she and Zachary Hale would be trapped forever.

She had only confusion as a reaction to that.

An hour later, she showered in an area so confined, her elbows and knees thumped against the sidewalls, and so cold she remembered bathing in mountain streams that were warmer. When she felt thoroughly clean, she put on a fluffy robe Zach had given her and hung her clothes in the breezeway to dry.

Zach had disappeared somewhere and it was just as well. It hadn't helped that he was polite and diligent when moving the family antiques. It hadn't helped that he had listened attentively to her suggestions and used the ones that would work. Wesley always seemed to be distracted, to never listen carefully to anything she had to say, nor she him as a matter of course.

While they were working, and try as she might to stop herself, she kept finding reasons to touch Zach, a hand on his arm, one on his shoulder. Once she stopped herself from rearranging the hair that lopped down on his forehead.

Each time he looked at her, paused to smile at her, she could barely keep the urgent beating of her heart in control. By the time they were finished, her whole body seemed sensitized to his presence.

Well, it was a fun ride. She discovered along time ago she enjoyed the sexual attraction. Sometimes those things could be acted upon and other times they were just passing fantasies to be enjoyed at a distance and then dismissed.

She snuggled into the robe. Zachary Hale needed to be the latter, to be kept at a distance.

She plunked herself in the stuffed chair near the fire and stretched her feet out onto the puffy ottoman. Her laptop sat on the end table beside her but she didn't reach for it.

What was she supposed to say? What could she report? Reporter Wants Swindler? It seemed wrong to even think of him like that now. But until…

The door to the loft opened and Zach strode in. There must be a shower someplace else, as he wore clean jeans and shirt. His sandy blond hair was tussled and pushed back, which made him seem more movie star than lumberjack.

ZACH HUFFED THE air out of his lungs.

Addy sat in the chair by the fire wearing only the robe he had given her. Her mass of blond hair looked damp, finger-combed and sexy as hell as it curled around her face.

Instead of leaving, he listened to a more base

need, his growling stomach. If he fed that need, maybe he could cool the other. He didn't believe it for a moment, but he pulled a cheese plate, a veggie plate and two bottles of juice from the refrigerator.

He'd spent the last hour trying to talk himself out of wanting the one person in the world with whom he should have no intimate contact. She was a reporter, an investigative journalist who had come to Bailey's Cove with the sole intent of convicting him in the court of public opinion.

It didn't matter that she had shown a side of herself he was certain she never meant to show, that she had put her heart into rescuing his family's treasures.

When the wind had launched her out into the darkness he had come to his senses and realized the things could be replaced. The person could not.

He had wanted to stop, but she was the one who would not leave the antiques to the raging storm. From that moment he had known there was more substance to this woman, whom his attorney had said be very wary of because she had a past she needed to make up for.

His brain kept ticking off the warnings—she could be doing all this for the story, she could be working him, she could have a heart as dark as a moonless Maine night.

But he had seen her in action, seen that she was not handing him a line and expecting him to believe her.

No matter.

He still should not want her. He shouldn't care that the swell of her breast filled the opening of the robe. That by the expression on her face she was not thinking about writing a news story. That her beautiful blue eyes never left his face as he approached.

He put the food on the coffee table and instead of picking her up in his arms and carrying her to his bed, he poked the fire and put on several more logs. When he was finished he turned and she was still watching him.

She could flee if she wanted to because he was sure his intent was written on his face, his body language.

She could stuff her mouth with vegetables to make her intent clear.

She neither fled nor picked up a piece of broccoli. She sat back in the puffy chair, feet on the ottoman. The robe formed a V at the neck and between her legs. Each one inviting. She shifted slightly and one side of the robe fell away from her knees.

He didn't trust himself to say anything coherent. There had been no women in his past who had stirred him so deeply and so quickly. He wanted her.

If she wanted him as much…

He closed the distance between them with two deliberate steps. Then he lifted his foot and straddled her knees, a leg on either side, standing over her. She looked at him and unless he was imagining it, one corner of her mouth slipped up in anticipation. He reached down, grasped the front of her robe and brought her to her feet. When she leaned into him, her breasts pressed against him and fire burned in her eyes.

CHAPTER SEVEN

ADDY STOOD, WEDGED between the chair and the ottoman. There was no space between them, her lower belly against what he was offering to her.

Zach released the front of her robe and let his hands drop to his sides. He didn't hold her. He didn't demand anything of her except perhaps an answer.

She stared into his eyes, a deep caramel brown in the shadowy light. Flecks of amber streaked the irises and thick dark blond lashes luxuriously framed them.

When he touched the mark on her cheek, she let her hands slowly snake up his chest and over his shoulders until they were locked behind his head.

Slowly, inhaling his scent, a thrill racing through her at the intimate touch of their bodies, she brought his mouth down to hers.

His arms reached around her back and pressed her body more closely to his, escalating the thrill, making her heart beat wildly.

His mouth devoured hers as his lips stoked her desire. The fire roared and so did she. All she wanted in the world right now was Zachary Hale, to explore with him, to find out where they could travel together.

When his hand reached inside her robe and caressed her breast her feelings exploded.

"Nothing has ever felt as good as this," she murmured against his mouth, surprised that she could feel so much, so deeply, so fast.

With one sweet move, he settled the top of her robe off her shoulders, so it dropped down her back, held in place by the belt. Naked from the waist up she saw herself as he must. Lit by the fire and full of passion.

He must have liked what the fire showed him as he tossed his shirt on the floor and drew her to him, pressing the nakedness of their bodies close. She suddenly understood hedonism. She shouldn't be feeling such pleasure in the arms of this man, especially after having known him up close and personal for such a short period of time.

All she wanted to think of right now though was the deep and thorough pleasure of his touch.

He undid the knot at the waist of her robe and let it fall behind her into the chair.

She held on to his solid shoulders.

He bent down and took her nipple between his lips and as he sucked and nipped, her knees buckled with pure desire. He caught her and lowered her into the chair.

"Put your feet on the ottoman."

"Why?"

"Just do it."

He leaned in toward her and kissed her neck, suckled her earlobe gently and reached with one arm down beside her. Suddenly the back of the chair dropped until she was almost flat.

She smiled and pulled him down on top of her. "Ahhhh."

He trailed kisses down to her breast and drew her nipple into his mouth again. Lifting her chest into him she begged for more, and he responded by taking her in deeper and smoothing one hand down her ribs to her hip. Then he slid his fingers to the inside of her thigh, pressing with his palm.

Her brain and her body had never felt like this. No man, no occasion of joy had touched her soul the way he touched her with his gentleness.

They were two alpha primates and this could be a test of wills, but his ego so easily shared power. She could eat him up just for that.

When he made a treacherously glorious trail

of kisses down her belly toward where the core of her fire burned, she panted in anticipation.

Then when she thought she would melt with the sheer pleasure of his touch, he stopped and looked up at her as if waiting for her to protest. All she could muster was a smile and a jut of her chin toward the zipper of his jeans.

A moment later, he was stripped and standing before her with the firelight bathing his skin, making the curls on his chest almost sparkle, dancing in the sun-blond tips of his hair. The flickering light made the planes of his muscles stand out and lit up his need for her.

And she was gratified to see how much he needed her.

With him standing, she felt like the conquered and he the conqueror, but she knew differently. If he felt as she did, all she would have to do was crook her finger and he'd switch positions with her.

And so she did.

When he was under her with a condom in his hand, he looked up, his lips in the twist of a "come on" smile. She nodded her approval.

Then with the touch of his hands and his mouth, he crowded her senses, made it so she could not think. In fact, she didn't want to think about anything but having him, kissing him, feeling him inside her.

She had no idea what her heart was feeling, but she rode with her soul until she found true joy with a man for the first time.

When his world shook beneath her, she knew Zachary Hale felt as she did because no matter what the movies said, faking it didn't look like this.

He pulled her down on top of him, and stretching out her legs behind her, she rested the tops of her feet on the soft ottoman and her cheek on his chest.

The storm roared outside and at first their breathing seemed to match its pace. After a long while when the heat of passion cooled, he pulled the quilt on top of them and she fell asleep.

ZACH LISTENED TO the sound of Addy's soft breathing.

Their union had been glorious. Neither one of them seemed to be able to avoid it, but he knew it changed nothing on the outside world, didn't change her rabid need for a story. Didn't change what Hale and Blankenstock appeared to the world to have done. It only changed the tiny, time-limited world of a woman and a man trapped in a loft.

There was something about Adriana Bonacorda, something strong and honest. She seemed driven to get to the truth. When he had kissed her the first time, it had been because she showed this vulnerable, true side of herself. Few people in orbit around him ever showed that side of themselves.

He almost always had to leave the rarified sphere of his moneyed world to find those who called him friend and meant it. Finding those people was difficult, except in Bailey's Cove.

Addy was one of those people. She might want something from him he wasn't likely to give, but with her there was no subterfuge.

He put his arms gently around her, smoothed her hair back from her face. He was certain his attorney wouldn't think much of his having sex with a journalist, but that was the outside world.

She looked up at him, her adorable, beautiful face full of sleep and amusement. "Is it a truce when you make love with an olive branch in your hair?"

He gently ran his fingers over her gloriously frizzy golden hair. "You don't have an olive branch in your hair."

"*I* don't have any branches in my hair, but you do."

He reached up and brought what he found down so they could see it. "Not an olive branch."

"Okay, so it's a pine twig." She nuzzled into his neck and left kisses.

"I think a pine twig is a good stand-in." He kissed her ready lips and felt his need arise quickly.

She grinned and the corners of her mouth made her cheeks crinkle. "Then I assert that having sex with a pine twig in one's hair is a declaration of truce until such time as the trucees—"

"Hey, is *trucees* a word?"

"When pine twigs in one's hair are involved, *trucee* will suffice as a word."

He hugged her closer.

"—until such time as the trucees decide to dissolve such truce."

Addy put her hand on his chest, smoothing the curling dark blond hair as she ventured toward his ridged stomach. "Are we alone up here on this mountain?"

"You must be a flatlander if you call this a mountain."

"On this hill?"

"Medium- to small-size hill."

"It seemed like a big one, as in Olympus-size, when I was chasing you up here." She pressed the tip of her index finger to the middle of his chest. "Are we?"

"If I said yes, would you be afraid?"

"Should I be?"

"I think you should." At least for her job.

"Because we're in bed now, but we thought we were enemies. And that makes one or both of us insane?"

"One or both of us. There is a neighbor about a half mile farther up the road if you think you need help."

"Is he as scary as you?" She pressed a palm down his cheek.

"He's not scary at all. Forgetful and a bit on the negligent side, but a friendly sort of guy."

"Tell me."

He covered her hand with his. "We're going to run out of power before this storm lets up, even if we conserve."

"He's usually responsible, always making sure there's enough fuel to last what—several days?"

"He mows the grass, plows the snow and fuels his and my equipment with my stock to keep the gasoline rotated."

"But other than being a negligent gas-can filler he's harmless?"

"Harmless as a lamb. Now about my being scary."

"Billionaire. Philanthropist. Business mogul. New England's most eligible bachelor."

"Is that what they're saying?"

"Doesn't sound too scary, but are you a scary man?"

"I don't want to be. Never meant to be."

Neither of those options was a definite no. She wanted so badly for him to say no. To tell her he didn't do any of the things he was accused of, that he was innocent.

He didn't. He wasn't guilty. He couldn't have lied to and cheated those people or she would not be lying naked on top of him at this moment, would not have kissed him, made love with him.

She had to believe he was innocent.

And she did, in her heart.

"TRUCEE, WOULD YOU like to take a shower?"

Zach took handfuls of her hair and drew it away from her face and brought her lips to his for a long kiss before he let her answer.

"If that's an offer for more sex, yes, even if it means going in that tiny stall with the cold water again."

He chuckled. He could get used to that, had almost forgotten what it was like to laugh with someone when the motivation was personal and not political or mere professional courtesy.

"I can do better than that. Much better. It won't be glamorous, but I can guarantee hot."

"WHAT IS THIS PLACE?" she asked a few minutes
later as he led her across the rear of the garage
past the old car that had been one of the first
off an assembly line and the antique buggy
that had served the family before the inven-
tion of the auto.

Dressed in the matching robes Cammy had
insisted he needed in his closet, he pointed toward a door in the far wall. Then he followed
her. Cinched at the waist, the robe swayed with
the gentle rocking of her hips. He wondered if
she even knew she did it, let alone how sexy
it was.

She opened the door and he reached in and
flipped on a pair of low-energy ceiling lights,
and then he waited while she stood in the door
gaping.

He gently pushed her through and closed
the door.

Instantly, the warmth wrapped itself around
them. With glee she shed her robe and handed it
to him, then dashed into the multihead shower.

A spray of warm water shot out at her and
Addy let out a sigh of indulgence. "Join me?"
He smiled and hung their robes on hooks by
the door.

She lathered the bar of soap between her
hands and sniffed the bubbles.

"Flowery. A woman picks your soap?"

"She chooses everything in the loft that seems as if a woman picked it."

"The wall hangings and cushions?" She raised her dark blond eyebrows in question.

"The sheets and quilt for my bed, even my pillows and the place mats we ate soup on."

"But she's not your mother."

"Not in a million years."

"Then I don't need to know. It's just that, at your age, if your mother picked things out for you on a regular basis, it might be a little too creepy."

"At my age?"

"You know. Upper-corporate-management age."

She started to slowly soap her body starting with her arms and then her perfect breasts. Her nipples peaked, and he almost grabbed the soap to do it for her, but the show was too enticing.

When the bar of soap slipped between her legs, he reached around her and hugged her soapy body against his. Warm and slick she brought him to peak at a dizzying pace.

Later when they were sitting on the floor of the shower, she turned and wrinkled her nose. "This where you went earlier to get cleaned up?"

"It is."

"Then how did you get a pine twig in your hair?"

"I went to check the generator."

"How much time do we have left?" She turned quickly and put a hand up. "Wait. I don't want to know. It doesn't matter, anyway."

"You looking forward to sitting around in the dark?"

She put a hand on his chest. "I'm looking forward to lying down on that big bed with you and nothing but firelight."

"You make it sound so sexy."

"It will be."

All he could muster was a growl.

She held a hand up in the stream. "Is it my imagination or is the water cooling off?"

"If we keep changing the hot-cold mix we've got about ten minutes to icy."

She nodded, got up and soaped up one more time before rinsing and then held out the soap to him.

When he reached for it she snatched it away. "I'll do it—for...you." The huskiness in her voice betrayed her intentions.

She started down his chest with long strokes of the soap bar. "Why did we have so much hot water? I would have thought you'd have a small water heater here where the fuel had to be hauled up a mountainside."

"A small hill. And no stopping for idle chit-chat."

"Chitchat?" She made a face at him. "All right, a hill, but this tank must be huge."

"Not as big as you think. It's only a hundred gallons. The fireplace is set up to heat it." He grunted and grabbed her roaming hand, which had begun to soap places he'd better soap himself.

"So it's been heating since we arrived."

"Essentially." He put the soap away and rinsed quickly as cool was beginning to stream out of the showerhead.

She fell silent and he knew what she was thinking as she rinsed her hands. Tomorrow the storm would have moved off. Tomorrow they could go to their separate corners and the next time they saw each other, they would have to come out fighting.

"It will be hot again tomorrow morning." He toweled her mass of blond curls, her arms, her shoulders and when he crouched to dry her legs she put her hands in his hair and massaged softly. "Does this mean we don't have to fight over who sleeps on the couch tonight?"

"Don't worry. I can find you some sheets and blankets. You'll be comfortable there," he said as he stood.

She narrowed her eyes and he grinned at her,

loosened both their towels until they fell to the floor and pulled her warm body against his.

The light above them flickered for a moment and then died. They both laughed. Whatever they would be to each other when the storm passed, they would spend tonight in each other's arms, by the light of the fire.

"I guess that's how much time we have left on the generator."

ADDY SAT BESIDE Zach on the soft gray sofa near the fire finishing the last of the fluffy blueberry pancakes he had made for breakfast by heating the griddle in the fire.

When she finished the last bite, she placed her plate on the coffee table, snugged the luxurious robe closer to her body, and turned to put the bottoms of her feet against his thigh. The night had passed all too quickly with periods of sleep and glorious episodes of lovemaking. When the morning was full-on with its dreary light they had showered again.

Zach had checked the generator and reported there was gas, but he couldn't get a spark of life from it.

"How's our storm doing?"

"Still banging on out there."

"How wrong is it for me to be quietly thrilled to have another day of isolation?" The firelight did it's magic on the angles of his face, on the color of his hair.

"We are an odd pair," she said after a while.

"We are that."

He faced her. As he studied her, she wondered if he saw the blue eyes her mother had given her, the small straight nose from her grandfather, her out-of-control hair, or if he saw into her confused and fractured soul.

"I mean," she continued, "we would never have spoken more than a few words to each other—ever, if you'd had your way. We would have had a long and detailed interview if I'd had mine. Instead of either one, we had incredible sex."

He stared at her without a single twitch. She had expected an eyebrow lift, a lips curve or even a shrug, but she got nothing. After a moment he leaned closer. His lips covered hers and roved to take in her bottom lip and when he released it, his tongue swept in and she curled in against him.

When he broke the kiss, he said, "We are so good at option three."

Laughing, she put her feet on the floor again. The light of the storm, leaking in around drawn drapes, was dim and shadowy, and seemed to help hide her original goal from her. One thing was missing today. The utter dislike she had harbored for Zachary Hale. "I cannot even wrap my brain around what I'm supposed to be doing. The rampage inside me about you is gone or at the very least, hidden, and I'm almost relieved."

"I can't say I've dwelled on how to get rid of you in hours."

"Yup. An odd pair."

Without the rampage she could collect facts, weigh judiciously what she was told. Get to the truth.

She disentangled herself and went to the window and watched the rain pour down in sheets and rivulets.

If only she could speak with Savanna, grill her again because Addy had questioned her thoroughly until her sister had cried and asked if Addy thought she was making it all up.

At that point Addy had known her sister truly believed the accusations she was making. Believed in her heart that Zachary Hale was solely responsible for the wrongdoing perpetrated by the investment firm of Hale and Blankenstock.

After the Afghanistan fiasco, Addy could not let herself be convinced by her sister's tears. Then Savanna had told her of the files she'd seen over the last few months.

When Addy had asked her to make copies,

Savanna had refused, saying she wasn't going to get into trouble because of Zachary Hale, but she said the evidence against him had been unquestionably damning.

Savanna's plight had fired Addy up into an unrelenting simmer of nervous energy. The inspiring sensation of being on the hunt for a big story had empowered her to charge into a hurricane, to follow a man to his hometown, to invade his private space.

She turned away from the window. "I still need to know things about you," she said against the backdrop of the storm and the crackling fire.

"My great-great-great-grandmother made the quilt we left drying on the kitchen table."

"Not that kind of info. Tell me how Hale and Blankenstock got started. I have all the public documents about the start-up, but I have none of the emotional angle, you know, personal interest."

"Grandma Hale was born in Maine. Her parents were born here, but her grandparents on her mother's side were both newcomers. That made her a newcomer. She was both proud and afraid of her heritage, so she wrote Colleen Fletcher's diary, made it up. It's not written very well, but it's racy enough to make cheeks turn red. Some of it's fact and some of it's fiction. Said it gave her a better understanding of the woman and her motivations."

"Go on." Human interest, she told herself and then she realized she liked hearing this less polished, less politically correct version of Zachary Hale speak.

He held out a hand to her and she returned to the sofa to sit beside him. "It turns out Colleen Rose would not accept any more of the treasure than the few trinkets because she didn't want her father to have any reason to think badly of Bailey. Apparently the treasure was buried here in the cellar at one time. The details are sketchy but when it was moved, Colleen didn't want to know where."

"She didn't want it, really?"

"She didn't want it and she never wanted it found."

"Where do the people here look for it?"

He laughed.

She gave him a sideways look. "What?"

"A few pieces were found recently buried deep in the sand in one of the caves on the shoreline. If it weren't for the hurricane, Chief Montcalm and his police force would still be turning away more potential treasure seekers after that discovery."

He trusted her with village tales and family lore, but he wasn't telling her about Hale and

Blankenstock. Was it possible he didn't see the personal side of the damage the investment firm caused?

"I have a family story, about someone who invested with Hale and Blankenstock. One woman, who admits she invested unwisely. Put all her savings, her retirement, her mad money, her children's college funds. She thought she had finally found a way to get by with the money her husband had left behind."

He looked at her for a long moment, staring into her eyes.

"There was an employee of Hale and Blankenstock. She worked at the data processing center. I'm sorry to say, I only saw those employees at the company holiday party and only very briefly." He paused for a moment. "Savanna Rorch is a relative of yours. You have the same eyes."

She wasn't surprised he remembered the name of an employee he'd spent less than sixty seconds with twice. "My half sister. The story is hers. She lost the money."

"I'm sorry for her."

He seemed to feel true sorrow for her sister. Did he feel remorse for what he had done?

"She might have deserved a knock upside the head for her wishful-thinking investment strategy, but she didn't deserve bankruptcy."

"I agree."

"You are defying your attorney's directive by expressing an opinion."

"Mr. Hale knew nothing about the questionable investments being made by Hale and Blankenstock" had been the mantra of the publicity firm representing him. His law firm had no comment.

"Extraordinary circumstances apply."

She turned and placed a hand on his shoulder, closed her eyes and inhaled his scent. "I've been telling myself for the past two days you are not the villain at Hale and Blankenstock. You are not the swindler. The man I met here in Maine is not the man I manufactured from the information available."

He didn't speak.

"And please don't say that I'm not the hardnosed reporter. I am. I truly am. I just like to think I can learn from my mistakes, though I might not be very good at that yet. I was convinced, and I thought with good reason that you were a bad person." She rearranged the collar of her robe and hunkered down inside its warmth.

"When I was chasing you," she continued, "one of the men at the bar told me you weren't the man I thought you were. And then you didn't act like the man I thought you were."

She put a hand to his cheek. "And then you kissed me and I kissed you back. From then on I… Well, I had to admit to myself I could be wrong."

"And a part of you wants to sing with joy at the thought."

"An aria if I could."

"And another part screams in agony."

She let out a soft snort. "The part whose career depends on you being the bad guy."

Maybe she was the bad guy in all of this. She pulled her robe closed tightly and stood.

"ADDY, DON'T GO." Zach stood blocking her exit and captured her hand in his.

Her hand went limp as she sighed. "Zach, I don't know what I'm doing."

He picked up her other hand and turned her to face him. "I'd laugh out loud if it wouldn't hurt your feelings."

She wrinkled her nose. "Hurt my feelings. Hmm."

He squeezed her hands. "There are things I used to understand. Most of them had to do with integrity and justice. In fact, most things were crystal clear. I used to get up in the morning and know exactly what I'd be doing each day. Right down to the dishes I'd wash after breakfast."

"Wait." Her lips curled in a smile. "You washed dishes."

He grinned with relief at her humor and pulled her into his arms. She came easily and put her head on his chest.

"I liked breakfast to be my time of day. The part that never had to change unless I wanted it to."

"I guess I ruined that."

"Changed, not ruined."

She let out a long breath of relief and he could feel some of the tension between them lift.

"My grandfather told me my good nature would get me into trouble one day."

"And that day is here?"

"In spades." He didn't now why he was saying this, going against what Hunter Morrison had told him about not speaking with anyone about what had happened at Hale and Blankenstock.

Except that he trusted her. God help him, he trusted this woman.

She pulled him back down onto the couch and sat silently looking at him. Her warring thoughts raced across her features until she came to a hard fought for decision.

"Listen, Zach. About this weekend, I need to consider anything we said and did from yesterday on as off the record. If I want to use something you say here on Sea Crest Hill, I'll clarify with you."

"I'm sure Hunter Morrison doesn't think 'off the record' is safe enough."

"He's far away in Boston."

"You're very good at prying out peripheral information. He's here. Has a small office in town and works out of Chicago."

She smiled in acknowledgment. "Like I said, I won't use anything you've told me since I arrived on Sea Crest Hill."

"Circumstances might change your mind in the future."

"It's the best I have."

She watched him for a reaction. He had trusted her to help him and she had not let him down and she had trusted him right back.

"When did you first know?" she asked, her gaze not wavering.

"Three weeks ago I heard the first rumblings."

"That something was wrong or that there was a Ponzi scheme going on at Hale and Blankenstock?"

He let the irony bubble out in a laugh. "I still don't know that there is investment fraud of any kind at Hale and Blankenstock."

"How can you say that?"

"All I have are allegations and since I didn't do it, and there is no other person at the firm with the power to do it besides myself and Carla Blankenstock, I'd have to accuse a woman I've called a friend for fifteen years."

Her expression lightened toward a smile. "Well, there's perspective for you."

"I have to guess exactly when it started because all the records have been confiscated. My attorney is working on getting what he can. It might have begun as long as five years ago."

"Why then?"

"That's when Carla Blankenstock started to behave differently, to pull back from our friendship. She explained it at the time as her husband wanting her to keep her married life and her business life separate."

"And you didn't believe her?"

"I believed her up until three weeks ago when I questioned how she was offsetting the risk of one of the portfolios. She gave me a vague answer about a few stock options. I didn't like the sound of that and started looking into her side of the business."

"You found clients and Carla Blankenstock did the investing."

"The arrangement worked well for us for a long time."

"It's said you set the business up in such

a way that you could take advantage of Ms. Blankenstock, so that you could blame her."

He grimaced. "The Carla Blankenstock I knew when we started the firm was no one's fool."

"Is she now?"

"I don't have any proof of that, but she changed after she got married."

He wondered if the change had all been Carla. He had been accused of being aloof, removed from the dirt and grit of the real world.

"What is it, Zach?"

He looked into the fire.

"It was me."

CHAPTER EIGHT

THE TONE OF his voice spoke unyielding restraint and Addy's chest suddenly tightened until she had to force in air.

Not because he may admit all his wrongdoing off the record and unavailable to her, but that he might have done the things he had been accused of doing.

"What do you mean?" she asked even though she wasn't sure she wanted to know.

He was going to tell her something important, something that would give her answers, help her understand more about the man and his company.

She wanted to know the man, what drove him, what troubled him, what made him the man she wanted to spend time with, maybe fall in love with.

Well, that was crazy. They had been thrown into close quarters and had acted on feelings they never would have considered had they met in his office or on the yacht in the harbor. Her fantasy man was tall and dark with a part of his soul taken by evil forces that he battled every waking hour. He… Oh…

None of that mattered. The man who had unexpectedly touched her heart, offered her his humor, his thoughts, the real Zachary Hale, was closing up in front of her eyes.

The seconds passed, and as they did, his expression changed to something like hard resolve. She had seen that look on his face, when he was trying to get rid of her, when he barely spoke to her. She couldn't let things between them go back to clipped answers and historical presentations.

"Zach?"

He looked over at her. "You can't be involved in this."

"I already am."

"It will swallow up everything you want. Back away now. No one in Bailey's Cove will tell anyone you're here. When the storm lets up, go. Be the objective reporter of facts."

"Zach, I don't need protecting."

"Everyone needs protecting once in a while."

She suddenly wanted to be protected— protected by him. Being so might somehow make the hard days easier and the long nights less fretful. What would the world be like if someone had her back, if she could leap and someone would catch her?

She cleared her throat. "The best stories aren't found along the garden path or from the shelter of a bunker."

"If you're too close to this, it will ruin things for you."

"I've been sticking my neck out for a decade now."

"Much longer than that, I suspect."

"Agreed. Talk to me."

He gave her a look that said that wasn't going to happen.

"So who else are you going to talk to besides Hunter Morrison?"

He smiled at that and she let him sit with it.

"Carla is a brilliant woman." He began speaking slowly and deliberately. "We used to talk for hours about what we'd do when we got out of college, the businesses we'd start whenever we could put together a plan investors would buy into. Because of family commitments, I went on to my grandfather's shipping business, but she was always into the markets. And what made her good at it was that she loved the game."

He wasn't looking at her, wondering what she thought. He was speaking from some deep memories, from places she wanted to know about.

"Carla must have been aware someone

would do jail time if the amount of the fraud was big enough."

"That's why you think she's being influenced?"

"There were other things she could have done, other ways to steal money. She wanted to get caught."

"How did you feel when you found out?"

He stopped. "When I realized I was a source of outside investors and feeder funds that channeled assets directly into a scheme like that, it made me want to take up a lumberjack's ax or a fisherman's lobster traps as the tools of my trade."

"How could you not know what she was doing?"

"You've heard of a Potemkin village?"

"It's a facade, built up to look like the real thing in case someone came snooping around."

"Without the records I don't know for sure, but Carla must have set up a bogus paper trail of transactions and accounting reports. I should have been there for her when she began to get into trouble."

"What did you mean when you said 'it was me'?"

Pain flashed across his features before he began to speak. "I was the last line of defense the investors had. All I had to do was open my eyes. I could have seen Carla's misdirection, not at the outset, but eventually, in time to stop her, in time to turn things around. I was as responsible as anyone for the failure of Hale and Blankenstock to protect its clients."

Relief rushed through her, unwarranted because the admission or the realization obviously caused him such pain, but gave her a reason to confirm her suspicion that he was not guilty of the wrongdoing at Hale and Blankenstock.

"You said Carla pulled back."

"We were close friends until she got married."

"Do you want to talk about that?"

Zach had not expected to like any reporter, and he particularly had not expected to like one who chased him from another state.

"Your turn. You're a freelance reporter and you have a sister who used to work for Hale and Blankenstock. What else?"

While she thought about what to say, he got up to put another log on the fire and then turned back to where she sat looking lovely, sexy, in the fluffy robe. Perhaps her clothing was dry now, or he could find something that fit her that would make her look less attractive. Once he'd had a taste of her, he couldn't seem to get enough. If she weren't so bright and so inquisitive, so open and honest he would have been able to resist her. Heaven knows he should have, anyway, but it was too late now.

He sat down beside her and pulled her against him.

"I don't suppose you've ever heard of Celeste Rile?" she asked.

"Celeste Rile was a woman from Connecticut whose son insisted she be kept alive by extraordinary measures in the hospital so he could collect her Social Security payments and live in her home. Your series about her launched elder-abuse and social-security-fraud investigations all across the country."

He could see her surprise. He'd read the story and had been disgusted by it. Yes, sometimes people did desperate acts; he could even have sympathy for them, sometimes.

"And what about Rasa's World? Are you familiar with that story?"

He studied her for a long moment. The woman in Afghanistan, the whole story had been a lie. Then he said, "You're her."

"I am. And my tale of woe is an example of the bigger you are the harder you fall." She snapped her gaze to his. "I'm so sorry."

Having her feel sorry for him was the last thing he wanted.

He started to get back up when she grabbed his hand and pulled herself closer until her nose nearly touched his. Right now was when he needed to make the break between them. He needed to distance her from all this.

"Well, honey," she stated in a matter-of-fact tone. "Welcome to my world. It's lonely scraping one's butt at the bottom of life's barrel and I'm glad for the company."

Sharp laughter burst from him, and she grinned and kissed him lightly on the lips.

"If I recall correctly, Rasa was the Afghani woman whose tale captured the hearts and pocketbooks of so many Americans and even gained international fame and backing."

"Yes, scrape. Scrape."

"The sound of your butt on the bottom of the barrel?"

"Ah-yuh. That's what you Mainers say."

"Ah-yuh. So tell me how your involvement with Rasa got started."

"Do you miss nothing? Forget nothing? I said to you, 'Tell me how Hale and Blankenstock got started.' You're using my own phrasing to get me to talk."

He gave her a let's-hear-it flick of the eyebrows.

"When I was embedded with an army unit, I had been so focused on researching army life, the needs of the soldiers and journalist survival in the country, I didn't get very deeply into the culture.

"Rasa was the wife of one of the more radical warlords. Actually, I'm not even sure to this day if that was her real name."

"How did you find out she made it all up?"

She frowned. "I should have been smarter. I should have listened to Jimmy. He was one of the soldiers assigned to assist me with the locals and warned me I could be taken in. Jimmy was a black-and-white kind of guy. Right or wrong and no in between, so I took him with a grain of salt. Rasa is the one I should have been suspicious of."

She got up and poked around in the fire until the log fell and sparks shot up. "I heard crying coming from a house that had been blown up. She said she had lived there with her family, a husband and three children. She told me the others had all died when an RPG meant for an American convoy hit their house instead. She was angry with the insurgents, angry they had taken her family away from her.

"She said she held her small daughter in her arms while the child died of her wounds." Addy put her hands to her head and began to pace. "It was all told in such detail. The blood, the dirt, the pain. The American convoy had not stopped. She said the confusion was so great that people ran all about while her child died. No one helped her. She said I was the first one who had ever inquired about her child and that she was grateful.

"She said it would have been different if her child had been a boy, her friends, her neighbors might have helped her."

"Have you ever told your story?"

"You mean about Afghanistan?" She shook her head without waiting for an answer. "Once the counter-story broke with irrefutable proof that I had been duped, no one wanted to hear what I had to say."

"I'd like to hear. What happened next?"

She sighed and sat down beside him. "Rasa blamed her daughter's death on a group of insurgents no one had heard of before. I thought I was doing a great service. I uncovered a new group of the enemy and I was helping bring the plight of the Afghani women to the world.

"A lot of people followed me. I had over three hundred thousand followers on social media. I was such a fool."

She crossed her arms protectively over her chest and as all the Adriana Bonacorda bravado left, her shoulders slumped. "There was no faction. I thought I might be spared a bit because the Afghani woman's plight is still accurate. The story of these women in jeopardy was tainted by my telling it."

"A fine mess."

She looked up at him and he smiled. The strength it took to go on after the story in Afghanistan and to chase a swindler up the coast still lived in her.

"A fine mess," she repeated. "And you were to be my way out."

"And now I'm not?"

"Zach, if I'm not reading you correctly now, then I might as well pack it in."

"I hope it never comes to that."

"Do you mean you'll give me a juicy exclusive that I can put into print?"

"A man can't give up all his secrets in…" He pointedly examined the calendar on his watch. "In less than three days."

She looked thoughtfully at him.

"Let's see what that would be in real-world time." She sat up on the edge of the couch so she could see him. "As strangers meeting for the first time, we would have spent from, say 5 minutes to three hours together a day—and that's being generous. I'd say, we've spent weeks together in real-time relationship terms. We're the opposite of geological time. Every one of our days is in fact a week or so."

"There might be an odd sort of logic to that."

He studied her face and wondered if there was any chance for a relationship with her in the real world.

A dark dread clenched his gut. There was no way he would ever drag anyone else into the fray that had become his life.

He reached out and lightly traced her jaw line. She was so ferocious and that lightened his heart. She had survived a lot. She'd survive him.

"It's time to check in on the real world."

"How so?" she asked, her forehead wrinkling.

"I've neglected the house too long. A quick look around shouldn't take more than a few minutes."

"Nope."

"What *nope?*"

"You're not leaving me behind. It's scary here by myself."

He laughed. "You scared?"

"All right. You are my forbidden fruit. I can't let you out of my sight. We have to check the house, together." She kissed him then, took another taste of his mouth and he could not help himself; he tasted her back.

"Addy, I have never wanted anyone the way I want you. I can't get enough." He stood, holding her in his arms, but then set her gently on her feet.

He found them dry clothes, sweatpants which Addy could tie around her waist. The shirt bagged down around her thighs.

"You look adorable."

She glanced at her appearance and then up at him. "You have a terrible sense of style."

He chuckled and plucked at the shoulder of the baggy shirt. "I don't think so. I like what's under the baggy stuff."

"Wanna check it out?" She wagged her shoulders back and forth in mock innocence.

"I'm leaving you here."

He walked away quickly, but before he reached the door, she was holding on to his arm, dancing at his side.

He would miss her a lot when she had to leave.

AS ADDY ACCOMPANIED Zach she realized she was in deep trouble. Being with him was the thing she wanted the most since they first made love—no, since their first kiss. She had not known she could feel this strongly, let alone this quickly. Maybe there was something to be said for love at first sight—no, that was out for them. How about soul mates?

Were they soul mates destined to find each other?

Did she now believe in fairy tales, too?

Everything they had carried to the breeze-way was safe and drying slowly. Her clothes hung on the line, her jeans stiff and her bra a sexy blue with just enough plunge and the right amount of lace was hanging out there in plane sight.

When Zach put a finger under the ever so slightly padded cup of the brassiere she poked him in the ribs.

"Just checking to see if it's dry."

"Is it?"

"No. You'll have to go without it for another day."

She took the bra down. It was dry, completely. "You are such a liar."

He continued toward the door to the kitchen. "So they tell me," he said, and then sighed exaggeratedly.

She nudged him again.

"What was that for?"

She gave a big answering sigh and he smiled and planted a fast kiss on her lips.

"I just need to see to the cellar for a minute. If you check the rooms on this floor, I'll join you upstairs."

The kitchen was secure. The quilt draped over the table and chairs almost dry.

Addy moved through the east rooms on the first floor quickly. Minor water damage was visible on the ceiling near the outer wall in the parlor below the four-poster room. That was expected and could not have been prevented in light of the tree having its way with the house.

The west face of the house was sheltered but she examined it, anyway. Though it was raining and blowing hard, she could see the hill behind the mansion. No doubt a month or two of rainfall had come down in the past few days. The trees spaced out over the landscape of the terrain would prevent any mud or rock slides from occurring.

A slide could put the house in danger, especially the cellar.

The cellar was an old storage space hacked and blown out of rock and dirt, Zach had told her, by some determined settlers with access to lots of black powder for explosives. On the second floor she was relieved to see the tarp held, and now that the storm had lost some of its rage, it would most likely hold until the damage could be repaired.

In the beam of her flashlight she could see a new pile of debris in the middle of the room. When she shined the light to the ceiling it was easy to see why. The damage from the tree and moisture from the storm had taken its toll on the floor of the attic and the ceiling of the bedroom.

Plaster and chunks of wood were strewn over a few feet of the floor and something, maybe a box, was lying in the midst of the rubble.

CHAPTER NINE

THE BOX ABOUT twice the size of her palm and a few inches tall, half buried beneath plaster and chips of ceiling paint. Almost instantly, ideas of what might be in the box filled her head. Gold? Jewels? No. More likely a child's treasure chest of found objects, a fossil, a feather from a blue jay. A lock of hair or a locket. Not much because the box was so small.

She slowly approached the debris, never letting the beam of her flashlight waver from the target. Maybe it was a treasure map? Bailey's Cove had it's own pirate. Oh, but he died before he could live in the house.

She squatted down and reached for the box, but pulled her hand back. She knew she could snatch up the box, hide it in the baggy clothing and whisk it away.

Ye-ah. With it, she could whisk away the last of her self-respect.

What if the box held a story as big as Zachary Hale?

What if she just took a good look and then

ran with the story of what she found, never taking the box from the room...

She was depraved.

She reached for the small box released by the devastation from some long-ago hiding place. No one had lived in the house for over thirty-five years, Zach had told her at one point. His mother had told his father she would not live in a museum and Zach had been raised in a home on the south side of Bailey's Cove.

Maybe the box had been hidden by Zach's grandmother.

As Addy cleaned off the surface of the box, something inside rattled. Carefully she brushed away the rest of the dirt and dust still stuck to the box's intricate surface.

Addy examined the box. Roses, hand carved with care covered the lid. There was no label adhered to the surface. It could be a one of a kind, made for a beloved, she speculated.

Addy gently shook the wooden box again.

A clink and a small thud answered.

"Addy?"

She nearly leaped straight up in the air.

Zach looked troubled in the shadowed light.

"What's wrong?" she asked.

"There's at least five feet of water in the basement."

"Oh, no. Were there any antiques down there?"

He shook his head.

"I'm so sorry." She took a step forward. "I don't know how much this will help ease the burden of your basement, but…"

She held out the box. She already knew she was no hard-nosed journalist when it came to Zachary Hale. This proved it without a doubt.

"What's this?"

She pointed to the ceiling and he stepped in to look up at the damage.

"This," she said, "came down with it."

She pushed the box into his hands and he examined it carefully.

"We're done here," he said quietly and turned away.

Addy had expected more of a reaction from him. People continued to surprise her.

She scrambled after him and expected to follow him to the loft but on the first floor he detoured into one of the back rooms serving as the mansion's library.

From one of the lower shelves he took a leather-covered volume. The careworn pages had sketches and photographs attached with handwritten explanations beneath them.

She held up her flashlight so he could better see the images.

He flipped back and forth among the pages

until he came to a sketch of a box, a wooden box covered with carved roses.

"Oh, my goodness."

Under the drawing several lines were written using a quill and ink.

Hand-carved box belonging to my beloved mother, Colleen Rose Fletcher McClure. She said a dear friend gave it to her, and I always speculated the box came from my father. Not Mr. McClure, but the man everyone but my mother denied had fathered me. The box, in which my mother kept a few of her secret treasures, disappeared sometime during my childhood. I credited one of the servants with thieving the box, but my mother asked me not to be so hard on people. How could I be else. It's a harsh world when your grandfather hates your father and gives no quarter to a grandson who wants only to know what happened to his real father.

It was signed.

Rónán Uilliam McClure

They silently stared at the sketch of the box.

"Apparently, the pirate's son was not fooled by the subterfuge. So we can speculate the box was hidden away by Colleen Rose? Can we open it?"

He grinned. "Down, Ms. Journalist."

"I mean, how casually interesting a find. Should we go eat dinner, wash the dishes and go to bed?"

"I'm not averse to going to bed."

"Very funny."

"All right. I am hungry."

"We aren't going to open it at all, are we? You're going to wait until the pirate's descendants, Daniel MacCarey and Heather Loch, are there. No, you'll give it to them because the box most likely has treasures from the pirate, their relative, not yours. How could I ever have thought you were a crook?"

He smiled ruefully and sadly and then kissed her on the mouth in forgiveness. "I don't know, maybe because everyone else did, because your sister no doubt still believes I am."

He carefully closed the book and put it back on the shelf. "I wasn't kidding about being hungry."

"Me, too. How about we go see what we can find to warm up over an open fire?"

"You gave up easily."

"I'm not finished. I'm regrouping. There could be a story in that box. Maybe not an international sensation like you, but something of interest as least to the people of Bailey's Cove."

"The good folk of Bailey's Cove will find out soon enough about the existence of the box and soon afterward the contents. Ms. Loch shares eagerly."

THEY ATE THEIR fireplace-heated dinner at the coffee table in the envelope of warmth from the flames. The box sat on the dining-room table all by itself and unmolested.

When they were at the sink doing dishes, using bottled water pumped from the hand pump in the house, Addy turned to look at the box.

"We could just take a peek."

"Or not."

"The box is technically yours."

"Only technically."

"I could take a look inside and not tell you what I found."

"I could read about it online. Reclusive Maine man finds love letters from long ago?"

"And you're a romantic. I do love that facet of you, but be careful. You're beginning to speak in taglines."

"Where did *your* mind go first?"

Not to love letters, that was for sure. Did that make her unromantic? She parted her lips to speak and he captured her mouth with his. And when he was finished with his plundering told her, "The truth, not the corrected version."

"Okay, a treasure map. I thought of a treasure map."

"And what would you do with a treasure map if you found it?

"I would have given it to you, of course." She tilted her chin up at him in challenge.

He coughed out an abrupt laugh.

"You don't trust me." She feigned insult.

"I was sure I didn't trust you when I met you. That's why I almost left you in your car in a ravine while I sought refuge from a hurricane in my nice, safe loft."

"But you came back for me." She dried the last plate and put it on the stack in the cupboard. "You yanked me out of my car and practically carried me away. I do owe you."

"The storm is letting up," he said as he wiped down the sink.

"That makes my heart hurt."

When he smiled at her she could see the questions in his eyes and the pain. He had a world of hurt waiting for him. Even if he eventually proved he was not responsible for the financial collapse of Hale and Blankenstock, he'd have lost his friends and his business.

Who would trust him, to have been so close and to not have seen what was going on?

She pushed the tip of her index finger gently into his chest. "I have an idea."

"Some of your ideas are quite good." He captured her finger and drew the tip into his mouth.

She snatched her finger back and curled her hand in to a protective fist around it.

"You'll like this one."

He followed her to the lower level to the shower room. She left a trail of clothing in her wake. With each ugly, unflattering item she left on the floor, the sexier she felt. By the time she reached the door to the bathroom, all she had on was one sock.

Once they were inside the warm room, she leaned against the closed door and held up the foot with the sock on it for him to remove. He obliged. Then he lifted her leg higher and kissed the bottom of her foot. Sexy, so sexy and it was just a kiss on her foot for heaven's sake.

Her heart wanted to burst with the aching feeling that soon this would be all over. The world would want Zachary Hale and he was already pulling away from her.

He kissed the inside of her ankle, her calf, knee. Each kiss made her unreasonably sad and brought her closer and closer to ecstasy.

How could she have gotten herself so close to the story, too close for there even to be a story?

"If we keep this up—" the words seemed to grind out of him "—we will run out of condoms at some tragic time."

"Not absolutely necessary." Her words as breathy as his had been guttural.

He paused for a moment.

"Don't stop." This time her words sounded like panic. "I have my end covered, so to speak."

"As far as I know I'm all right."

"Then I suggest to you if that desperate time comes, we will consider ourselves safe."

He trailed kisses along the inside of her thigh and all she could do was keep from melting into a puddle of need at his feet.

"Zach, you make me feel so…well, and all you did was take off a sock."

He brought the trail of kisses up her body until he pinned her to the door and covered her mouth with his and let his fingers work magic.

After he had his way with her, she took off his clothing and kissed each area she uncovered. All this might end tomorrow, but right now she would take everything from him she could get and she would love it. She would love him.

She was a crazy fool to let her heart take

in this man, to have opened herself so far she may never be able to recover from emotions that ran so deeply.

Soon the hot water of the shower cascaded over them and there was no world except the one filled with steam, soap bubbles, a reporter without a story and Zachary Hale. From somewhere came a deep moaning Addy couldn't seem to stop. Never wanted to stop.

As she took all of him inside her, she had to salute her heart for it's great taste. She loved him. She loved Zachary Hale and nothing good would come of it and at this very minute she didn't care.

ADDY THREW AN arm over her eyes and when she couldn't shut out the light, rolled over in the vastness of Zach's bed and groaned. It seemed as if they had barely gone to sleep. The shower had only been the beginning.

And now someone had gone and turned on the lights.

Lights?

The electricity was back on? How was that possible? Did the electric company work during hurricanes to have the power back on so soon?

She didn't want this new development— at all.

"Zach." She reached out and when she couldn't find him, she sat up and pulled the sheets around her. Light streamed into the room from all the east windows.

The sun.

The storm was over.

There was no way she could stay with him and have any kind of credibility when reporting his story.

There was nothing for the two of them outside the confines of this estate.

The pain became emptiness.

"Zach?"

When he didn't answer, she flopped face down on the bed.

She was alone in the loft.

Alone.

How she hated alone.

Alone was what she had been when Rasa's deception and her gullibility broke over the internet. The goal of the faction Rasa's husband belonged to had been to prove how stupid and easily persuaded she and other westerners could be. When the story burst onto the news scene, it had shown Addy's photo alongside one of Rasa, or whatever her name was. While they had somehow gotten a college yearbook photo of Addy, the woman sat in an armored vehicle with many armed men and they were all laughing. The caption read, "How can these foreigners be trusted with our lives?"

Her friends had all been journalists and they scattered as though she had cholera. Two years before, she had left her family and other friends behind when she chose to pursue Afghanistan and parts east.

She remembered that first night on the futon in her condo with no story to work on or anyone to call. Even the guy at the newsstand on the corner had given her the stink eye when she had gone down to get something to read. She had to shut down her computer because it could not stop showing stories of the journalist about whom there had been Pulitzer buzz. Depending on the slant, she had been duped/stupid/arrogant/too fluffy even to be read, choose one or all, or make up one.

She pulled the feather pillow over her head. No matter what had gone on in her life, nothing would ever be as bad as having this man walk away leaving behind a greedy emptiness.

Zach wasn't gone yet. He'd comfort her before sending her off to face the world. In the meantime, she'd keep the Huns at bay with a pound or two of down feathers in a pillowcase.

After a few minutes and through the feathers, she heard men's voices.

Shock almost made her leap from the bed.

For three days she had been holed up with Zach, no outsiders to intrude. No reputations in ruins. No jocular ridicule or accusations or, perhaps the worst, pity.

When she heard footsteps on the stairs she sat up. A moment later Zach entered the loft.

His smile was wan and spoke of things she was sure she did not want to hear. He sat on the edge of the bed and then leaned back until his head rested in her lap.

Oddly, she was reassured because it seemed he felt the way she did.

She soothed the sun kissed hair back from his forehead. "Who were you talking to?"

"Owen Calloway. The man from the place farther up the road. He took a wrench to the generator to get it to work and filled it with fuel."

"Ah." She had hoped fervently that Owen had come to tell Zach the road was washed out, that they could go back to bed for the rest of the day, maybe the rest of the week.

Zach smiled up at her. "Not that we needed light to do what we did."

"I've never been more grateful for a power failure." She bent down and kissed his beautiful mouth.

He nestled his head against her belly. "I wish my life wasn't redlining."

"That reporters weren't hounding you, chasing you even to your family's estate."

He lifted his head and captured her gaze with his, his expression earnest and searching. "I've never met anyone like you, Addy."

"That's a good thing I trust."

"This might be the last thing I should say, but I'm glad you came. You are the only person I could imagine that could make all this worthwhile. I have no idea what my life will be like when all this shakes out. In today's world, the truth is only a point of reference. I could be in jail. I could be broke. I might have to live here because it's all I have left."

"And after I've gotten so used to all the luxuries in your life."

"You really don't care about all that stuff, do you?"

"Not so much."

Addy breathed into the silence, pulling back every time she wanted to cry. She didn't cry. She'd seen true heartache and pain. Not a disgraced reporter or a dethroned king of finance. She'd seen real pain, and hers was nothing to cry about.

"Maybe we don't have to chuck all that we've been to each other these few days," she started slowly, not sure where she would go with the thought, only knowing she could not let this all go away forever.

"There's too much uncertainty for the foreseeable future."

She stroked his hair. "We could meet in say ten years and see if we're still attracted to each other at Boston Common. You know, à la *An Affair to Remember*."

"Ten years from today? I'll have gray hair by then. My father had a full head of it by the time he was forty. You wouldn't even recognize me."

Addy tried to crush down the feeling of sadness that suddenly tried to overcome her. He wanted to take the sane route, to say goodbye.

"I think I'd recognize you no matter what." She couldn't keep the tears from her voice.

He turned and sat up. His soft lips touched one eye and then the other and then gently kissed her lips. "I haven't had enough of you either, but I can't let you into my life."

"I've already crashed and burned in my own. How could it get worse?"

"Journalism is rough. The world of finance is take-no-prisoners cutthroat. There's no caring, no compassion."

She put a hand to his cheek and he continued. "It could get worse if you're connected to me in any way. You'll have no credibility, and you've already had more than enough condemnation in your career."

He stroked her arm from shoulders to fingertips, but said nothing. There was only one thing to say. Goodbye.

"So, ten years from today it is, in the Common. I guess since the park has been there for almost four hundred years, it will still be there in another ten. Shall we say, noon?" she asked as she joined hands with his.

CHAPTER TEN

ADDY STOOD ON the front steps of the old mansion on Sea Crest and let the view take her breath away. The sky, a rare and brilliant blue, hurt her eyes after so much time spent in semi-darkness. The road that had seemed so destitute and so long when a hurricane was blowing up, now looked like something she'd enjoy on her bike. A good workout with great scenery.

She could not see Owen's place for the trees and another bend in the road. On his trip to town, the older man had notified O'Reilly's her car needed to be hauled from the ravine. About the people from the town he said, "Ah-yuh, town could be flatter 'n a pancake and those folk 'ould be out there whistlin' while they work." But he said the damage was severe on the south-most end of town and everybody was working hard to put things right.

Below her and spread out at her feet, the village of Bailey's Cove stretched mostly to the south along the Atlantic Ocean. The homes on the hillside below her seemed intact, but she could see only the leeward side of everything. There might be damage on the southeastern aspect of the homes and businesses, the side that faced the winds. There might also be water in their basements.

She pulled her wrinkled but clean jacket closely around her. Considering the destruction that must lie at the bottom of the hill, her heart went out to the struggling town. Zach had told her how Bailey's Cove was in a battle to keep its identity and to grow at the same time. This storm would be devastating to their timeline.

From high on the hill, she could see the yacht still floating in the harbor but it seemed to list a bit to one side.

As she watched, a line of trucks and cars filed down Church Street from the north. Some of the vehicles in the parade turned off and others kept moving forward. The whole line halted when the lead truck stopped and threw a piece of debris into the truck bed. When they came to a large chunk filling half the lane in the road, people from several vehicles leaped out to help.

Soon there were people scurrying everywhere. Hugging, shaking hands, cleaning up.

Today, instead of repairing and tidying up, she planned to go out and begin to expose Zachary Hale's innocence or his guilt in the news media. Without a doubt other journalists would be heading to Bailey's Cove and, no matter what she did, Zach's private life was going to be under scrutiny.

Zach stepped up behind her and put a hand on her shoulder.

She turned toward him. "So we go back to our corners."

He offered her a small smile. "No regrets."

"No regrets," she responded and gave him a slow, lingering kiss that spoke of goodbye and good luck.

"I'll walk you down to your car."

She held up a hand to stop him. "I could not stand it if you did. O'Reilly's tow-truck guy will take good care of me."

She grabbed her bags and started down the road, walking away from the man she had gone from hating to loving in three long days and nights.

Goodbye, she said silently because she couldn't bear to say it out loud.

Her shrunken red moccasins hurt her toes as she left Zach and went toward her old life. She had transferred money to her sister's account and after that had steadfastly refused to open her computer. There was nothing on the outside world that could compare with the man she had come to know. Her voice mail was full apparently mostly from Savanna, most likely about the money, but she made one call, to the Three Sisters bed-and-breakfast, to get a room. Thankfully, the number was a mobile phone. Christina Talbot, the owner, said they weren't really open for business yet and that they didn't have electricity. Addy said she'd bring her own candles and offered to help with cleanup.

Christina's response had been a big welcome to the Three Sisters B and B, and she gladly accepted Addy's open-ended reservation.

She glanced over her shoulder once to see Zach still on the porch watching.

He waved and she waved back.

The thing about the loving part was it felt so good and the excruciating part about actually leaving was the emptiness.

Each moment that had passed had nearly undone Addy. The big, brave reporter, who could face down a slum landlord in New York or a robed man with a military-grade weapon, could barely even think of facing the world where Zachary Hale was not her lover and not her friend.

Patty O'Reilly, the tow-truck driver, opened the door for her and soon the cab of the big red flatbed truck with her poor, damaged rental car rocked from side to side as they made their way slowly down the hill toward town.

Patty was extremely polite to her but did not say one word to her once they were in the truck. The driver made a call to give the person on the other end of the line their ETA as seven or eight minutes.

Addy could only guess what kinds of rumors had already flooded the town. "Reporter unjustly hounds one of our own" or "speculation runs rampant as reporter holds up in hideaway with beleaguered billionaire."

ZACH RETREATED INTO the house. He doubted either of them would stick to the bargain of no regrets. He wanted to be innocent and she'd want to fry him in the media for being a crook when she heard the news his attorney had sketched out for him in an email this morning.

As soon as she found out, they would no longer just be adversaries, they'd be enemies.

Shaved and dressed in business casual, he headed into town to see Heather Loch at the old church. The box with the roses on the lid sat on the seat beside him. As curator of the local museum, Heather would not only know how to open the beautiful box without harming it, as a descendent of both Colleen McClure and Liam Bailey, she deserved to open it. Beside the box sat the old leather-bound book with the box's provenance. The two should not be separated.

His phone rang. Markham Construction returning a call to talk about getting the water out of the mansion's basement.

"Henry Markham here."

Zach told him the problem and Markham said he'd get there this afternoon. Zach didn't have to tell the contractor the doors would be unlocked. Everyone's doors would be unlocked while the world was forbidden to enter the town.

Zach checked for damage as he drove. The road on Sea Crest Hill was rutted from flowing rainwater. The homes along the way looked mostly intact. No trees had fallen on top of them. Although a number of them would have water in their basements. Markham had said they'd stop in the neighborhoods en route down from Sea Crest Hill and pump out any basements that needed it. A systematic approach, Henry had said, would make the contractor's contribution to remediation more effective. The company would no doubt be busy for a couple of years demolishing and rebuilding. The old mansion alone would take a month or more after the supplies arrived.

As he drove down Church Street, Heather Loch waved to him from the doorway of the old church-turned-museum.

"You okay?" he asked as he approached her

in the arched doorway of the old church. Her gray frizzy hair had been tamed by a couple of clips today.

"We got through. Some are not so lucky. Kimi's potter's studio got clobbered, but Kimi was at her mother's in Bangor, so she's all right. She's back now and trying not to be devastated. Pins and Needles, the yarn shop, got the roof torn open and water poured in. Might give those two something more to do than gossip. Braven's, Pirate's Roost and Morrison and Morrison are all right. The Three Sisters, except the middle house, the one Christina calls Cora, has damage to the new porch she had added. Other than that, I don't know yet. How's the old home on Sea Crest?"

"Damaged by a tree fall."

"Ah-yuh, so Owen says. Did you lose much?"

"I'll have to bring a few things down for you to restore, but most of the loss is to the structure and that can be repaired." He wanted to tell Heather it was thanks to Addy he was able to salvage and save everything, but he had decided not to discuss the journalist with anyone.

"Owen said his house and yours got water in the basement."

"About five feet deep, and it's receded a bit. Nothing was stored down there and I don't expect much structural damage."

"Guessed as much. Jennifer Markham was down at the Roost this morning, said they were headed upward toward you later this afternoon. The Roost is feeding anybody who needs food for as long as their generator lasts. Said they'll cook anything you need cooked from your freezer or refrigerator. Mandrel's Café is doing the same thing. And the kids who run the deli found the funds to reopen the Dawn of Ham, cheesy name, but the sandwiches are good and they are out on the streets already handing them out. They are serving whatever they can get their hands on. Braven's will heat up anything you bring in until they run out of power."

"It's a good town, Heather."

She chuckled. "They let a crazy old woman come and live here."

"You're not so old."

She tagged him lightly on the jaw for the slight.

"There's a lot of damage on the south end of town where the wind seemed to sweep in harder, causing a tidal surge. I knew they built those condos too close to the ocean. What were they thinking? We'll get through this. You wait and see." She pushed at the strands of hair the wind was loosening from the clips and then she pointed at the box under his arm. "What have you got there?"

He had carefully wiped and cleaned away the plaster, but left much of the accumulation of age. Heather would clean that away with loving and skillful hands.

"Something I think you and Daniel Mac-Carey should see."

"Then let's go inside where the wind isn't so chilly and you can tell me all about it."

Inside the old church with its cathedral ceiling were display cases and exhibits where the pews had once been. The walls were covered with paintings, sketches and photos in a progression that showed the town's growth over almost two centuries. The museum was less than two years old and already it was crowded.

Heather took out a white cloth and put it on top of a display case.

Zach placed the old book on the white cloth and held the box out to her.

"This fell from the attic onto the floor of the four-poster bedroom."

She turned it around carefully in her hands, lifted it above her head to look at the underside. Shaking it gently, she listened intently to the sounds coming from inside. Then she rubbed her fingers over the pattern on the top of the box.

"Roses. Fell from the attic, as in hidden under the floorboards in the attic? The Goldens would love to hear about this."

"Is that group of senior-citizen treasure hunters still intact?" he asked.

"Livelier than ever, especially since the find in the caves."

"My grandfather was part of that group."

"Do you suppose the box is hers? I wonder if it's hers. Do you think it was hers?" The excitement quickly raised the tone of Heather's voice until she couldn't speak anymore.

"It was hers. Whether she kept it hidden or someone else did, I think only the contents will tell us."

"How do you know?"

He opened the book with Rónán's drawing and note about the box.

Fire lit in the older woman's eyes as she read the words.

"Maybe she hid it herself. Maybe it wasn't stolen."

"I'll leave it to you. When you look inside, you can find out."

She grabbed his sleeve to prevent him from walking away. "Not so fast. I've been thinking about you."

"A lot of people have been thinking about

me these days," he said suddenly feeling the weight of millions of people wishing him harm.

Heather let go of his sleeve and waved a hand dismissively. "Not that stuff. Since I found my long-lost relative, I've been thinking of Daniel MacCarey as my younger brother—all right, much younger. I like the feeling a lot. I don't have any close siblings and neither does he. I *feel* like his older sister, you know, even cried at his wedding to Mia."

"Rumor has it he's fond of you."

"Isn't that great?" She waved her hand again. "I was thinking since our common ancestor was a half brother to Liam Bailey's son, maybe you'd want to be our half brother."

"I don't know, Heather." He took her outstretched hand and held it. "You know they are trying to pitch me in jail for bilking billions of dollars out of people's pension funds. And I might end up there."

"No you won't, and like we care what *they* think. Those same folks tried to tell us Bailey's Cove should be abandoned to the sea, and those folks said the Three Sisters bed-and-breakfast would never even get completed and it opens next week. Heck most of *them* don't even believe in the treasure of Liam Bailey. Heck twice if you want in on the sibling deal, you'll get to be an uncle to Danny and Mia's children when they have them."

Zach found himself smiling at Heather's pragmatic manner of looking at things. "An uncle." He thought about his older sister who at forty still held fast to her vow never to marry or have children, so much like their mother who was born in an age where you had children because you were married.

"They'll have to let me be a granny because I look the part." She pointed to her head of gray hair. "Anyway the segue is that I don't want to wait to open the box until Daniel gets back in town this weekend from the university. If you'll stand in as a brother and witness, I'll open it now."

"Will that be all right with Dr. MacCarey?"

"I spoke with Daniel about you being our half brother and he said bring it on. Not in those words, ya know."

"Before or after the Hale and Blankenstock scandal broke?"

"Because of it. We were thinking you might need to know there were some people solidly in your corner."

"I'd be honored, sis." He loved this town.

She grinned big and hugged him.

Then she placed both hands over the box, and closed her eyes. It seemed as if she were trying to feel any energy the box might be emanating. Knowing Heather Loch, that's exactly what she was doing.

"All right, let's have at it." she said when she opened her eyes.

Donning cotton gloves, she pulled a brass key from her pocket and held it up. The key had the same pattern as the keyhole cover and hinges on the rose covered box.

"Where did that come from?" The woman was very new age or just plain spooky.

"I got it at a rummage sale here in town where they advertised antiques for sale. The key, probably the only antique worth anything and I got it for a buck. A bargain even though I never knew what it was for until I saw the box."

"Lucky coincidence."

She glared at him.

"Not *lucky* or not a *coincidence?*" he asked feeling reprimanded.

"Coincidence is just listening to that small, quiet voice inside your head."

"Does everyone have a voice like that?"

She nodded, concentrating to see that lifting the lid did not cause any harm to the box or its contents. "If you just stop listening to the loud one in there yammering on and on, you can hear the small one."

Zach shook his head and stood back a few

steps to let Heather have the first look into the box.

She pulled out a ring and slipped it on her index finger.

"Wait. Let me see that."

"Like yours," she said without looking up at him.

His grandmother had a matching ring specially made for him. Told him it would bring him the greatest love if he wore it. He hadn't taken it from the box on his dresser in years.

"It must be their hearts," Heather continued. "The two red stones represent their hearts. Those subtle lines in the gold down the side of the band represent the bottoms of their two hearts. See?" She outlined a heart using the two stones and the lines.

Then she pulled out a letter.

The seal had already been broken, so she carefully unfolded the letter and held it closer to the oil lamp she had lit.

She glanced up at Zach and then began to read aloud.

I have built a wall around my heart to protect it from those who think it best that I forget. I will never forget. The wall will crumble long after I'm gone, but it will not matter. Bless you who have opened this box. You are children of my heart and I pray of his. He would have loved all of you as he loved me. His heart had grown so good, so generous, so loving. Liam is not gone far. I can always feel him at my side. My father will have had something to do with his disappearance. Killed him most likely, and though my heart grieves most sorely, I will keep the secret of my father, so I can raise my son to be the man his father was and not be sent away from this, my beloved's town. I have kept out the ring, his ring, which Rónán Uilliam, my little 'Liam should have someday worn. After his heart, his son is the greatest treasure Liam Bailey ever gave to me.

May the love of God keep all who come after us safe.

Colleen Rose Fletcher McClure
Who was always Rose Bailey in her heart.

"OMG" was all Heather could muster, and then, "OMG. OMG."

"What else is in the box?"

"Nothing, but don't you see? It's a riddle."

CHAPTER ELEVEN

PATTY FROM THE O'Reilly service station didn't look up from her paperwork when Addy asked where the Three Sisters bed-and-breakfast was. She pointed. "Treacher Avenue."

Addy had kept her smile to herself and started out on foot toward the downtown. Treacher must be there somewhere. The town was laid out between the hills that rose behind it and the ocean. If she walked down Church Street, she was certain to run into that particular avenue eventually.

She didn't have that much to carry—her notebook computer bag and her tote bag. She had shoved her clothing and the candles and lighter Zach had given to her into the tote. "You don't want to be in a coastal village after dark without some kind of light," he had told her. He must have expected the lights to be out for days.

Anyway, she wasn't sure she would be able to light the candles because each time she did she'd think of him. Though each minute she spent in darkness, especially darkness broken only by firelight, she'd think of him.

He had offered her a jacket, but she insisted the coat might connect her to him and what she didn't say aloud was she didn't want to be reminded of him every second she wore the coat. At this chilly moment as she hiked down Church Street, she was a bit gloomy she hadn't accepted.

As far as she knew, there were no other journalists in the town. According to Owen's news from the Pirate's Roost, the state and local law enforcement were out near the highway checking identification and if you didn't live in Bailey's Cove, you didn't get in. With only one road leading into and out of town, it wasn't hard to maintain the security shield protecting the town from ne'er-do-wells—like Wally Harriman and Jacko Wilson.

Zach's being up here during a hurricane might just turn out to be his lucky break. With the sun shining down on her, she could believe, it might be hers also, if she wasn't so cold.

Cars and trucks passed her by and she looked longingly at them. She wondered if any of them would even hesitate, let alone, stop for the reporter. Patty had clearly known who she was, so word must spread quickly even during a hurricane.

Addy jumped. A cold nose had put itself in her hand and scared her nearly to death. The nose was attached to a sleek brown dog that looked up at her as if he knew what her life was like.

"Hello, boy," she said as she stopped and ran her hand across the top of his head. He pressed against her thigh as if to tell her to hang in there and things would be all right. She felt a sob clog her throat.

"Yeah, doggy. My life is a mess. Thanks for understanding."

A car stopped on the street and the driver leaned over to roll down the passenger window to speak to Addy.

"Going my way?" the woman asked.

The driver was a stunning blonde. The kind who could shun makeup even for a black tie event because she didn't need any.

Addy turned to say goodbye to the brown dog, but he was gone, trotting up the street.

She turned back to the woman in the car. "I'm looking for the—"

"Three Sisters. I'm Christina Talbot and not a single other car is going to stop for you because you are an 'outsidah causin' trouble.'" The woman laughed and reached across the seat to push the door open for her.

Addy climbed into the sleek gray car and closed the door.

"Don't worry about them. They shunned me for a month and all I did was move away for a couple of years and then come back."

"They might have good reason to shun me. And thanks for the ride."

"Pitch in as if you are trying to save your own grandmother's house and they'll love you soon enough."

"You know I'm a journalist and you know I'm here for a story on Zachary Hale."

"Good man. He should have married me when he had the chance. Too late now."

Addy jerked her gaze away from the gorgeous woman and stared out the window down Church Street.

"Ah, so it's like that."

"It isn't. It's… It's…"

Christina put her hand on Addy's arm. "Not to worry. The opportunity for Zach to marry me came when I was six and he was fourteen. I thought I'd make the prettiest bride and why wouldn't he say yes. Alas, he asked another woman to homecoming."

She made a sharp right onto Treacher Avenue and stopped about halfway down to the docks. Addy had already been on Treacher Avenue once before, the day she'd arrived in town.

"Meet Cora, Dora and Rose." Christina pointed first to the slightly larger middle house and then to the houses flanking Cora. The gorgeously painted Three Sisters had stood tall against the storm.

"They're wonderful."

"Thanks." Christina beamed. "And welcome. Go in and pick any room upstairs in Cora."

"Are you not coming in?"

"At the bottom of the hill is Kimi Applegate's pottery shop. It was almost blown down and she needs help salvaging what's left. Her husband was Freddy Applegate and he's gone, died in Afghanistan."

The world was a small place, Addy thought. "Can I help?"

Christina looked Addy up and down.

"There are some extra clothes and shoes in the back closet of the reception hall, boots if the shoes don't work for yah. And pick out anything warm you can find."

With that she was off. No exchange of phone numbers. No "I'll see you at dinnertime" or any indication when she would return. Addy decided whether or not this town liked her, she liked it.

Inside the lovely home, Addy found herself in a reception hall that ran from the front to the back of the house. The hall was spacious enough that it had a matching pair of chandeliers and a fireplace. The paint was a muted blue color and the portraits on the wall were oil paintings of the harbor.

Addy smiled. Plugged into an outlet were several power strips with all sorts of mobile devices attached, including one rechargeable razor.

Addy dashed upstairs and dropped her laptop on the bed covered by an old-fashioned chenille spread with pink roses and green leaves. The dark blond oak of the furniture stopped her abruptly.

Like sandy-blond.

She wanted to stop and think about Zach but refused to go that way. From the downstairs closet, she quickly picked out a few warm items. Soon wearing faux-fur-lined boots and a quilted jacket she was ready to work. With friends in the town she might get background information like no one from the outside world would have.

And by lending a hand she might not feel like such an opportunist.

Across the street and down a few buildings sat a damaged yarn shop. Two women carried large boxes of yarn to the curb and set them beside a hand drawn sign that said FREE. One of the women poked the other and the pair of them stared at her.

Addy waved and hurried on, not waiting to see if the women returned the wave.

The hike down the hill was short; the entire time she could see the place where she first met Zach. She could imagine him looking like a fisherman, see the red hurricane flags flapping and feel the rain pelting them all.

The boats had already been lifted upright and secured. Only the outline of the shed gave a clue there had been a building where Zach had parked his SUV. What was left of the structure was scattered in chunks and splinters on the pavement.

The wind blew briskly as she arrived at the ruins of the potter's studio.

"Hi," Addy said to a petite woman with straight black hair. "I'm here to help."

The woman greeted her with surprise.

"Do I know you?"

"Only by reputation if at all. I'm Adriana Bonacorda, Addy."

"Ah, the reporter." The smaller woman grinned.

"That'd be me."

"I'm Kimi Applegate. I was the owner here. And I welcome your help, Addy."

As they spoke, a pickup truck of stout

produce boxes arrived at what was left of Potter's Paradise.

The driver leaped out and helped the two of them unload the empty boxes, several bags of newspapers, a pot of coffee, two ceramic cups and a paper bag.

"Good luck, Kimi. I gotta go help Mia at the Roost next," the big man with the baseball cap called as he leaped back into the cab of the truck and sped off.

"Goodbye, George," she called after him.

A waving baseball cap shot out the window and then pulled back in as he continued up Treacher Avenue toward where the Pirate's Roost restaurant sat at the top of the hill.

"I hope you like your coffee black."

"I like it all ways." Addy remembered the rich black in Afghanistan and the milky pale her sister made. Didn't matter, she drank it. "I just like some better than others."

Kimi laughed in such a charming way.

The two of them worked solidly together and time passed quickly. Over the sandwiches George had brought in the brown paper bag, Kimi talked and Addy memorized.

Turned out, Kimi wasn't from Bailey's Cove.

"You must have a story to tell," Addy prompted.

Kimi stopped and examined Addy as if trying to discern a motive.

"Sorry," Addy said, "I am first and I suppose always a journalist."

"Be careful about poking some of the old sea dogs around here. Some of them can get pretty snarly. I do have a story. I met my husband in London. When he first brought me back here, there was quite a bit of staring. Then a man in town did some— Well, Freddy called it 'butt kicking' and, anyway, the man told a few of the loud ones, I was a person just like them and because I was Mrs. Freddy Applegate, they should honor and thank me." She stopped and blushed.

"Wow, I'd like to meet that man who did that for you."

She laughed again and Addy wondered where this woman got the courage to laugh so much when her husband was gone and her means of making a living had been reduced to a freestanding kiln and pots strewn about.

"Your wish is about to be granted."

Kimi put the pot she was wrapping into the nearly full box and hurried over to the squad car that had stopped with a crunching of gravel a few yards away.

The man at the wheel hopped out and stood by the door of the car. Addy got the feeling

Kimi would have run over and put her arms around his neck if he would let her.

He didn't look much like the kind of man who got hugged, at least not in public. He stood straight and tall. He was probably five-ten, but he seemed six foot three. His salt-and-pepper hair was trimmed neatly and combed a bit to the side, very cosmopolitan like. She'd bet he didn't hale from these parts, either.

"Chief Montcalm," Kimi said as she dragged Addy by the arm toward the man, "this is Addy Bonacorda."

He shifted his uniform hat from both hands to one and reached out to her. His firm handshake lingered a moment, gauging her, and she knew he had come to see her, not Kimi.

"Addy, this is our police chief." The chief gave her a stern look and Kimi stepped forward. "Addy's assisting with the cleanup of my shop."

"I'd like to have a conversation with you, Ms. Bonacorda. If I may."

She followed the chief and got into the squad as he held the door for her. He didn't get in, but went over to speak with Kimi. She looked fretfully at Addy, nodded a few times, and smiled wanly.

Then the chief strode to the car and got in. Addy had thought they would share their few words in the squad car, but the chief apparently had other ideas as he put the car in gear and backed away from Kimi's shop without a word.

She had time to glance out at Kimi who gave her an encouraging smile. What did she need courage for?

Addy's mind started taking inventory. Had she done anything that would interest the law? The chief put her in the front seat with him, so that should mean something unless they transported all criminals in the front seat.

Ridiculous.

She folded her hands in her lap. When the chief didn't speak at all, Addy realized this was a game of wait and see. See what she'd confess as he drove along Church Street.

Zach—did he do something, say something, file charges against her for trespassing or a crime she didn't know she committed?

Ridiculous, again.

As they drove silently down Church Street Addy could see both the charm and the devastation in the town. The redbrick buildings that looked a hundred years old held up well, like the one with "Morrison and Morrison" spelled out in poured concrete above the door. Across the street a strip mall with a taco store and a dry cleaner's and a few other businesses had been nearly flattened.

In the next area of town, the buildings were more modern, but not so modern as to fail to show wear. They seemed like they were from the nineteen forties or fifties. The police and fire stations and the city hall sat side by side. At the other end of the block was a clinic with many cars in the lot and an ambulance at its emergency bay with its lights still flashing. Across the street from the police station was Mandrel's Café, the town diner where workers were setting up outdoor grills. They were also unloading a truck that said O'Brien's Grocery on the side. A quickly scrawled sign said simply FOOD.

As the chief parked his squad in front of the police station, it had become a war of wills with her not asking why she was here and his not telling her. Maybe she'd end up behind bars without so much as an accusation.

He leaped from the car and she was certain he would have opened her door if she hadn't popped it open herself. Instead, he waited for her to clear the door before he closed it firmly without slamming it.

He held out a hand for her to precede him and she did, into the small art-deco lobby, finished in gleaming wood. Across the way sat a auburn haired woman behind glass.

"Hello, Chief." The woman greeted the man

with a professional smile that told her nothing, but greeted Addy with a look that broadcast Public Enemy Number One.

Clever of the police chief. First he made Kimi tentative and then he brought her in so this woman could glare at her and make her quake in her boots. *Too bad, Chief,* she thought, *these aren't my boots.*

"Melissa, I'll be in my office," he said to the woman who looked at him and then at Addy and smiled all satisfied, like the cat that just ate the canary.

Small-town law. She'd run amok with more than one sheriff who thought their power was bigger than the next guy's, police chiefs whose version of law went to the highest bidder. One tribal chief in the Amazon had made her his wife without her knowing she was getting married and then tried to keep her captive. She got out of that one by miming that she was already pregnant. He hadn't seen that as a boon to his position and turned her out of a village on the river without a boat. She'd waited two days with only four breakfast bars and a gourd half full of questionable water before a boatload of tourists came along and gave her a lift.

He could do that. This chief could take her out to the police barricades and abandon her to find her way back to Boston.

"Right in here," he said as he gestured for her to go ahead of him down a corridor. They came to an open door with Bruce Montcalm, Chief of Police, Village of Bailey's Cove written in three lines.

She glanced inside the sparse office and doubted the wordy door was his idea.

She took hold of the chair nearest the door, adjusted it so he'd have to turn his chair or turn his head to look at her. He was not the only one who could play the nonverbal signals game. To beat that he would have to stand over her, but there was no dignity to be had by looking uncomfortable in one's own office.

He went around the desk and sat down. He might have even nodded slightly in acknowledgment as he swiveled his chair in her direction.

"Chief Montcalm, I'd like to know why I'm here."

The chief folded his hands on top of his desk and stared at her without malice.

She sat back and folded her hands in her lap, when what she truly wanted to do was to look back and see how close the door was, and what the chances were of her getting her chair outside to jam under the knob to slow his pursuit.

She took in a breath and raised her hands palms out. "I give up. This chair is too heavy for me to drag out the door and it doesn't take much imagination to guess you could leap over your desk, nothing but air."

His expression did not change. "I brought you here because I wanted to express my deep concern that you might stir this town up."

"Stir it up?"

"The town is broken at this moment."

"On the record, sir, I'd like to hear about that."

"For the record, the burden the folk will bear is to rebuild, with their own hands. The coffers of Bailey's Cove will not hold up under this onslaught even if they do and even with the aid the government is about to offer."

"All right, I hear you saying there is too much damage for the town to recover from."

He gave a single nod.

"And you brought me here because I can make it better—" she paused and waited and when she got no response "—or worse."

The nod came again.

Zach had told her everything she needed to know under the bond of "off the record." She would free him of the mess if she could, but she could not. Her career, her livelihood depended on her finding an angle sensational enough to keep the readers happy, or at least her editor. "I don't yet know what I'm going to write about Mr. Hale. The world believes him to be a crook, but there is no real evidence he has done anything wrong.

"When the blockade is lifted," she continued, "reporters, photographers and camera trucks will descend on the town and snatch up the scoop on the country's latest financial fat rat. If that happens, if I lose the exclusive that Zachary Hale is not to blame, I might as well start my new career—motel maid in Toronto or dishwasher in Wisconsin. Worthy jobs and I'm grateful someone does them, but they are not why I got a degree in journalism."

A warm feeling flooded her. She believed. When under pressure, she truly believed in Zach's innocence. Since he was innocent, the two of them could...

The chief sat, still waiting.

"Mr. Hale was kind enough to let me stay at the mansion on Sea Crest Hill during the storm. He takes very good care of the place. I can see that it was a lovely home at one time."

"This is not about Mr. Hale."

CHAPTER TWELVE

"NOT ABOUT MR. HALE."

Addy sat opposite Chief Montcalm attempting to grasp what the subtext must be. "There is no other reason I'm in Bailey's Cove than to get an interview with Zachary Hale and to get a bit of background about the town where he grew up. What I'm here for is all about Mr. Hale."

Obviously the waiting chief was still wanting her to admit to something.

"What else do you know about the town of Bailey's Cove?"

A tack. If you couldn't get the answer you need, go at it from another angle.

"Yeah, a fair amount. I know that the mansion on Sea Crest Hill and Mr. Hale's family are deeply imbedded in the town's history."

"Go on."

"Established by the pirate. There's a child attributed to the pirate. Mr. Hale has half cousins, so to speak, in town in the form of the pirate's love child's descendants."

There wasn't anything shocking anymore about the liaison of the pirate and his Colleen Rose. They should have been born today. Their life could have been just fine. Was Zach the pirate and she Colleen Fletcher?

She shuffled around in her brain looking for the thing she was supposed to be admitting.

"I met a brown dog on the street. He didn't seem to be a stray. Told me he understood things about me. Said I'd be just fine. Oh, wait. Did I really say that out loud? Sorry. He didn't tell me anything. Sorry."

When she clamped her mouth shut she was surprised and relieved to note the chief wasn't even looking at her as if she were crazy.

She went over the past three days in her head and found the box from the attic.

"The box. I know about the box."

This got a full nod.

"Okay. News travels fast around here. All the cell phones must be back up. So then you know a tree fell on the house and the damage caused a box that had been hidden in the attic floor."

"After you found the box…?"

"I gave it to Mr. Hale." She stopped studying her fingers and snapped her gaze up. "You want to know if I peeked inside the box."

His head tipped sideways in question. "You didn't look before you gave it to Mr. Hale."

His tone did not accuse, but she wondered how hard it was for him to sound neutral.

"I wanted to. I didn't want to give it to him at all until I had thoroughly examined the contents."

"But."

"You've met the man. He sort of emits a hypnotic 'trust me' aura, and he walked in just after I found the thing. Frightened the wits out of me and I just gave it up without a fight."

He softly huffed out a breath. Now he had to decide whether or not he believed her.

"Oh! The treasure. The treasure. That's why all the privacy. Driving me here to the station instead of questioning me at Kimi's where she or someone might overhear. Subterfuge. But do I know more than the average townsfolk about where it is? No. I'm a treasure-know-nothing. I know a pirate loved his sweetie until his death by her father's hand. Well, I know the rumor. I know there is much speculation about the treasure and that many believe it's gone. What do you believe, Chief Montcalm? Tell me."

"Ah-yuh, that's not going to happen," he said in clear relief.

"Ah-yuh." Addy guffawed. She couldn't help it.

He laughed with her, as she somehow knew he would. "Chief Montcalm, I will not tell your secret. I will not tell the citizens of your town that there is a nice guy under that stern stuff you put out as your face to the world."

He looked all stern again and Addy wondered if she had gone too far.

"There is a ban on noncitizens being in town, Miss Bonacorda, unless they have someone from the town sponsoring them and they have to be here for the purpose of assisting the town, not creating a burden on the limited resources."

She got a sinking feeling there was going to be no one sponsoring her if the chief didn't think she should be here. She could ask Christina or Kimi, but they had only known her briefly.

And what if the news she had to write about Zach turned out to harm the town? Would Christina and Kimi be held accountable, be sorry for helping her?

"I'll get my things and head out." On foot if no one would give her a ride. Maybe the brown dog would keep her company, at least until she got to the edge of town.

"I can't bend the rules designed to keep the town safe. Wait in the lobby. I'll have an officer drive you to the Three Sisters. You can have your car-rental company send another car."

Addy rose slowly from her chair and turned toward the door.

This was it. She wouldn't be reporting what she had learned about Zachary Hale, that he had a birthmark on his inner thigh, that he had a devastating way of treating a woman as if she were a precious treasure to be adored, that his lips were as soft as crushed velvet.

And though she had said goodbye, she hadn't truly meant it. If it weren't such a devastating thing, she'd ask to have the hurricane back, if it meant she got to spend more time in close quarters and semidarkness with Zachary Hale.

AVOIDING REMAINING chunks of debris, Zach drove down the main street toward the offices of Morrison and Morrison. He and Heather had discussed the riddle over lunch. She told him his attorney's offices had weathered the storm with only one broken window. The old warehouse behind it, which had been tied up in an embattled estate for years, sat at a dangerous angle and would be torn down allowing the back of the law firm to face the ocean.

She had talked about other developments in town and he had listened politely though he didn't recall a thing.

Adriana Bonacorda. Addy. He saw her face as she said his name in ecstasy. When she teased him, it made her wild hair seem even wilder. When he had surprised her with Colleen Rose's box in her hand, she had been the most beautiful of all. She had been totally honest and he wanted to love her on the spot.

Love. There probably was never going to be a time in his foreseeable future for love. He certainly could not bring Addy into the mess in his life that could take a decade or more to clear up. If some people had it their way, he'd spend all of that time in jail.

Even if Addy said she'd wait, he'd have to refuse. The next ten years of her life were going to be great. She'd get her career restarted and who knew, maybe launch the next biggest news media outlet or get that Pulitzer she had been in line for.

She might even start a family. That thought hurt the most. She would find a man who could love her and be there for her. She deserved all the happiness she could find.

Morrison and Morrison Attorneys, a century-plus-old law firm was south on the main drag. Hunter Morrison worked with the other soon to be Morrison, his fiancé, Delainey Talbot.

A jag of sharp pain shot through him and Zach recognized it instantly. It was jealousy.

Green-eyed and cruel. He was jealous of a man happily affianced to the woman he loved. Soon to have an instant family.

How much having a wife, a family, appealed to him came as a shock. He was the happy-bachelor type, a businessman glad not to have to share his day with a wife, let alone children.

He parked at the back door and let himself into the deserted offices. Almost deserted. Hunter would be there. The staff, Zach assumed, were home, tending to their families' well-being.

"Up here." Hunter called from the second floor.

The lobby of the old building was painted in muted hues but there was nothing subtle about the wood trim. Mahogany, shipped in at great expense, outlined the doors and windows and, he knew, paneled the walls of the conference room.

He jogged up the steps and from the landing could see Morrison at his desk, dressed for doing odd jobs rather than office work. Knowing Hunter, he'd helped with the cleanup before he came here to meet him.

He stood and shook Zach's hand.

"You should be in Boston or New York, holed up in a hotel, not come crashing through a hurricane to get here. Not enough excitement in your life?"

"I'm afraid there's more."

"The reporter. Should I ask?" Hunter's lean body fit his name and now he sat hunched over his desk in worry.

"She ran off the road into the ravine near the house. She wasn't hurt, but she stayed with me for the three days."

"Close quarters were a problem?"

"Not until a tree crashed into the house." He shrugged one shoulder.

Hunter grimaced. "So really close quarters."

"I'm afraid so."

"How much did you tell her?"

"On the record, I told her about the house and the past residents. The usual historical information. Off the record, I told her the truth as I know it about Hale and Blankenstock."

"Do you think she believed you?"

"At the time she seemed to, but there's a lot to be said for who might influence her now."

"Will she keep to the 'off the record' agreement or was that a ploy?"

Zach rubbed the back of his neck. Helping him be smarter was why he hired Hunter, but sometimes the man had his work cut out for him. "I believe her when she says off the record. She didn't seem like a player."

"Are you going to see her again?"

"I don't think that would be wise." It would be downright stupid, but he couldn't help thinking of holding her in his arms.

"I'm glad to hear that because I have some bad news. My people have it from a reliable source, the Bureau has information about damaging files from the records department of Hale and Blankenstock."

"Files they found in the ones confiscated? The FBI doesn't usually show their hand so quickly unless there is something to gain. Why release information like that so early?" Zach tried to think of any files that could pose a problem for him.

"It wasn't the FBI. It was an independent source."

"Who? What did they have?" Not Addy. It couldn't be Addy.

"A data processor from the Hale and Blankenstock offices had access to the files she labeled suspicious."

Zach had known it wasn't Addy, but he felt relief nonetheless.

"There isn't anything in my files that would be a problem."

"These are incriminating, and they are reportedly yours."

"They can't be." This was the one thing in life Zach was certain of. He did little of the actual investment of people's money. Mostly he found people to let Hale and Blankenstock invest their money.

"I'm having the person investigated as we speak to see if we can tie her to Blankenstock outside the normal office relationship, we might have something with which to fight back."

Zach got a bad feeling about this person. "Do you know what she says she found?"

"Fraudulent investment transactions signed by you and communications from you to Carla Blankenstock insisting on her buying stock in several dummy corporations set up by you. Blankenstock, of course, has been quick to say she's sorry, that she didn't know the corporations were not real. Says she trusted you."

"Can we get copies of these files and can we tell if they're forged?"

"I've got the Chicago office working on it."

Zach put his elbows on his knees and dropped his head into his hands. When he thought of losing everything, he thought of losing any chance of having Addy in his life. The money was only window dressing.

"Don't start to doubt yourself, buddy. You've got help in your corner. We're solid."

Zach lifted his head. "Thanks."

"I know a bit about what you're going through. One day your world is spinning happily around the sun and suddenly you're out of control, wondering if there's any way for you to get back."

Zach felt as if he was confiding in a friend, not just talking to his attorney. "I heard about your trouble with a stalker. Is she still under lock and key?"

"For a long time, I hope."

"I saw Delainey at the recent weddings in town. She had a trail of hopeful admirers lining up to dance with her at both events."

"I'm a lucky guy. I could have lost it all if I hadn't wised up."

"Everybody is safe from the storm?"

"We weren't in any danger from the water, but we worried about a few of the trees ourselves. Delainey's house is surrounded by big pines and we're living there until the home we bought is remodeled."

"I haven't been any farther south than here. I hear things are bad down there."

"The condo I rented when I first moved here had the windows blown out and water halfway up the first floor. Several neighborhoods have significant damage. The house we bought is up on the hill sheltered by trees."

"You look happy."

"I never thought I'd have anyone in my life like Delainey. She makes me deliriously happy. Her daughter, our daughter, Brianna, is the greatest kid. What can I say?"

Zach smiled. He was happy for the man.

When Hunter's mobile phone rang. He glanced at the caller ID.

"I have to get this one."

Zach nodded.

"Hello, Chief. What can I do for you?"

As Hunter spoke, Zach got up and wandered over to the window. Across the street were several police officers and a slim woman with her hair tied back under a scarf. They were all carrying bags of what looked like clothing. Then he remembered the dry cleaner's was across the street. The owner, Monique Gardner, had been one of the brides at the double wedding. Her husband was a police officer, Lenny Gardner. That might explain the crowd of uniformed men and women helping her.

"Have her stay there in the lobby, I'll deal with her." He paused for a moment and then said. "It shouldn't be too long."

Zach turned back. "Do you have to be somewhere?"

"I do." He put his hand out and Zach took it. "You'll be all right. We'll get things sorted out."

Zach hoped so. He hadn't been able to see a light at the end of the tunnel since the day the FBI first showed up at his office and demanded his computers and his files, froze most of his assets and told him not to stray too far.

Things didn't seem much brighter now and the best he might wish for was that he hadn't dragged Addy too far into his mess.

"Thanks for all you're doing, Hunter."

"You go back to Sea Crest."

"Henry Markham is pumping water out of the basements in the neighborhood. I'll go and see if I can lend a hand."

"Where you won't see her."

Zach chuffed.

"You have it bad, man. I was there. I am there." Morrison glanced at a photo of his fiancé and her daughter.

"If I can avoid her questions for right now," he said, and kissing her and making love to her, "I might find some answers of my own."

"Call if you need me, Zach, I'll be checking in on the man I bought Morrison and Morrison from. He and his wife have some flooding in their basement. And don't worry, law enforcement will keep any other reporters out of town and, for your own peace of mind, don't go online. I'll call you if anything else develops."

More of the same, Zach thought as he headed for his SUV, or worse. What was in the files the data processor had seen? The person was almost certainly Addy's sister, and did Addy know?

CHAPTER THIRTEEN

ADDY SAT IN the lobby of the police station swinging her feet like a bad child in time out.

The punishment seemed unfair. She shouldn't have to leave.

She had lived through the hurricane. Who else to better tell the stories of these people?

She pushed up to the edge of her chair. Chief Montcalm had asked her to wait in the lobby. He didn't say she had to sit quietly. There were a dozen fine citizens of Bailey's Cove present. Each had a story.

She patted down her hair and then leaped to her feet. "Hello, everyone."

She waited until most of the people were looking at her. "I'm Adriana Bonacorda. I'm a reporter for a Boston paper and I'm looking for anyone with a story to tell about the hurricane."

No one said a thing. She scanned the room. If these people were seeking help from the police, there had to be a story.

"Anybody?"

Blank stares.

Tough crowd. To prime the pump, she often started with a related tale of her own experience. The only one she could think of was about Zach. No, she could not tell them about the sweetness of making love to him and being torn away because there would never be credibility for a story she reported about her lover. She had been discredited and justly humiliated once and she was not having that again.

"Ma'am." A high voice broke through the anguish, and her eyes snapped open. A boy, five or six, aimed pleading eyes in her direction.

When she smiled at him, he gave a tentative glance over his shoulder at a woman with long dark hair sitting in a chair, her heavy wool coat wrapped around her thin body. The dark-haired woman urged the boy on with a flick of her hand.

"I'd love to hear your story. Thank you." She looked at the woman in the wool coat for permission.

The woman waved an okay and Addy patted the chair next to her. "Sit right in this chair beside me."

She waited as he climbed up and situated himself.

"What's your name?"

"Bradley Dillon," he said and puffed out his chest.

Addy scribbled. "What happened to you in the hurricane, Bradley?"

"My pet is gone and hasn't come back."

"Is your pet a brown dog?"

"No. He's a white cat named John Barleycorn and I let him go so he could find his own safe place."

"You let him go?"

"You know, like they do the horses in the movies, in case the barn blew down, but it was a house I live in."

"And he hasn't come back?" Addy asked.

"Not for two days." His hand came to his face and his eyes brimmed with tears. "I promised I'd take good care of him, so Mommy said I could have him."

"And you're here to tell the police so they can look for him?"

He nodded.

"Maybe these people here would look out for him, too."

The boy faced the group in the lobby. Every one of them had been listening to his story, except for one woman huddled in the far corner.

He stared at the small crowd and smiled. "Will you help me find John Barleycorn? He got his tail got caught when he was a baby and it's a little tail so you'll know him."

"I'll help." A dark-haired girl raised her hand.

The old gent a few chairs down nodded his willingness.

"I'll help and I'll get my kids to help," said a woman on the far side of the room.

"Thank you, Mrs. Quizzenberry." The woman looked very teacherlike in her flats and khaki skirt.

It wasn't long before almost everyone in the lobby had agreed to participate in the search except one elderly man whom Addy suspected was hard of hearing and the woman in the far corner with the collar of her coat turned up against her frail neck.

"What?" the elderly man asked the person next to him and she explained close to his ear.

"Oh, I can do that, sonny," he said as he grinned at the boy with a mouth full of pearly white teeth.

A gray-haired woman raised her hand. "We were scared to death. The water made a car smash into our house, and I couldn't think of any place safer than the police station."

No one argued with that.

"Is everyone in the town accounted for?"

"Are you really asking if everyone is all right?" Mrs. Quizzenberry said, looking pointedly at Bradley still sitting in the chair beside her.

"I was."

"Mrs. March is waiting for her husband to come back from his errands," the teacher continued, this time looking at the woman in the corner who didn't seem to notice.

Addy nodded. She got it. At least one person was missing, possibly dead.

After two minutes or so of dreadful silence, another woman spoke up. "I'll tell you what I saw. The clouds were a terrible gray green and they seemed as if they were going to come and just eat the town up. I never been so frightened in my life. My husband wanted us to leave, but I said I was born here and I wasn't running away 'cause the weather. I'm here, er, well, my husband is in there, reporting our lawn mower stolen."

The woman's face suddenly split in a wide grin. "I think it just floated away. It was old. Keeping the awful thing running was kind of like a hobby for him and I'm glad it's gone."

One of the men grumbled.

Another woman sat up on the edge of her chair. "The water, it just started risin'. I was out in the street a few blocks from my house." She pronounced water as 'watah' and 'ah' was I. "As I walked, it got deeper. It went over the tops of my shoes and then up to my knees. I was afraid. I couldn't tell where my feet were when I was trying to get home. By the time I got there, the water was almost at my front door."

She took a breath and continued.

"We should have gone. I should have made my husband leave. Everything on the first floor of our home is washed away. When it wouldn't stop coming in the downstairs, we ran up to our bedroom. I felt so helpless because we had to run upstairs with only food and water and not everything that was precious and dear to us." Addy's sympathy went out to the woman.

"The urn of my dear first husband must have floated around for two days," the woman continued, "but he's still snug inside his brass home. Thank God he picked out a brass one and not the pretty ceramic one I liked. He always was good with details."

Addy tried to look industrious and not amused when she recorded this one.

"Did you see Brown Dog?" asked the man with the hearing aide. He looked expectantly and seriously concerned as he did a visual poll of the crowd.

"Um…I saw a brown dog." Addy held a hand out to the brown dog's height. "About this high. Leather collar, no tags. Sleek coat, eyes that sort of have a way of—um, seeming like they can see into your soul?"

A little cheer went up.

"Big George must have bought him a collar," somebody said.

"Did he come up to you? Did he touch you?"

"He put his nose in my hand, scared ten years off my life, and put his head on my thigh so I'd pet him."

"Oh!" chorused around the room.

"Does that mean something?"

"Brown Dog wanders around town, never causing trouble and always being friendly." People looked at one another. "He doesn't really belong to anyone. George who works up at Pirate's Roost takes care of him mostly."

"If he touched you, it means you're lost," this from the woman in the corner who had finally looked up and seemed to be able to identify with that fate.

Lost. It sounded right and no one seemed to judge her for it.

Addy heard so many tales of fear and hurt she gained a much better understanding of the plight of the millions who had suffered because of hurricanes. Homes demolished. Every belonging scattered over a wide area. Hours, days of dread and heartache as everything was ripped from them. Being left with desolation and feelings of utter confusion as to what to do next.

Addy hunched over her notebook of little gems. She knew there was a lot more to tell in this town than tales of a man caught in a web of subterfuge and lies.

"Subterfuge and Lies." That had a quiet yet sinister ring to it. A good working title for the first article about Hale and Blankenstock.

She wondered how Zach was doing, what he was doing? Had he made a run for Boston where he could hide in a swanky hotel under an assumed name? No. He'd stay here and help.

She stretched out the length of her body against his and the warmth of his bare skin against hers...

Ye-ah, think of something else. The box. What was in the box? I should have looked, she thought—the reporter in her was mad.

A pair of brown Italian leather shoes appeared in front of her.

She looked up and her jaw almost unhinged. Drop-dead Gorgeous was wearing a frown aimed directly at her. Lucky the woman he smiled at.

He almost got a word out.

"Wait. Wait." She held up a hand. Zach would have gone to see his attorney and his attorney would have come to make sure she was escorted from town—in fact, he had come to do it personally.

The man studied her from head to toe.

She raised a finger in his direction. "Hunter Morrison!"

He nodded and Addy knew her stint in Bailey's Cove was up.

HENRY MARKHAM, the man next to Zach in the old cellar, stood slightly hunched because of the low ceiling, arms akimbo in the muddy mess that had been the basement of the historic mansion. The place smelled of dirt and wet rock with a patina of age. The only light down there was whatever was carried in. Candles, lanterns and, today, flashlights.

The flashlight in the man's hand illuminated the nearest wall. "Sorry, Zach. The water is still trickling in. I'll leave one of the pumps set up, a couple blowers and an exhaust fan. When the emergencies are settled and we can get supplies and materials, I'll bring the guys up here. Where we start will depend on what materials we can get first."

The basement, large by early-nineteenth-century Maine standards, was outlined with a series of structural supports carved from hardwood tree trunks, the marks of the ax still present after almost two centuries.

He and Markham were in a small, heavily damaged room at the far end of the basement.

The floor of compacted soil meant this room had been the root cellar, the place where winter fruits and vegetables were stored.

Henry had been taking digital flash photos as they moved through the basement in case the insurance company needed them. He took photos of each wall, each section of the floor, giving attention to the areas of the walls that bulged.

When Markham touched the area of split stone, the wall lost its cohesion and slumped, making both men retreat. Large hunks of rock landed with thuds and muted clatters on the floor.

"Sorry, man. I guess demo will be relatively easy."

"No harm, but look at this."

As the wall collapsed, something yellow had spilled out from behind the rock.

"What is that?" Zach asked as he shined his flashlight on the smidgen of color.

Markham hunched closer. Then he picked up a shard of something and laughed. "Welcome to a mid-eighteen-hundreds garbage dump. A shattered teapot and a couple of broken plates. I suppose useless stuff had to go somewhere.

"Listen, Zach. We can put the stone back up and seal it tight or we can pour concrete, whichever you want. In either case, we should install drain tiles with a sump pump. I can make the space dry and usable for storage."

As they inventoried the damage, Markham had pointed out several other areas where the rocks were ready to fall away as they had done in the root cellar room. "I should have had that pump installed a long time ago, anyway. If I do, I can get Heather to set it up to look like it would have been in the eighteen hundreds."

"She'll be tickled."

"Ah-yuh, I gotta run." Markham directed his beam toward the cellar stairs. "The guys are finished up at Owen's and starting on the neighborhoods below. Time to get my hands dirty."

"Can I help?"

Markham's gaze went to Zach's hands. Zach laughed and held them up.

"Yes, they are a bit too neat looking and soft for your kind of work." His fingernails, though not as professionally manicured as Carla Blankenstock's were, were neat and trimmed short. "The only calluses I have are from exercise equipment."

The contractor smiled. "If you have old clothes and boots, come on down. You won't miss us. We're loud and we're messy."

AT NEARLY MIDNIGHT, Zach knew he should be tired. He had worked with Henry Markham's crew, clearing Hurricane Harold's damage. His hands hurt, but thanks to the spare gloves Markham kept in his truck, were not blistered.

Sleep should have been the easiest thing in the world.

Then why was he still staring at the ceiling?

He knew exactly why. Every time he closed his eyes he saw Addy. He saw her in her drowned-rat look the day he met her.

When he had heated up the soup, he remembered how she almost drooled wondering if he was going to give her any.

He closed his eyes as he thought of her in the shower, her soapy hands slipping smoothly down her chest, her belly...

He threw off the covers and got up.

There had to be something better to do than to torture himself.

In the breezeway, he dressed in the already muddy work clothes and shoes and began carrying the rock that had fallen at Markham's feet. By the time he'd made his third trip outside, he had created a makeshift trail that may never be able to be scrubbed away. Indelible, just like Addy was in his mind.

He trekked up the cellar stairs with two more stones. The moon showed his way to the pile of hewn rocks. Along with the rocks he had started a separate pile of broken dishes, porcelain shards, a small bent spoked wheel maybe from a baby carriage and several other unidentifiable bits of life. He'd tarp that pile in case there would be pieces of interest to the museum.

He must have been carrying stones for a couple hours when he sat down on the stoop to have a glass of water and clear his head.

He drank half the water in a single gulp and closed his eyes. When an image or a thought came to mind he breathed and let it float off into oblivion. He welcomed the blankness of the space between the stars and let it fill him with nothingness. Peace descended upon him.

Oh, Zach, come to me.

His eyes popped open.

So much for nothingness. He chugged down the rest of the water and went back to work.

He used a hammer and an old railroad spike he had found in the garage to loosen stones that had not yet been liberated by water and the ravages of time.

When he chipped away a few stones in one particularly solid section, he could see something red. More pottery? When he removed another stone, it seemed to be a piece of oilcloth—if a twenty-first-century guy could recognize oilcloth. He pulled on the corner of the piece, but it would not come out.

I have built a wall around my heart... The wall will crumble long after I'm gone... Colleen McClure.

He grabbed his hammer and spike and chipped away at the mortar with renewed energy.

CHAPTER FOURTEEN

ZACH TOOK A step back and surveyed the open area in the rock face of the basement wall. Most of the exposed area in this section wasn't rock or dirt but mottled red-brown oilcloth.

By the time he had enough of the stone removed to see the size of the wedged piece of the cloth, he had removed approximately three square feet. And the cloth was not merely wedged in place. The very old-fashioned waterproof cloth covered something.

As far as he could tell in the insufficient light of the battery-operated fluorescent lantern, the mottled cloth covered a box of some kind. At the very least something rectangular-shaped approximately two feet long by fifteen inches tall. How deep it was, he had no way of knowing.

The cloth covering the box had been, at one time, tied with lengths of rope or twine. Only small chunks of the ties remained. When he pulled back the layers, it was clear to see the cloth had been a deep red at one time.

This could be a significant find and he wanted to share it with someone.

He wished Addy was with him.

He should get Heather up here. What if it was Bailey's treasure? It was supposed to be buried up here somewhere. He'd just never known where and he hadn't needed to dig for treasure.

If it was the treasure…

Addy had to be back in Boston by now.

He'd call her. She'd like to know, and with her safely in another state with a blockade between them, it couldn't hurt. His hand instantly reached for his mobile phone.

Of course his pocket was empty.

He hurried up the steps from he cellar and shed the muddy clothing.

Having given himself permission to talk to her made doing so suddenly seem like the most important thing in his life.

He raced to the loft, grabbed his phone from the charger and dialed the number Addy had given him.

"Zach?"

As the sound of Addy's voice swept over him, his heart hammered like a tenth-grader with the homecoming queen on his arm.

"Zach, what's wrong?" she asked when he had been too struck to speak.

"Addy, sorry. You must have been asleep. Go back to sleep, I'll talk to you later."

"You'll talk to me now," she said, her tone concerned, not cross. "What's wrong?"

There was so much wrong he almost laughed out loud, especially since the most ridiculous wrong thing was he missed her and now called her in the wee hours of the morning.

"I found something."

"In the middle of the night. You found something in the middle of the night. Why aren't you sleeping?"

"You."

She laughed. "What are you talking about?"

"You're down in Boston sleeping away. You wouldn't understand about being lonely in Maine"

"I do...understand...about being lonely in Maine." Her voice broke with sudden emotion.

She'd be back to her life, with the distractions, the people. "But you're not lonely in Boston?" Why should she be?

"I'm not in Boston."

"I must be too tired because I can't put that together so it makes sense. Hunter Morrison said he'd take care of you."

"Of getting rid of me? Booting the journalist out of town? Muzzle freedom of the press? Keep you sequestered from prying minds?"

He could hear the teasing in her voice as if she were running a finger down his cheek as she said the words. He smiled and a dawning hope rose in his chest. "Something like that."

"Well, you'd better get a new attorney."

"Because you're still in town."

"Not only am I in town, I have been vouched for by one of the town's finest dressed, but I've been given a stern warning that I must earn my keep."

Zach laughed out loud. "You are really here."

"I rescued pottery this morning and cleaned up shards and a splintered building in the afternoon."

"Can I come and pick you up?"

"It'll be quicker than if I walk up that mountain. And it's kind of dark out there. Did you know this town only has streetlights on Church Street and, of course, none of them are on."

"Where are you?" He pulled on his jeans as he spoke.

"Cora. I'll get dressed."

"Getting dressed is optional. I'll be there in seven minutes."

"Seven minutes… You gotta love a small town."

He snapped his jeans and slid on a shirt. At the doorway he nabbed a cap and headed down the stairs.

Halfway down he stopped.

What in the hell was he doing?

His career, his life as he knew it might be over if he could not extricate himself from the mess at Hale and Blankenstock. By getting too close to Addy, he might well be ruining her chance of restarting her career, repairing her life.

His phone rang. Maybe it was Hunter calling in the nick of time to save him and Addy.

It was Addy.

He let it ring again.

And again.

"Hello."

"You had better not be having second thoughts, buddy. I know where you live and I have my ways of getting to you."

Her tone made him smile. "I don't want to ruin things for you." He started down the steps toward the row of shoes in the breezeway.

"I'm afraid you already have."

"What do you mean?"

"You are such a guy."

"Thank you. I thought I knew what that meant, but enlighten me."

"As an extremely rich man who also happens to be incredibly good-looking, it might be over the top to tell you this, and I hate to feed your ego too much, but you are amazing in bed and, well, out of bed."

"Now what am I supposed to say to that?"

"That you'll be here in six minutes."

"Five and a half." He slid on deck shoes, put his phone in his jacket pocket and was pulling out of the garage in another ten seconds.

As he stopped in front of Cora, she ran down the stairs, her nightgown trailing out from under the tail of her jacket and her clothes stuffed in a wad under her arm. She was sexy and beautiful and adorable all rolled into one and he couldn't wait to hold her in his arms again.

He climbed out of the SUV and she hurled herself at him. He caught her against him.

"I missed you. I missed you," she said as she clung to him, her feet dangling in the air.

"It was hard to tell."

She pressed her mouth to his, her lips and tongue hungry and exploring.

He smoothed down the tail of her nightgown and held her close.

"So now do you believe me?" She smacked her lips to his one more time.

"I do and I think I might have missed you, too."

"You think? You might?" She pressed closer. "I think you know you did."

"You are a crazy woman." He kissed her again and then picked her up and deposited her in the passenger seat of the SUV. "I had no idea I liked crazy women."

"Only one crazy woman, please, and we're being watched." She pointed to the porch of the Victorian home named Rose, the first of the Three Sisters as approached from the sea. "Brown Dog has something to say."

"So you've been here in town, what, one day?"

"One and three quarters very long days."

"And you've already been convinced the stray dog has powers."

"He had me pegged."

"Pardon?" He made a U-turn in the middle of the empty street and headed back the way he had come.

"He apparently finds lost people and helps them be found."

Zach reached across the console and touched her cheek as he turned from Treacher Avenue onto Church Street.

He'd like to be the person that helped Adriana Bonacorda feel found. Tomorrow, in the light of a new day they might feel differently, but this morning, they had found each other and that needed to be enough for now.

ADDY SMOOTHED THE sheer fabric of the night-gown and tried to repress a shiver.

Zach flipped a switch and in a few moments, warm air poured over her. When he put his hand on her thigh, she wanted to insist he stop the car and make love to her. But she was sure Bailey's Cove had some of the same rules about such things in public as the bigger cities.

"What have you been up to?" she asked to distract herself.

"Mostly getting covered with mud."

"Without me?"

"I thought about you. Didn't want to, but I did."

"All the time?"

"Most of the time."

"Good. I thought about you, Zach, but all the wrong kind of thoughts. I should have been thinking about how to pin your ears back, about how to trim your sails, about how to put you in jail for decades."

"But you weren't."

"I don't want to do those things anymore. I don't believe they are right anymore."

"Does a journalist have to believe in a story?"

"I do. I tried for several years to give editors the line they wanted, sometimes the truth bent to someone else's moral code, but those stories always came out flat. I have some extremely dreadful clippings in my filing cabinet."

"I'd like to see them."

"I'm burning them tonight."

Being with Zach again excited her beyond belief. She wanted him, but she also liked him. A rare thing for Adriana Bonacorda and men.

She loved him. Crazy, so crazy. "Are you driving as fast as you possibly can?"

"Faster." He turned the last corner and drove the SUV inside the garage in quick time.

They opened their doors as the SUV stopped and he met her in front of the SUV's grill. The air warmed by the engine engulfed them. He reached under her nightgown and ran his hands along her naked hip to her thighs.

"I almost couldn't wait to do that," he said in a breathy voice against her ear.

"I thought it would never happen."

He snatched her up into his arms and carried her up the stairs. By the time he lowered her to the bed she wanted him so badly she hurt with the ache of anticipation.

As he undressed, she slipped her jacket off and reached for the nightgown.

He caught her wrist. "Leave it. It's incredibly sexy."

"To have sex with a woman while she wears another woman's nightgown? Have you ever?"

"I'm going to now."

He was naked by then and she held her hand up when he started to lower himself to the bed. "I just want a moment to admire."

After a split second he asked, "Had enough?"

"Not nearly, but show-and-tell is finished."

He obliged her by stretching out full length on top of her. When she groaned her appreciation, he moved against her.

"You make me hot," her voice so wispy, she hardly recognized it. "Am I on fire yet?"

He smiled and then covered her mouth with his. After long, uninterrupted minutes, his searching lips kissed her neck and on down to her chest. He sucked her nipple through the fabric of the gown and she was wild to have those lips against her skin again.

Murmuring sweet words, he bunched the material of the nightgown in his fists and raised it up to her hips. Nothing had ever been better than having Zachary Hale make love to her. Nothing. She closed her eyes and gave herself over to the homage he paid to her as he lowered his mouth, inching hot kisses along her belly until, he lifted her and pressed his hot mouth to her center.

Stars exploded behind her closed eyelids as

she arched into him, letting the waves of pure pleasure wash over her again and again.

"Oh, Zach. The things you do to me."

She must have spoken aloud as he ran his hands up her belly under the gown and pressed his palms to her breasts.

"More," she said when the pleasure ebbed.

He moved away and swiftly put on a condom. When he was pressed to her in every way, he kissed her breathless again and she took all of him willingly. As he began to move inside her, she let herself rise with him, keeping him as close to her as she could.

She wanted him close, always close.

THE FIRE FLICKERED across the room when she opened her eyes to find Zach's face next to hers. "Did I fall asleep? I didn't mean to sleep."

"But you're so beautiful when you sleep."

"I'd rather be beautiful and awake. I want to spend every moment I can enjoying you."

"How about now?"

"Now is perfect."

"You're perfect."

"Nearly." She put a hand in her out of control hair.

He drew her hand away and kissed her on the mouth. "Completely perfect."

"We might have to agree to disagree on that

one. Now about this adventure you spoke of earlier. Oh, the box. You saw Heather and the two of you opened the box."

"We did, but it's not about the little box. You'll have to get dressed."

She realized for the first time he was dressed. "I don't even know where I dropped my—" She stopped when he held up her jeans and shirt.

"I brought this for you also." Now he held up a plaid flannel shirt.

"Am I about to get cold?"

"If you do, let me know. I've discovered the best method to warm you up."

When she lifted the gown over her head, he leaned in and teased her nipple. As he went on to tease the underside of her breast, she leaned back on her hands and let him have his way.

"Yes, you have discovered wonderful methods to keep me warm." The words came out strained as she struggled for air.

He suddenly pulled away and with shocking swiftness popped her shirt on her and followed that with the flannel one. Resigned to getting dressed, she lifted her feet, and her panties and jeans followed. Left sock and then the right.

"You really mean business here."

"Come on, you lazy thing."

She stood and stretched, raising her arms

above her head. "The sun is nearly up," he pointed out.

"The sun. You are insane."

"Come, anyway. You like me because I'm insane."

"I like you because you are rich."

He chuckled. "And I've brought you to such luxurious surroundings as you've never experienced before."

"All right, because you're handsome."

She ducked under his arm and snuggled close. She liked the warmth of his body against hers. She had missed him desperately even before she climbed into Patty O'Reilly's tow truck.

"Hunter is handsome and you didn't throw yourself at him."

"Maybe I did. How do you know?"

"Because you're not on the slow bus back to Boston by way of Newfoundland."

"And glad of it."

He led her down the wooden steps from the loft and then down the stone steps to the cellar.

She stopped. "Wait. You didn't demand that I come here so you could put me to work, did you?"

"How's it going so far?"

"Well, so far so good. Why are we going to the basement? Isn't it wet down there?"

He shrugged. "Wet and, in the right spots, muddy."

She pulled away in mock horror.

He took her hand again and continued down.

"Duck," he told her.

"What?"

"Oh." At the last step, the ceiling to the basement came up really fast and if he hadn't had his hand out, she might have struck her head.

He picked up a lantern from the bottom step and lit it. The walls of the place were rock and dirt.

"Whoa, cheery place you've got down here."

"You will not mock me when you see what I've brought you here for."

"You didn't just bring me for…" She paused and waited for him to look back at her and then pointed upstairs and winked.

"That, too."

He stood up.

"Stop!"

He slowed enough to prevent crashing his head into the wooden beam but did impact with a slight crack. "Ugh."

In horror, Addy reached for his head and felt for blood.

He laughed that sweet sound she would never tire of but would love to get the chance to try.

He took her by the hand, stooped and led her to the far end of the cellar.

In one excavated section there was a two-foot area in which there was something that looked like reddish-brown plastic. He carefully lifted the edges, several layers of it; the inner layers were pure red. Nested under the layers of the old cloth was a chest, an old wooden chest.

"You've gotta be kidding me." Addy could barely catch her breath as she spoke.

CHAPTER FIFTEEN

ADDY LIFTED A drooping corner of the red cloth, revealing more of the box. By the grain, it appeared to be oak. By the age of the surrounding cloth, it seemed to be as though it had been walled up here for a long time.

"How old do you suppose it is?" she asked quietly.

Zach laughed soft and warm. "Old enough."

She touched the box. The surface felt oily and cool. "Do we get to take it out of there and see what it is?"

"It should be removed by someone like Heather Loch, someone who knows what they're doing. Heather might not even touch it. She might defer to someone from the university or a larger museum who has more experience."

"How long do you think that would take?"

"Days to weeks depending on how long the barricades stay up outside town."

"Don't you think they would let someone

from the university inside the roadblock to take a look?"

"They might, but I don't think Bailey's Cove could withstand that." He answered as quietly as she had spoken and then leaned closer with the light. "The town's in a vulnerable state. If treasure seekers descended on us, the essence of Bailey's Cove might be destroyed forever and the townsfolk have been struggling with this for a long time."

"So what do we do?"

"Take it out of the wall." He leaned in and opened the layers of oilcloth again so they could see the wood of the box. "Looks like a hasp, a closure mechanism."

She put a hand on his shoulder and stood on tiptoes. "Life with you in it is so exciting."

He put a hand over hers and turned so he could see her face. The emotion she saw there almost took her breath away. When he kissed her slowly and tenderly, she melted against him.

He pulled gently away, the longing of a lifetime etched on his face, "Addy, I—"

"Zach, I know." She studied his face, the features, the lines, the secrets told by his eyes. She would remember this man for every day of her life. Reaching up she put her palm to the smoothness of his cheek. "Now tell me, is the hasp like one might find on a treasure chest?"

He smiled and so did she.

"I guess one of us had to say it. Treasure chest," he said shifting back to the work at hand.

"Hold the light," he said as he tugged at the cloth. The chest didn't move. "Seems as though two hundred years of house settling has caused an issue."

"If I carve out the dirt above it, I might be able to slide the chest free." He worked carefully with a hammer and the railroad spike.

Twenty minutes later, he was able to bring the box forward.

"It's heavy."

She rushed in. "Let me help."

He brought a knee up to support it and hefted the chest in his arms so he had a better grip. "I've got it, I think."

"Can we take a peek now?"

"We could, but I'd like to take it up to the loft. If you'd lead with the flashlights, that would be helpful."

"We can open it in front of the fire, see it the way a pirate might have seen it, at night by firelight, after everyone else has gone to sleep."

"In secret," he whispered.

She led him through the darkened basement

and breezeway. At the top of the stairs she held the door.

He carefully placed the still-wrapped box on the dining-room table and slowly removed the red oilcloth.

Addy moved around the table, looking at the box from different angles without touching it, excitement bubbling up inside her. "Not a very fancy treasure chest, but I guess they couldn't order one from treasurechests.com or…"

He looked up at her.

"I know. I know. I'm like a kid. I want to rip it open, but then I don't want to open it at all. I couldn't stand it if there was no treasure or just a few trinkets and a bunch of meaningless documents."

He retrieved a rag from under the sink. "You wipe it off and I'll move the couch and chair so we have plenty of room."

By the time she had the chest mostly cleaned off, Zach had spread a light-colored blanket between the couch and the fire and placed a towel near one edge.

Addy tried to lift the box. "Wow. It is heavy. I suppose I could carry it if I had to, but I've got you."

She grinned at him, trying not to think of how brief her time with him was going to be.

"You do have me," he said and kissed her

with what felt like regret and longing. She understood those emotions.

Zach carefully placed the box on the towel to keep the blanket from getting any of the oil on it. They sat down on the blanket and she leaned against him. Neither one of them reached for the box.

Plain lines, polished oak with carefully dovetailed corners. The hasp and hinges appeared to be brass. There was no lock on the hasp. Burying a box behind a rock wall must have been considered enough of a lock.

She put a hand on his arm. "Thank you, Zach, for thinking of me. I'm honored you wanted me to be with you when you opened this...this whatever it turns out to be."

"You seemed like just the right amount of adventurer and crazy person to get the most out of it."

He looked at her for a good long time. He wasn't thinking about treasure.

"You're thinking about Hale and Blankenstock, aren't you?"

"I should be in Boston seeing what could be done about getting to the truth."

"The FBI confiscated the paper records and electronic versions and they asked the two of you not to handle anyone's money for the time being or to do any kind of investing at all. Your assets are frozen and they instructed you not to contact your investors. Plus your attorney told you to get out of town." They both knew there was little he could do. "I, on the other hand, could be back in Boston, seeing if there is anything I could do from there."

He put his hand on her shoulder. "I appreciate you wanting to enter the fray on my behalf, but the battle is not yours. Carla Blankenstock and I are going to have to go head-to-head on this one. She thinks she has all the advantages, but there is still some game on my side."

The fire crackled merrily as they sat in silence.

"What do you say we ignore the rest of the world and open this mystery chest, Addy?"

"I don't know. What if it's not treasure? What if it's old golf shoes?"

He grinned. "Too heavy for that."

"Lead bars?"

"A decoy? And the treasure might still be out there. Then we can't let the town find out. They've had their collective hearts broken for two centuries and this would have been their best and biggest hope." He reached out a hand only to pull it back. "I don't know if I can take that kind of disappointment right now, either."

"Well, we both can't chicken out," she teased him. "You don't have to look. I'll do it and if it's disappointing, I won't tell you, I'll just take the box with me and you'll never have to see it again."

She started moving toward the chest.

"I've got it." He caught her and she laughed. "Go sit back there where it's safe."

"In case it has asps or a deadly chemical spray or something equally dangerous."

"Something like that."

He sat cross-legged in front of the chest. When he lifted the hasp it made a tiny groan. To protect her, she supposed, he had placed his body between her and the box.

A Galahad, an Arthur, a Lancelot, a throwback of the finest sort.

He lifted the box lid slowly and looked in and without turning he asked, "Is there any town lore that you know of about someone losing their head?"

"Head? No. Do not tell me there is a head in that box." She charged over to his side and scrambled around so she could see.

He lifted the lid completely until it rested back on its hinges.

The contents of the box sparkled and glittered in the firelight.

"Oh, my." Addy sat back on her heels. "Liam Bailey, you dirty dog."

Zach laughed out loud. "That old devil."

"Legend says he denied ever being anything but a law-abiding privateer." She curled up beside him.

"Colleen must he have hidden it away from her father and husband knowing either one of them could have legally taken it away from her and spent it as he pleased." He dropped a kiss on her shoulder.

"You've been sitting on pirate treasure all this time."

"There's more irony in this tale. My parents turned over ownership of what my mother disdainfully called 'the family mausoleum' to me when I was twenty-five. Said it would do me good to take responsibility for something, even if it was just an old wreck barely worth caring for. My mother wanted nothing to do with the old mansion and my father always acquiesced to her wishes. I've been seeing to it since then."

"So the place belongs to you, and everything in it. Hmm."

She put her arms around his neck and brought his mouth down to hers.

He broke away. "There's a pirate's chest treasure sitting beside us and all you can think of is kissing me."

"I have you in my arms. I can't think of anything hotter than being surrounded by gold, jewels and man." She put the tip of her index finger over his heart. "This man."

The light from the fire glistened off the treasure and soon off their naked bodies.

All that glitters, Addy thought as she tumbled over the edge, bringing Zach with her.

When the fire had burned low, he raised himself up on his elbows. "Are you a witch?"

"Have I cast a spell on you so you'd forget the treasure and make love with me instead?"

He rolled to one side and then got up to renew the fire. When he returned he grabbed a hand of glittering gold and gems.

She gasped at the cold and the pleasure when he placed a golden necklace dotted with green stones on her chest. Then she closed her eyes when he began to arrange the elegant jewelry with the tip of his finger.

After he had settled the long strands of the necklace on either side of her neck and the large, sparkling gem between her breasts, she opened her eyes and glanced down at herself.

"You look lovely in emeralds and gold. I knew you would."

"You've thought of such things, have you?"

"You make me think of many things I've never thought of before. I would always see you in emeralds if it were up to me. And then I would see you out of them."

If he didn't stop, she was going to have to have him again, but he sat up and found two more blankets for them. "Digging into a box of treasure while wearing only a blanket. Kinky. I like it." She reached into the chest and pulled out a handful of coins. "These rectangular ones are somewhat tarnished. What does that mean?"

"There's less gold in them."

"How do you know that?"

He looked sheepish and then shrugged.

"Oh, yeah. You're rich. I forgot."

"Did I tell you that's one of the reasons I like you?"

"Because I don't mince words?"

"Because you don't care that I'm rich."

Now it was her turn to shrug.

She aimed a smile at him. "It's not your wealth that impresses me." Wrapped in her blanket, she moved forward. "Although what would impress me right now is knowing what else is in that box."

He tipped the chest so the contents spilled out. "There are heaps of stones, set and unset, of all colors, and coins—many, many coins— a few chalices, several crosses, miscellaneous things and one crown."

"Imagine being some ill-fated king or queen

out there in history who lost their crown to a pirate."

Zach pulled the crown, a circlet of gold with crudely faceted stones roughly attached, from the box and set it gently on her head. "I think we've discovered what your hair is for. Holding a crown in place."

She felt the crown in her hair with both hands. "I like it. Maybe no one will notice if I keep this one."

"You can have it."

"I don't think so." She could not think of having anything so precious to always remind her of what she had and lost.

"It's mine to give." His look answered hers with, he'd give her the world if it was his to give.

"Don't we, I mean, you, have to return everything to the owners?"

"The contents of this chest are over two hundred years old. The chances of identifying any of it and connecting it to an owner are remote. With its clear provenance, it's mine to give to you."

She took the crown off and put it back in the box. "Crowns aren't much use when digging up news stories."

"I guess it's just as well. I can see Heather having a heart attack right now because we've been handling these things without the standard precautions." He held her gaze with a smile. "Imagine her reaction if I started giving it away willy-nilly before she got a chance to examine it and catalog everything."

She could hear the same regret in his voice that she felt. He was saying goodbye again. With care, she put the coins back in the oak box. When Zach returned the emerald necklace and the rest of the treasure, she closed the lid and lowered the hasp until it clicked into place.

"What are you going to do now?"

"You make walking away so hard." She kissed him on the mouth as she squeezed his hand.

"Stay with me for now. I'm going to ask Hunter and the chief to come up. It's best if whatever I do is open and aboveboard." He kissed her hard, almost desperate, but stopped abruptly. "With a few exceptions," he said.

She was an exception. She had always been an exception. It had started when she was a kid. Her hair was an exception. All her siblings had glossy, straight hair. She was the exception when she fought ferociously to have the journalism club she started in sixth grade treated with respect. She was certainly the exception when she took on the types of stories that interested her and not always the ones the editors were clamoring for. Suddenly being an exception was a bad thing.

She wanted to love Zach openly and freely, to tell him.

JUST BEFORE NOON Chief Montcalm looked from one of them to the other. He shook his head. Hunter Morrison sent the two of them with a questioning smile. They were all standing at the dining-room table in the loft. The unassuming treasure chest sat in the center, lid closed under the single fluorescent lightbulb hanging from the ceiling.

"The old folks in town have a bit of oral lore handed down from one generation to the next," the chief said. "It goes… 'Today Mama took an old box from a hiding place only she knew about. She wrapped the box in red cloth and tied it up. Then she took James and Mr. Michael to town and I never saw the box or those men again.'"

"The old folks. Do you mean the group that's called the Goldens? How do you know what the Goldens talk about?" Addy asked.

He stared at her dead-on.

"You're not going to tell me. Okay." Addy frowned. She'd love a crack at interviewing this guy for his life story. She was sure there were some doozies there.

"You saw the red oilcloth on the workbench in the garage," Zach said. "We found remnants of the twine it had once been bound with."

The law officer carefully undid the brass hasp. He slowly lifted the lid, stopped halfway and opened it all the way. "Well, I'll be damned."

"Wow, Chief. That was a pretty emotional outbreak for you."

The other men looked at her.

"What?" she asked, just beginning to realize how deeply the chief had built his reputation on being a closed-off kind of guy.

"Zach, we are going to have to keep this quiet," the chief said distracting everyone.

Hunter leaned in closer and then he straightened.

"Very quiet," he said, and then and gave Addy a pointed look.

"It must be worth millions," Addy said when she peeked in for the hundredth time since this morning, which seemed to be days ago, but was only a few hours.

"Many millions if it's real."

The chief looked up when Zach commented. "The evidence points to real."

"What are your plans now?" Chief Montcalm asked.

"I thought I'd see if they'd put it in the vault in the bank, but I wanted your opinion."

Before he spoke, the chief stared at her as though assessing how much he could say in front of her that would or would not show up on the front page of a newspaper.

"I know George Heinz at the bank," he finally said. "He'll want an inventory and there are many mouths at that bank. Mr. Morrison is right. This needs to be kept very quiet."

The chief looked at her again.

She shrugged. "Okay. Okay."

"I'll keep it here," Zach told them. "This place has been searched several times over the years, and the folks in town are busy with other things."

Addy's phone rang.

"Excuse me."

She left the three men discussing the fate of the box and stepped out of the loft onto the landing outside the door.

"Hello, this is Addy." The caller ID already told her it was Richard Smally, her previous and soon-to-be editor at the Boston paper.

"Addy, I'm waiting. I need what you've got on Hale or I'm going to have to let Wally and Jacko duke it out over the story. That would be a shame because you could always find the interesting angle."

"I'm working on just such an angle right now."

"Well, you've got until five p.m. tonight and then I'm going to send out the hounds. Oh, and Bonacorda?"

"Yes."

"Don't let me down."

He didn't need to say it, but the great big *again* was not very silent inside her head.

"Five p.m."

CHAPTER SIXTEEN

ADDY KNEW RICHARD SMALLY well. If she didn't get something viable to him by the deadline, she'd miss her chance of ever getting back her journalism career. Soon she would fall outside the implied, but never spoken of, age bracket for breaking out of the pack. The world changed slowly, some corners more slowly than others.

Addy retreated to the couch wondering what she could say about Zach and the situation in Boston or here in Bailey's Cove that didn't qualify as off the record.

The three men stood around the treasure, discussing how to get the word out. She wanted to raise her hand but was certain they didn't want it to come to the town via her.

She could go to the Pirate's Roost and ask questions for a great human-interest sidebar, but she'd have to be cagey or they'd catch on that she had been tipped-off by the chief.

Wait. Why should she care? She was a journalist and a reporter. She got leads and info from many places, people who never knew she got leads from them, from people who were miffed they had spilled the beans. Or spoke on a subject because they were angry with someone.

Other than Zach, she hadn't promised any of the people of Bailey's Cove she'd keep mum about what they said…

Until she accepted their invitation to be one of them.

By staying, by helping, by letting them trust her, she had more or less said the secrets of Bailey's Cove were off the record. The legends of Bailey's Cove belonged to them until they wanted the world at large to know.

She was done for.

"Do you need a ride back to town, Ms. Bonacorda?"

Addy looked up to see the three of them watching her with great interest. The chief had asked the question.

The chief had donned inscrutable. Hunter had that questioning smile again. Zach's expression said a noncommittal goodbye, and Addy couldn't stop the feeling she was fading away. Soon she'd be nothing but a point of interest in local history.

"I was thinking of asking a few more questions—"

"I'll take her, Chief." Hunter Morrison

stepped up and interrupted her. "We have a few things to discuss."

Asked and answered Addy thought. "I'll pack up my things."

She slid the laptop and power supply into her bag along with her paper and pens and Christina's nightgown and headed for the door. She spared a single goodbye glance at Zach.

Walking away this time was so much harder because she knew it wouldn't kill her. It would just make her suffer forever. No, maybe only for ten years, until they met in the Boston Common.

She trudged down the steps with Hunter behind her. It was time she headed back to Boston.

"I get it, Mr. Morrison. Everything said on Sea Crest Hill except the published historical information is off the record including any personal information about Zachary Hale and the treasure of Liam Bailey." Tucked into the passenger seat of Hunter Morrison's car, Addy gave him the speech he was most likely looking for.

"Hunter, please. Call me Hunter. We are in Bailey's Cove after all, and it's mostly informal here."

"Can I quote you on that?" She tried hard to keep the sarcasm out of her tone.

He laughed, a pleasant laugh with no hint of derision.

She leaned her head back against the headrest. "I get that you're protecting Zach."

"He's pretty good at protecting himself, but he tends to believe the good in people and overlook the bad, so I do my due diligence on his behalf."

"What do you want to know from me? Shall I list the evil side first? I sometimes chew my fingernails. I don't drink the milk out of the bottom of my cereal bowl, but I do drink dirty martinis. At this minute my bed at home is unmade and I can't tolerate people who are two-faced. The last one is my favorite."

"Are you finished?"

"How much time do you have?"

"I know. You still eat fast food in spite of the guilt and you ride your bike the wrong way on one-way streets."

"You've been following me around?"

"No, but I'm a good guesser. Listen, I didn't volunteer to drive you back to Christina's so I could elicit promises from you or put you on the stand."

"Then why?"

"I wanted to let you know I understand how hard it is to love someone who, for crazy reasons sometimes, cannot love you back."

"What are you talking about?"

"You, how you look at him. Your body language around him." He paused and glanced at her. "How you worry your fingers when the subject comes up."

She instantly stopped and put her hands flat on her thighs. "Very funny. I've known him less than a week. How can I be in love with him?" So much in love with him.

"Time isn't relative when it comes to that kind of thing. Think of how fast you learned to hate him."

She couldn't argue that. Ten minutes into Savanna's story, she had loathed the man.

As Hunter drove into town, busy workers were everywhere. The sound of hammers and chain saws could be heard even through the car's windows. "You're engaged," Addy said. "How long did it take you to fall in love and buy her a ring?"

"I fell in love the first day I saw her in the sixth grade." His tone was matter of fact.

"That was fast and young."

"I asked her to marry me almost seventeen years later."

"Commitment anxiety?"

"Divergent paths."

She leaned forward in her seat belt as if she

could see the future better. "Don't tell him. He doesn't need that kind of pressure in his life."

That must have been the correct answer as his features lost some of their tenseness.

"I won't tell him anything. That's up to you, but don't give up hope."

"Why are you doing this? Why are you telling me these things?" She had to stop the finger worrying again.

"People around town are talking about that reporter woman. Apparently she's not afraid to get her hands dirty and she's pretty nice for an outsider. And Delainey never stopped loving me."

"You're a lucky guy."

"Hang in there. He'll get through all this."

Hunter turned the car from Church Street onto Treacher Avenue. As he pulled up in front of Cora, her phone signaled a text.

Sorry. Thought it was the right thing to do, her sister wrote.

Now what was she doing?

"Trouble?"

"My sister. Apologizing for something. I'd better call her."

She got out of the car and he came around to meet her.

"Thank you for the ride."

"I know unsolicited advice doesn't usually

sit very well. Just trying to payback my luck by passing the message forward."

She reached out and hugged him. "Hunter Morrison, I'm glad you have Zach's back."

She left him smiling as he got back into his car.

"Answer your phone. Answer it," she said as her sister's phone rang and rang. By the time she got to her room and voice mail was about to click in, Savanna answered.

"That was quick," her sister said. "I thought I'd have to wait forever and then one more day."

"What did you do that you're sorry for?" Addy didn't feel like jocularity at the moment.

"I had to do it. You're investigating him, aren't you? You're trying to get the truth about Zachary Hale, aren't you?"

"Why? What have you done?"

"I've told the FBI which files have the incriminating stuff. The exact ones, so it won't take them long to arrest him now."

Proof. Real evidence. And the FBI had it. Before, all she had was a base from which to start a story, hearsay, so to speak.

Addy stopped. Nausea swamped her. And confusion. "Why did you do it now?"

"I started feeling guilty and I just had to. What if he got away? What if he left the country? I couldn't let that happen when he took all my money and spent it on who knows what."

Addy listened to her sister, and yet Addy had so much of her own evidence that Zach was not that man, although none of it would stand up in court.

Addy had to force herself to breathe deeply in order to be able to breathe at all. "Are you absolutely sure the documents are authentic?"

"Are you all right?"

"I'm fine." Addy slumped onto the bed.

"Fine. Anyway, you already asked me and I told you that they looked authentic to me."

Addy stood.

She was Adriana Bonacorda and that meant something.

Addy thought for a minute. This was her sister. She would at least have electronic copies. She was proud of what she had done and why shouldn't she be? She thought she was protecting herself and her girls.

"Email copies to me." Her sister often pretended to be scared, but usually she was the slyest one in the room.

"I don't have any copies, Addy. I didn't think it would be a good idea. I have my girls to think about and raising them from jail would kill me."

"Savanna."

"What if he comes after me? He could send his thugs or something. He could try to hurt my girls."

She had copies.

"Savanna, he's not in Boston and I'm pretty sure he doesn't have any thugs. You and the girls are safe. Send me the files."

Savanna heaved a sigh of resignation and then Addy gave one of relief. If she was going to ask the really hard questions, she had to have hard facts.

"The FBI told me I was interfering with a federal investigation and it's a felony with jail time if I, well, interfered again. He frightened me, so no, I don't, and as it turns out, I'm protecting you by not having them."

"What? I don't need protection, Savanna."

"Why is it you're the only one in the family who is capable of taking care of herself? The rest of us, according to you, are…are somehow lesser beings.

"Well, I only need you," Savanna continued, "because I can use your talents to expose this man, this monster who takes away people's lives, makes it so people will have to work until they die trying to keep their families fed and clothed, with no help for college or any kind of nice stuff. You knew, Adriana, with the money that man promised I'd earn, I planned on sending Yasenia and Cecelia to college. Now I'm just trying to figure out what to cut from their schedules so I can begin again to save money.

"Let's see. Yassy was going to get a new leotard for gymnastics, but even gymnastics is out. CC needs…"

"Savanna, I'm—"

"Trying to help? Trying to help yourself."

"Is there something wrong with that?" Was there something wrong with wanting to become the best investigative reporter? Was there something wrong with her whole lifestyle? Her sister answered, but Addy wasn't paying attention. Nothing her sister said on the subject of Addy's career meant anything.

She had to figure those things out for herself.

She had started out chasing Zachary Hale because of her sister and because the man had hurt so many investors. Those were the things she told herself. She tried to think back to remember why she had chosen one story lead over another. Tibet over Sri Lanka, Argentina over Alaska. Every single one of them was to further her career.

Was that wrong?

"Thanks, Savanna, I have to go."

"Wait. What should I do?"

"There isn't anything for you to do. Just look after yourself and your girls."

"I'm taking the girls and I'm going to Mom's."

Of course she was. Their mother would dote on the children while Savanna got a therapeutic mani-pedi.

Addy put a hand to her forehead.

When she was with Zach it all felt like an outright fabrication by her half sister.

Zachary Hale.

Who are you?

Which man are you?

Addy wasn't afraid. She was angry.

Angry mostly at herself. She should know for sure the answers to these questions.

She wanted to go back up Sea Crest Hill and demand Zach tell her about the files Savanna had directed the FBI to.

Her sister would make a great witness. Single mother, two children, sweet, petite, sleek dark hair. She had lost everything but she had identified the files that would convict the big boss, the wrongdoer, the guy who assured she'd work until she died and she'd still die in debt.

Addy pushed herself up and paced. After a while, she stopped and stared out the second-story window. She could see the wreckage at the docks, the pottery studio and people across the street using whatever supplies they could find, most likely parts of destroyed buildings, to temporarily patch the roof of the yarn shop. More rain was coming.

The sudden clear horror of it all dawned on her. Savanna knew, Hunter Morrison knew—why else would he be so adamant that she hang in there, stay in town where he could watch her? The chief knew for sure. And she had been too blind to see.

Did everyone in Bailey's Cove know Zachary Hale was a crook? Is that why they protected him so much? Did they all benefit from his scheme?

Everyone who knew must have also known Zachary Hale had the reporter up on Sea Crest Hill to convince her of his innocence, or at least assure her silence.

There was something she could do.

She had to calm down.

She had to think, to figure out the truth. She had an article to write.

And then she could go help the people of Bailey's Cove because no matter what she thought of a few, most of these people would be good, innocent folk.

ZACH STRODE OVER to the fireplace and poked at the dying embers. At the dining table, Hunter Morrison had been making phone calls since he returned an hour ago. Chief Montcalm had returned a few minutes after Hunter.

"Is the file threat real and does Ms. Bonacorda know anything?" Zach asked as he stopped worrying the fire and went to the refrigerator for a pale ale. He offered Hunter one. Hunter nodded and when Zach came over to the table, pointed to the chair opposite to him.

"Addy didn't volunteer knowing about them and I didn't bring them up." Hunter said after Zach sat down. "If she doesn't know about them, I didn't want to tip her off."

"How could she not know?" Zach demanded, then quickly held up a hand of conciliation and continued in a neutral tone. "The woman's her sister."

Hunter slugged back a few swallows of the ale and then put down the bottle gently. "Half sister. I understand they haven't been close until recently. I don't know when they started sharing the files from Hale and Blankenstock, but I think you're right there could be no possible reason for Savanna not to tell her sister."

"We're doing what we can to find out what's in the files. Tomorrow or the next day we should have copies."

"Carla had to have planted the files in the first place. I still can't believe she would slip so far down without saying anything to me, without my knowing." Zach felt the pain of betrayal many times over because Carla had not spoken up and when she did, she blamed him.

"There is the possibility she's being played by someone else." The chief spoke with his hands on his hips. "If she is, then Carla Blankenstock would believe you're guilty, because she knew she was not."

CHAPTER SEVENTEEN

IT RIPPED ADDY'S heart to pieces to believe anything so immoral about Zachary Hale, but the truth was before her in black and white.

All she needed from him was denial and she'd believe him.

They were in the loft. Adriana Bonacorda on one side, Zachary Hale, Hunter Morrison and Chief Montcalm on the other. The fire had gone out. The electric lights all burned brightly to keep the night at bay.

The proof in the files was so clear it could barely be debated, yet she wanted to believe it was all lies.

Zach stared at her, his expression cold and distant. She had never seen this side of him, not even when he was trying to get rid of her in the beginning. Was this the side of him that could have stolen the fortunes of others?

Addy didn't know what to say. She had wanted so badly to believe him, but she had laid out all the proof against him and he had not denied the wrongdoing.

The chief of police trusted him.

Hunter Morrison not only defended him legally, he defended the man morally.

"I just need you to tell me it wasn't you."

What she truly wished for was that none of this happened and that she had met Zach at some charity event and she was reporting the event as a *good news* story. That Hale and Blankenstock had never taken a wrong turn, never made a questionable investment.

The three of them loomed over her, Zach and Hunter in their meticulously tailored business suits and Chief Montcalm in his uniform, starched and pressed to within an inch of its life.

Each one of them seemed to be daring her to continue. Each one of them had an expression that looked as if it was made of stone.

As one, they took a step toward her.

Fear tore at her from the inside out.

Addy sat up in bed.

Her room at the Three Sisters was dark and she was in her underwear on top of the chenille roses on the old-fashioned spread.

Finding out she was alone in her room, she breathed a generous sigh.

The exchange had been a terrible dream. If the real one turned out like that, she would ditch journalism because that would confirm without a doubt that she could not read people at all, that she might as well give up her aspirations. Her mother always told her she should be a teacher. A worthy profession, maybe she'd go study for that.

Groggy from lack of sleep and aching from working all day, she yawned and stretched.

Voices filtered up from downstairs and Addy remembered Christina had invited her to a late dinner with her friend Gregory Miller and a group of other hungry workers.

Thirty minutes. She'd been asleep for only a half hour, although it seemed so much longer.

Her muscles protested as she rose from the bed. If she hadn't hurt so much she'd laugh. *Out-of-shape reporter works with citizens to clear debris left from Hurricane Harold and now she can't move.* Maybe she should have taken time in her previous life to lift a few weights or at least walk around the block.

Helping to clean up Bailey's Cove had made her many friends and given her a few muscles, albeit sore ones.

Before she dozed off, she had emailed her editor an article any other journalist could have written, but with a few specifics about the town in which Zachary Hale had grown up. She didn't mention how he spent precious free time in Bailey's Cove when not in Boston. She did tell a circumspect account of him and the others saving boats belonging to the townsfolk. She said nothing of the yacht in the harbor. She said nothing about the files her sister spoke about to the FBI.

For her efforts, she got reamed out in a blistering email from Smally. He reminded her how close to the edge she was skimming, but the editor did not turn her loose, she knew, because he was still hoping for details none of the rest were able to get.

Addy forced herself into the shower, which consisted of soaping everything and then splashing for a furious sixty seconds in water that was just a bit warmer than freezing.

She came out the other side feeling quite refreshed. Whatever Christina needed her to do, she would do.

When she got down to the kitchen, hot food was being prepared for a table set for a dozen.

"Greg Miller," said a man standing at the sink peeling carrots. Greg was good-looking in that casual bad-boy sort of way, the kind who didn't seem to notice or care that he turned heads. He nodded, not holding out a wet hand for a shake that Addy was convinced would be firm and friendly. "And you would be the much-spoken-of Adriana Bonacorda."

"Oh, no!" Christina cried and pointed at the stove. "Addy, get the pot."

Addy dived for the lid just as water started bubbling onto the stove top. Inside the pot, potatoes jumped and jostled in the boiling water.

"Thanks."

"Thanks for inviting me," Addy said smiling at the bustling group of people around her.

"Ha-ha, we just wanted your help," Christina said with a warm grin. "We're so lucky." She continued to cut stacks of carrots into sticks.

"How so?" Greg asked as he added another peeled carrot to her pile and she held out her hands toward the bounty of simple fair spread out in the kitchen. "Compared to other areas of disaster where the population is dense, we have enough resources to go around. Dinner may be meat and root vegetables, but we're eating well."

"How is it," Addy asked, "that everyone had enough stocked away for such an occurrence? You didn't expect a hurricane."

"There won't be any stock left at the grocery stores when this is over, but the O'Brien's wouldn't horde a crumb. The Crandalls were a little reluctant to open their doors at first, but they've come around. The O'Brien's convinced them the townsfolk are good for it. Kind of an 'eat now, pay later' plan."

Dinner was soon ready and the table was almost filled with people who were fresh from the showers in the Three Sisters and as dog-tired as people could get.

"They found John Barleycorn, the Dillon boy's cat," someone said as Addy carried two bowls of hot whipped potatoes into the dining room. "Brown Dog herded him home."

The boy from the police station got his pet back. Addy felt all warm and fuzzy from the news. She found she liked the feeling and wondered if that was one of the motivations for living in a community—the warm fuzzies.

Harried and apologetic, a couple arrived and took their seats at the table. The man sat next to a blond-haired woman who could be none other than Delainey Talbot, Christina's sister, with her beautiful dark-haired daughter, Brianna. The child asked the man to move down one so her daddy could sit beside her. The man did so without hesitation, and then the child leaned against her mother with her eyes mostly closed.

As Addy approached with the filled and brimming bowls, Delainey gently sat her daughter up and stood to take one. Delainey seemed to be everything as wonderful as Christina was and that thought restored some of her shaken faith in Hunter.

Her steps faltered as she headed for the kitchen again.

Suddenly, it was all so clear.

Zach had not done anything to her to make her lose faith in him. She closed her eyes for a moment. No matter what, she would not doubt him again, even if he refused to see her ever again. He didn't do what they said he had.

Christina breezed in with the sautéed carrots with a mint glaze and stopped in front of Addy. "You all right?"

Addy smiled. "Just suffering a moment of clarity."

"Darn, those are hard." She leaned forward and kissed Addy's cheek. "Hang in there, sister. It's all worth it."

She looked over her shoulder at Greg, who entered with two platters, each carrying a roasted chicken.

"We are burning gas tonight," he said referring to using the oven for the chicken. "But the heat was well spent."

Christina continued, "We have everything. Come and sit down."

On cue, Gail and Sandy London, the twins from two houses down, entered carrying fresh butter and dinner rolls.

"Delainey, Addy, you two will know each other by reputation by now. And Addy, that bundle of sleepy gorgeous is Deelee's daughter, Brianna."

When Christina introduced her to everyone at the table she did not already know, including the late couple, the aforementioned O'Brien's. Smiles were passed around.

Included at the table were the bartender Michael Murphy and his wife, Francine.

"Hello again, Addy. Thanks for all you've done for the town," Michael said, his damp red hair slicked back. Francine seconded the thanks.

"Where's Hunter?" Mrs. O'Brien asked.

"He's up talking to Zachary Hale," Delainey answered.

"Can't they just leave that poor man alone," Mrs. O'Brien said as she brushed her straggling gray hair back from her face and gave Addy a sheepish glance.

With the group seated except the missing Hunter, thanks was given for the bounty and those in bad shape remembered. Two children and four adults here injured and had to be treated at the local clinic as inpatients. Mr. March was still missing.

Addy thought for the first time about the cohesiveness of the small town. Bailey's Cove, she knew from her research, was working to survive in the changing world.

"I was so happy to see the fuel trucks come back again today. Generators will hum once more," someone said.

Because Christina had heeded the warnings she had not run out of fuel. Every day mobile devices of all sorts could be found lined up in the reception hall of Cora plugged into power strips charging for owners who weren't so lucky as to still have fuel, or who had no power at all since Harold descended.

"I've learned my lesson well and good, ah-yuh," someone else said.

"How's Kimi Applegate dealing with everything? Does anyone know?" Addy heard the words but the speaker didn't register.

"Her husband's parents came and picked her up yesterday. She'll be staying with them until she can get back on her feet."

"Will she rebuild her pottery studio here in Bailey's Cove?"

The conversation continued around her.

"Oh, goodness, I hope so. When her husband died, I thought she'd leave, but I think she decided to stay because she liked our town and she said she loved the ocean. Of course things could change."

Addy admired the people, but didn't say so. The folks of this town seemed to truly enjoy each other. They weren't just residents; they were members of an extended family who cared for the welfare of each other.

And what she was doing could take away an important part of the community. Keeping Zachary Hale in people's minds, even in a good light, could lead to a devastating outcry if…

The doorbell rang just as Addy took a mouthful of the sautéed carrots. Christina got up but when footsteps sounded in the hall, she sat back down. In the doorway to the dining room, a woman Addy had never seen before appeared looking frazzled. Small with bangs and a dark ponytail, the woman's thin face showed worry lines, making her look older than she probably was. She searched the table until her eyes rested on Addy.

The table of people went silent.

"Did you think we wouldn't know, that we wouldn't find out that you were using us, pretending to be friendly when all you wanted was a news story?"

The woman plopped a computer down in the middle of the table so the others could see it.

The story Addy sent in a few hours ago would have hit the internet by now. If Richard Smally believed in nothing else, he believed in getting things in the pipe sooner rather than later.

She had given the story a working title of

Breaking Away from the Pack. It spoke of a man becoming a billionaire and living in a small town.

One by one, the faces turned toward her, all except the child.

Christina raised a hand. "Stella, there must be something more to this story. Addy?"

"May I see?" Addy asked standing up from the table.

Mrs. O'Brien turned the computer to face her.

"*Hale in Hiding* by Adriana Bonacorda with Jacko Wilson." The headline horrified her and sharing a byline with Jacko could only mean trouble.

The article started out with the edited question she had originally asked Smally. "Is Hale a stand-and-fight kind of guy or a flight risk?" She had posed the question to interest Smally, not to make any sort of accusation, but that is exactly what it seemed like she was doing.

And it would seem like that to all these people.

Jacko's edited-in part read "...and plots like the one Hale has been accused of often begin by a big ego thinking they can treat other people's money as their own. While there is no information as to why a billionaire would divert investors' money for his own use, it is only a matter of time until the motive, if it is there, will be uncovered."

It would not matter which part of the article could be attributed to Jacko Wilson, those words were going to harm Zach and leave her in a bad place with the folk of Bailey's Cove. Zach would know for sure she was here to get close to him and tell everything she found out.

"How could you do this?" questioned one of the twins.

Addy scanned the group, giving eye contact to those who would look at her, passing over the rest. The O'Briens looked at her as if she were a tragic figure.

Heaven help her, she might be.

"Will this get a lot of attention?" Mrs. O'Brien asked.

"Most likely, as it touches on two important developing stories. How the citizens of Bailey's Cove are doing after the hurricane and Hale and Blankenstock's alleged mishandling of people's money."

"Why do you care? Why should anyone care about Bailey's Cove? And why do you care about Hale and Blankenstock? Did you lose money? Is that it?" asked the inquisitive twin.

"As far as Bailey's Cove, people love to have someone to care about, someone to say prayers for, to wish well, people to help." Addy thought of her sister. "That's why they want to know about the town."

"You could be reporting on a missing jumbo jet or on the mudslides in Oregon. Why are you really here?" Michael Murphy studied her, reminding her these people were not sharks, but folks who cared about their town and about Zachary Hale.

"I came here searching for Zachary Hale. I wanted to hear his side of the story." Which was true now. "I'm glad I'm in Bailey's Cove because I can see and feel what's going on here, how the town works as a unit for the good of the community."

"Why—why do you get to decide what is news and what's not?" The frazzled woman who brought the story to this dinner table could hardly get the words out.

"I haven't got the power to make decisions like that. I don't get to decide which stories are news and which are not. The people who want to know make the decision, the readers. My editor puts it out there and the usual subscribers can see it if they are interested, but it's the readers who make the news go viral."

"But you can influence millions and millions to make the decision that he is someone worth hating." The twin.

"Yes, Addy. Why do you care about him?" Christina asked.

Why did she care about him? Because he was the kind of man who should populate the world. With their children. She sighed. She'd never thought about children of her own before, and now...she was so lost.

She needed to talk to Zach, needed to know how he reacted to this article. She would not beg forgiveness for Jacko's words, but for her need to write about his story, her need to put the truth out there at his expense.

"Excuse me." She stood. "Dinner was wonderful. It was a pleasure to meet everyone."

She grabbed her place setting and as she hurried away toward the kitchen sink, they invited the newcomer to sit in Hunter's empty chair.

"More than enough," she heard Christina say.

It occurred to Addy, there was nowhere she could not be as easily replaced. Her profession dictated what friends she would have and she found out after Afghanistan, for how long. They were gone. Her family had been fractured by her father's desertion from before Addy could remember, and her mother's many marriages. Savanna only approached her because, as a member of the press, she might have some influence. The hole, if any, she left in those groups closed up the minute she stepped out of the room, so to speak.

All she had left was Adriana Bonacorda.

She was not going to let herself down, ever again.

She placed her dishes in to soak and went to the hall closet where there were coats and shoes.

A light rain fell as she started up Treacher Avenue. She pulled the waterproofed canvas tightly around her and tugged up the hood.

On Church Street a few cars passed her. None was Hunter Morrison's car coming home and one was a police cruiser that turned onto the road leading up Sea Crest Hill. Zach would not be alone when she arrived. So be it.

ZACH CLOSED THE damper of the fireplace. The flames had gone out, the embers had died. Every time the flames had warmed him he thought of Addy. The loft had never been as welcoming as it had with her there.

Now that she was gone it seemed there was no need for the extra warmth of the fire. Power had returned to Sea Crest Hill, and the baseboard heaters came on to take the edge off the chilly air.

Nothing would ever be as it used to be.

"Micky Thompson, one of the town's teenagers is a ne'er-do-well, but surfing the internet appeals to him." Hunter typed into his computer as he spoke. "He's set up an auto search for Zachary Hale, et al, and has his system alert him to any new occurrences. He got a hit about forty-five minutes ago.

"The facts are truthful and spare and most of them are about Bailey's Cove and not about you, but the allegations are as good as accusations," Hunter said as he sat in front of his laptop reading what Adriana Bonacorda had written along with her cohort.

Zach came to stand over Hunter's shoulder and read the article.

"What's the reaction like?" Zach asked.

"It's getting a lot of hits."

"What about the comments? Everything you would expect?"

"You mean negative."

"I mean nothing unexpected."

Zach crossed his arms over his chest. "I feel as though I should answer, as if I should be out there with some kind of response, at least a presence with which people could interact."

"You might feel like that now, but there are too many legal and personal ramifications." Hunter turned and looked up at Zach. "You need to stay removed from the spotlight."

"How am I supposed to do that? Those

people invested because I advised them to. I assured them that they could trust Carla.

"One thing it's not is greed. She didn't need the money." Neither of them needed the money. Carla came into hers by way of a family trust. Zach had taken a small shipping company in Portland his grandfather had owned and steadily poured every earned penny back into the company until six determined years later, his corporation owned fleets of ships on both coasts, moving commodities across the oceans. He sold the company and opened the investment partnership with Carla Blankenstock; he had known they'd be good at it.

Dealing with people rather than always putting out fires in international shipping matters seemed like a kind of retirement. He had a great rapport with people and Carla was a financial genius. Their partnership started out well and grew quickly.

"I need to be back in Boston." He needed to speak with Carla.

"This isn't like every other problem you've faced with Hale and Blankenstock or anything you've taken on in your shipping company. This is personal. What's the closest the two of you have ever been?"

"You mean did we date, have sex, fall in love. None of the above. We had business lunches and dinners, but rarely without a client or two with us. We often traveled on different airlines and always had separate hotel rooms."

"She never behaved inappropriately?"

"She's married. I don't think it's personal."

"I don't think we should drop that as an option."

Zach knew his attorney had a lot experience and that he could trust him a hundred percent. "Hunter, I understand. There was one thing. I thought we should expand into real estate, but she nearly panicked when I brought it up and I'd never seen her like that before. I tried to talk to her, but she said she knew too many people who had gone down when the market crashed. It was as if she was afraid of something."

"Did that cause a rift?"

"I tabled the idea and it seemed settled. If she'd stolen the funds by then and knew that any irregularities were bound to show up, especially as we got into something new, like real estate, that might have caused her worried reaction."

"For whatever reason she's doing this, unless she's totally unhinged, she can't possibly think she'll get out of this unscathed. The FBI's forensic accounting team will uncover whatever is going on at Hale and Blankenstock."

There was a firm knock and the door to the

loft opened. Chief Montcalm entered looking solemn, hat in hand.

Zach recognized his flat-out disappointment and the harsh reality that he was left with. He had hoped, unreasonably, that the person at the door would be Addy.

CHAPTER EIGHTEEN

ADDY PUSHED THE hood away from her eyes and struggled up Sea Crest Hill. The road leading away from Church Street was steep and in spots slippery. More than once she realized she should have brought a flashlight or at least one of the walking sticks Christina kept in a pottery crock inside the front door of Cora.

She had been surprised to see more lights on Church Street when she left Cora, but even those did little good up the side of the hill. The houses along the streets had lights, but few front porch or yard lights reached as far as the roadway and walking was perilous at best.

When the grade steepened and her boot slid on the loose gravel, she stopped. She might be foolish to be racing up Sea Crest Hill on a whim. Zachary Hale may be guilty, but if she collected any more fair-weather friends, who would desert her at every change of fortune, she was crazy.

She started walking again and before long, the rain let up, leaving the air crisp and moist.

It was too late to care about how she looked when she arrived, but drowned-rat status wouldn't stop her from saying her piece when she got up the hill.

She pulled out her mobile phone and called her sister for distraction. The girls should be in bed by now and Savanna should be settling down with a book or a TV show. Addy was ashamed to say she had no idea what her sister did when her kids were asleep.

"Hey, sis," Savanna answered. "What are you up to now?"

"Walking up a hill in the dark and the rain."

"Are you always doing really strange things, or just when you call me?"

"Are you at Mom's?"

"No, I couldn't stand the thought of Mom telling me where I went wrong in life. Besides, you said I had nothing to fear."

"You have nothing to fear from Zachary Hale. Savanna, I was wondering if I can come and visit you and the girls in a few weeks."

"Uh. Something wrong Addy?"

"Maybe. I was just thinking that I might not be trying hard enough to stay connected with my family."

"Who of us does? I mean, I am so connected to my girls, I'd die if anything happened to them, but I don't keep track of my brother or you much at all." She chuckled quietly. "And since the grandchildren came along, I can't get rid of Mom. You ought to try it."

"I think I should, er, keep better track of all of you. Who knows, you and I might even be friends someday."

"You can start by telling me what's going on."

"I'm chasing a story."

This time Savanna barked a laugh. "When weren't you chasing a story?"

"Maybe I shouldn't be chasing them all the time. Maybe I should find something else to do for a living."

"What? And make me give up telling my friends my sister is some big, important investigative journalist?"

"Never mind."

"Adriana, I get it. Life seems to get so busy and people fall away." Her sister's tone was sober when she spoke. "I've grown up a lot. Being a mom does that. I'd like to have you as a friend. Call on us anytime. Come anytime. I can have the girls sleep with me and you can have their room."

"Thanks." Addy didn't know what else to say.

"They'd love to have Aunt Addy visit. You

and I could do pals stuff like lunch, you buy, and maybe even do something like an art museum. I've done enough discovery worlds and playdates to kill a sane person."

"I'd like that."

"I know you think you're immune to the frailties affecting the rest of us, but be careful. Don't catch pneumonia or anything, but go get 'em tiger."

"Savanna, do you think I'm going after these stories for the fame and, well, glory?"

Her sister guffawed loudly. "Sheesh, I'll wake the girls by laughing too loud if you insist on talking such nonsense. Many of your stories count, big sis. Toiling in obscurity so you won't make too much glory, as you call it, would not expose the unfairness in the world. I applaud you and all like you who stick your necks out so the rest of us don't have to."

"I never knew you felt that way."

"Mommy" came from the background from Savanna's end.

"Did so. If you ever listened to me. Now go collect news. I gotta go. Love you."

Her sister rang off after another muted call for Mommy, and Addy continued on alone in the darkness.

"Love you, too."

THE CHIEF HAD to take a call from dispatch almost as soon as he had arrived. Zach and Hunter waited silently as the chief spoke with someone to whom he respectfully referred to as "sir."

"Zach, Hunter," the chief said by way of a greeting, once he put away his phone. "Sorry about the call. Where are we?"

"We were discussing why Carla Blanken-stock would be doing what she's doing."

"Have you come up with anything?"

"Very little," Zach said. "We disagree as to whether or not this is personal."

"Does that leave greed?" the chief asked as he approached where the two of them stood at the window overlooking the road.

"Carla came into Hale and Blankenstock with solid backers and substantial personal wealth."

"What if something happened to the wealth?" the chief asked.

"She'd come to me and tell me."

"What if she felt she couldn't?" The chief assigned no blame with his tone, just curiosity.

"What are you getting at, Chief?"

"Just making sure all the bases are covered here. She married a man after knowing him for only two weeks."

Zach nodded, not surprised the chief knew

this about his business partner and friend's whirlwind romance, and then he pictured Addy. He never thought of himself as the romantic type until Adriana Bonacorda came along and changed how his brain was wired.

"I would have vetted him the minute she told me she was married," Zach said as he turned away from the window and headed across the room to the kitchen sink for a glass of water, "but she asked me not to. She said she needed something in her life to be real."

"Did you check him, anyway?"

"There was nothing I could do to check him that wouldn't betray her trust." He put the glass in the sink.

"If she was embarrassed."

"If she was embarrassed, I'd like to think she'd still feel as though she could come to me."

Hunter still stood near the window with his arms crossed over the chest of his white shirt. His suit coat hung over the back of one of the dining-table chairs. "I have people investigating all possible circumstances, including her personal financial status and the status of her marriage."

"She adored her husband from the moment they met."

"She may need to protect him for some

reason," Hunter said, a look of consternation on his face.

"How good is she at what she does?" Chief Montcalm asked from the middle of the room, halfway between Zach and Hunter.

"She has the broadest understanding of the world monetary markets of anyone in the field. There are few investors who are more savvy or, and I can't emphasize this enough, more honest."

"Then she's being influenced. Is it possible for her to cover any missteps she may have made?" the chief asked.

"If anyone could cover her financial tracks, it would be Carla Blankenstock," Zach answered.

"But as transparent as things can be made these days, that's how deeply covert they can be. I wish I had suspected something…"

"Why would you have known?" Hunter asked joining the other two.

"The only answer is, I should have. I made a promise to the people I talked into investing with Hale and Blankenstock." Zach grimaced. "About Carla's husband, after they met, I never saw Carla at any of the social events without him nearby. He traveled with her and he spent many a day in her office. She hired him as a consultant, though I left his job up to her. Perhaps, a bad idea in retrospect."

The chief's brows furrowed for a moment. "We need someone to speak with her husband."

"I can do it," Hunter volunteered.

"We met a couple of times," Zach said. "I can set up a meeting between the two of us."

"Neither of you are the gender I was thinking of. Hunter, you can't create that kind of conflict of interest without a judge throwing your defense out of court and possibly hitting you with an obstruction charge. Zach, you need to stay clear of any sign of impropriety."

"I still think I should do it," Zach countered.

"I have someone better in mind," the chief huffed. "You can't leave Bailey's Cove. The FBI came for you today. I convinced them we need you right now. Told them I'd bring you in myself when we could afford to let you go."

Zach shifted his gaze to see the chief studying him.

The door slammed and was followed a few moments later by hesitant footsteps on the stairs to the loft.

Most of the few people who had reason to come up to the tail end of Sea Crest Hill road were in the room with him now.

Addy...

A sharp kick started Zach's heart racing.

The ache surprised him and he retreated to the fireplace.

There was a knock on the inside door.

"I'll get it," Hunter said.

He slid on his jacket—out of habit, Zach thought—and answered the door.

Hunter scanned her as if looking for a weapon and then slowly stepped aside. Control the pace of an event and you could control the event. Hunter Morrison knew that one and so would she.

She pushed the hood of the coat off her wet hair and casually let her gaze sweep the room. She looked beautiful even with matted hair and raindrops for makeup.

When she spotted him standing beside the fireplace, she didn't alter her expression, though she'd know things had completely changed in the loft on Sea Crest Hill.

He let the feelings war inside him about her being there. She had trudged up the hill in the rain, looked cold, wet and tired. He wanted to send the other men away and to sweep her into his arms and restore the pink to her lips, dusky with the cold.

The three of them stared at her. The chief sized her up, and Hunter looked as if he was coming to some aha moment and Zach didn't like the other two men's reactions at all.

"What?" Addy asked as she shifted her gaze from one of them to the next.

"What do you know about files from the offices of Hale and Blankenstock?"

She stopped in the middle of the room and turned to face the chief who had asked the question.

"I'm not sure I know what you mean."

A standard dodge designed to keep the name of a source concealed, Zach thought. The chief recognized the diversion for what it was and didn't ask the question again.

Addy shoulders dropped and she stepped up and answered. "I have a source with documents, emails, etc. incriminating Zach."

Her gaze locked to his, she kept her voice steady as she delivered the condemnation, giving no indication of what she was thinking.

He held his face expressionless as well when she took a few steps toward where he stood. She stopped as if rethinking the move and then started again. When she was only a foot away she looked up at him.

The rest of the world faded away. He didn't care who was in the room. He didn't care about Hale and Blankenstock or the FBI. The spot on the glistening hardwood floor upon which he and Addy Bonacorda stood was all there was.

"I don't believe you did anything wrong."

She spoke the words as she looked into his eyes as if searching for a reaction.

His mouth opened. He started to protest. Her complete faith in him was not what he wanted. If she hated him, believed everything her source had about him, she'd walk away.

Even peripheral involvement with him could taint her as a source, especially in light of Afghanistan.

Then she sucked in a breath, nodded once and turned to address Chief Montcalm. "Sir, my source is reliable, but I have not seen the documents."

"The FBI has them." The chief studied her.

"I—um—know." She faltered for a moment and put a hand to her forehead and moved away. After a moment she spun on her heel. "Whatever I can do to help the situation, I'm here, I'm available."

The chief looked satisfied and Hunter circumspect.

The chief stepped forward. "I have something in mind that may interest you, Ms. Bonacorda."

"No! You don't know whether or not he's dangerous," Zach countered.

"Who's dangerous?" Addy asked quickly. There was almost an eager look on her face and Zach wanted nothing more than to whisk her to someplace safe…from herself.

At the same time he knew with absolute certainty she would not leave the controversy behind.

"Carla Blankenstock's husband," Hunter replied. "None of us can speak with him without interfering with or obstructing justice."

"And why are we interested in him?"

Zach felt any control he had slipping away.

"One theory is he's the motivation behind what Mrs. Blankenstock has done to Hale and Blankenstock," the chief answered.

"He seems to have her on a tight chain," Zach said. He heard the resignation in his own voice. He had to admit Carla had done the deed, committed the crime and she had to go down for it along with her husband.

"I'll do it."

Zach's heart seized at the thought of Addy in danger.

"No. Not for me. Not for Hale and Blankenstock."

Addy turned to him. "We can meet in public. If I get him to think he is going to get to further his wife's scheme to have you convicted instead of her, he'll jump at the chance."

"If he has the high opinion of himself I think

he does, he might not be able to keep from dropping hints," Chief Montcalm added.

"Is he dangerous?" Hunter stepped in.

"Caution should be used around any criminals," the chief added.

"Chief, you can't ask her to do this." Zach had to try.

She took a step toward him. "I'm volunteering."

"Not for me." He repeated the words, certain she would not listen to him and maybe that was one of the reasons he loved her so much.

She stood tall and faced him. "Ego boy, this is ego girl you're speaking to. If the story is big enough, I jump in with both feet and all fingers."

Zach leaned forward as the fury hammered a warning inside his head. "Don't do this for me."

"Sir, I'm in," Addy said sounding as confident as he was sure she felt.

Zach had to try one more time. "There are other ways to get to Carla's husband."

She held up a hand to his protest and turned toward the chief. "You'll make sure the men in black have my back won't you, Chief?"

"Why can't the Bureau do the job?" His words left his tongue feeling like lethal daggers. It had been a long time since he'd lost

this much control. "They must have someone
undercover, someone with training to handle
the likes of him."

"There are several reasons why it should be
me. I already have the credibility. As well as
the Bureau can build a backstory for their op-
erative, they can't alter the subject's memory
to recall something as big as the Afghani de-
bacle. Two, freedom of the press. They won't
stop reporters from talking to Carla Blankenstock's husband. I don't have to follow all their
rules and, well…" She grinned up at him. "And
I'm very good at what I do."

Zach's eyebrows drew together as he remembered she was good, very good at other things.

His whole body reacted to the sudden switch
and he had to take a series of back steps to keep
from dragging her into his arms.

Addy closed her eyes for a moment and he
could see she felt the same.

"You realize—" she addressed him alone
"—I'll do this because I have to, for myself."

Zach had already fought longer than was rational. "I want to be there."

"Not possible," the chief said. "I have to turn
you over to the FBI if you leave here. I can't let
you sneak past the roadblocks, and don't even
think about flying out."

"What do you want me to get the man to tell me?" Addy asked.

Zach bristled at the feeling of utter helplessness. He wanted to bundle Addy up and take her away...

...and he was equally certain she would not thank him for doing so.

CHAPTER NINETEEN

THE CHIEF HAD departed in his squad. Hunter had taken Addy back to the Three Sisters. They had left him alone to stay put, to suffer the indignities of helplessness.

"Take only the two of you to operate the *Zodiac* and make sure it's seaworthy," Zach said to the captain and chief maintenance officer for Hale and Blankenstock's yacht. "I don't care if we set sail with her listing heavily. I only need to get out far enough to have a head start. I'll arrange for a pick up as soon after dawn as possible and you can bring her back to Bailey's Cove or keep going to the shipyard in Bar Harbor to get the repairs finished."

"What's this about?"

"Nothing. You know absolutely nothing except that most billionaires are slightly unbalanced."

"But, sir—"

"And we pay very well."

"Yes, sir. We've been working on her, like you asked, since the winds let up. Give me six hours, if the navigation systems pass their last test, we'll be seaworthy, and the *Zodiac* is in top shape as ya know."

"As I know." The yacht's captain loved the vessel as if it was his child. He and his repair crew were some of the select group allowed in past the Bailey's Cove blockade. It had nearly killed the man to have been in Massachusetts greeting a new grandchild while the yacht weathered the storm.

"I'll meet you at the dock in six hours."

"Yes, sir."

Zach had six hours to spend. Five and a half of them he'd spend finding out as much as he could about Carla Blankenstock's husband, including, if he could, how the man treated Carla and what Addy might face when she met with him.

He had to admit Addy could take care of herself. As much as he wanted to protect her, she would always be an investigative journalist first. While she did what she had to do, interviewing Carla's husband, he planned to speak with Carla no matter what it took.

Addy would be safe. She had to be safe.

He leaned back in the chair where he had first explored her supple body, taken what she had offered and given her everything he had in return, where the sound of her joy had made music he would never forget.

She had to be safe.

SEEING ZACH'S FACE AGAIN, how much he cared for her, had made it harder than ever to walk away. She was certain he'd take the hit before he let anyone else be harmed by the scheme perpetrated at Hale and Blankenstock. Her heart fractured even more when he refused to let her stay close to him, had in fact, sent her away from him.

In her room in the Three Sisters, she pulled the soft chenille spread up under her chin and called her sister.

"Hey, Adriana, some of us go to bed at a civilized hour." Savanna's voice came out croaky and full of sleep.

"You could have told me when I called you the first time, Savanna, that you had hard copies of the files. You said you never had them."

"We were getting along so well, Addy. I thought I'd have time to tell you in person, you know, when your charming little nieces were sitting on your lap or something." Savanna sounded like their mother, always looking to subvert conflict. Maybe that wasn't all bad.

"You couldn't hate me," Savanna continued, "when those cute faces I created were giving you the ogle eyes of adoration. How was I supposed to know it might be important sooner rather than later, that you were out there falling in love with the enemy?"

"What are you talking about?"

"You know that reporter Jacko something or other."

"Wilson."

"Ya, that's him. He says you're up in Maine cozying up to Zachary Hale."

"I hate that man."

"Hale? Then it isn't true?"

Let her sister make of that statement what she wanted to. "I'm in Maine trying to figure out what happened at Hale and Blankenstock."

"Don't we know what happened?"

"There are credible people here backing Hale." Addy was sure she had never met men more upstanding then Chief Montcalm and Hunter Morrison.

"You mean lying for him."

"Not these people."

"It's true. You are up there, well, he said cavorting with the enemy. You really gotta see his blog."

"Jacko the Hacko puts out stuff that's just this side of libel. He gets a lot of readers that way and I can't knock that, but I've been busy. And I called to—"

"Chew me out."

"To—yeah—I did, and to tell you I'm coming back to Boston. I'm leaving at first light."

"Yippee," Savanna squeaked quietly. "Will you stay for at least a week?"

"I was there for several months last time."

"But that was before we were friends."

"I'll come and see you and the girls, but what I need to know from you is how did you know the FBI didn't already have the files you stole copies of?"

"Mr. Blankenstock—"

"Not his name."

"It's what everybody calls him. Anyway, he called me and asked if I'd seen any of the records incriminating Zachary Hale."

"And you told him yes."

"Sure, I said a few."

"Did he ask you for them?"

"He did not. He's a good guy. He didn't want them for himself at all. He didn't want any of the credit. He just wants that Hale guy to get what he has coming, so he wanted to make sure I'd turn them into the FBI."

"Of course he did." He had called to prompt a witness to come forward with the false information he and Carla had planted. If the material came directly from him, they would be suspect.

"I'm very concerned for you, Addy. You're up there with the enemy and you could get into trouble."

"You sound like Mom, except she'd never say that to me."

"Well, I am worried."

"You should be, but not for the reasons you think. Did you hand over all the files?"

"I may have held back a few."

"You are crazier than I thought."

"They're just unofficial documents, but they're originals. Stuff where Hale talks about what Carla has to do in order to support their biggest client, only he puts *client* in quotes." Savanna took a breath. "When you get here, I can show them to you."

"Why, why would you hold back from the Federal Bureau of Investigation?"

Savanna paused. "I was thinking they might be worth money."

"That's illegal, Savanna." Carla's husband would have been planning on her sister handing over all the files he and Carla had planted.

"It's not as bad as what Hale did. Mr. Blankenstock said he was calling all the employees who might help his wife before Mr. Hale buried her with his lies. He says he's going to help Mrs. Blankenstock get back as much of our money as possible. I might get some or all of it." She sounded so happy, but Addy knew if it were up to Mr. *Blankenstock,* there would be no money to give back.

"He's such a nice man," her sister continued.

Sociopath, Addy thought. He knew just how to stroke people to get them to trust him. He would have presented himself as earnest, confident and sympathetic. Zach had a hard time believing Carla would be fooled, but Addy knew what that was like. She hadn't fallen in love as Carla had, but she had nonetheless been taken in and made a fool of by Rasa and her husband.

A thought struck Addy that horrified her. "He didn't come to your house, did he?"

"He called me."

"If he does come, don't let him in and don't let him near the girls."

"You're scaring me again."

"It might be justified this time."

"Why? He's not the bad guy. You've got the bad guy up there."

"I need you to trust me on this one. Carla Blankenstock's husband is not going to help you get your money back."

"Okay, sis, we'll see. I tell you he's a nice guy. So tell me what he's really like."

"Carla's husband?" Addy knew what her sister was asking. What was Zachary Hale really like? Tall, strong, abs that beg to be touched, kisses that made her forget her own name. His smile slightly lopsided when he was relaxed. Honorable. A man she would like to spend the rest of her life with. A man who would not let her emotionally near him because he might be embattled for the foreseeable future. Couldn't he see she'd fight that battle at his side and love every minute? That she would not care about the unkind and sometimes evil things her competitors and erstwhile friends would write about him and sometimes her.

"Addy, Addy are you there?" her sister called.

"What?" She hoped she hadn't said any of that aloud. "I'm here."

"Hale. What's Zachary Hale like?"

"I don't want to talk about him." *I want him now and always,* she thought, *I want his arms around me.*

Talk was not good enough. If she got Carla Blankenstock's husband to give himself away, maybe this could all be over. "Go back to sleep. Thanks for the info."

ZACH SAT IN the chair across from Carla Blankenstock's desk while she paced on the other side. The midmorning Boston sun streamed brightly through the window.

"Carla, this isn't you. None of this is you."

"You have to leave, Zach. My husband will be here any minute and he'll be furious if he finds I've been talking to you."

She looked older than she had just a few weeks ago. Her dark brown hair seemed to lack its usual luster and her features were drawn in deep concern.

"He's occupied right now." Zach knew Addy would soon be deep into her interview of Carla's husband.

Carla strode to the window of her expansive office and put her hands over her face and cried. Zach didn't go to comfort her because the Carla Blankenstock he knew would summon her personal strength and thank no one who tried to help her.

After a few minutes, she took a deep breath and pulled her shoulders back. She held her hands folded lightly in front of her. It was her low-threat, high-power stance. She always used it when she was not quite certain of the position she had taken.

"I'm so sorry, Zach. So sorry. I've wanted for so long to tell you what was going on but I felt paralyzed and like a prisoner in my own life."

Zach felt sorrow for his former partner and how wrong her life had gone. For whatever reason she chose to be frank with him now, he was grateful. "Start at the beginning."

She barked a sad kind of laugh. "That's easy. I'm a fool. An embarrassed and stupid fool. I fell in love. Isn't that funny? Like a schoolgirl I fell for a sweet-talking guy."

Zach couldn't exactly call Addy sweet-talking but he understood the sentiment of love, something he had never quite grasped before Adriana Bonacorda and he couldn't let himself feel now.

"I thought he was in love with me. He said we were spending the money for us, our new home, our fabulous vacation home, an investment for our future children, our farm in France that would be our retirement haven."

Zach nodded, but let her continue.

"After we went through my money, he was angry at first to find most of my family money is tied up in trust. Our grandfather drilled into my sister and me if we ever lost the family fortune we would be failing the whole family. When I told my husband I could make any amount of money we needed, his words became so beautiful, his promises so sweet. I couldn't disappoint him."

"That's when you turned to Hale and Blankenstock for the shortfall."

She came over and took the chair next to his.

"It turns out I couldn't make money fast enough for what we needed. I know now no amount would have been enough. For the first year, there were no irregularities in our accounts because I set up a dummy company from which my husband could withdraw at will. He made everything he said, everything he got me to do, seem so plausible. 'Things will only be this way for a short time,' he would say."

"I'm trying to picture the Carla I knew in school making the first illegal transaction."

She gave a small derisive laugh. "It was so easy in the beginning. I knew I'd put it back in no time. I took a little here and there, but when the returns started to look subpar, I borrowed a little from the new accounts to pay the withdrawals. I should have stopped before I borrowed, but I didn't.

"The worst part of all this is that I knew it was happening. It wasn't as if I was drugged or unconscious or somebody had taken over my life. I knew each and every thing I did wrong was going to hurt someone. I knew that we were going to get caught and I knew we were blaming you. I knew all this and I did nothing. It was as if pleasing him was an addiction. I was always going to fix things tomorrow."

"You're doing something now. You're telling me."

"I'm a coward. I never knew it until now. I'm scared to death to face all this alone."

"You won't be alone, Carla."

"But I ruined it all. I ruined our wonderful company. I ruined our friendship and you did nothing wrong and I ruined your reputation. I can't take any of it back. I couldn't even refuse a date with the charming man I met at the country club." She laughed a sad sound. "I don't even know why he was at the club. No one seems to have invited him. When I found that out after we'd been married for almost two years, I asked him and he got elusive and then he got angry when I pressed. That's when he threatened me the first time. He said I was in too deep to get out and—" she looked up at him "—he said he'd have to take you down for the irregularities if I revealed anything.

"I let myself be convinced that you would not be ruined by what we were doing. You had enough money to buy your way out of anything. I guess some of what fed my idiocy was that I was jealous of your ability to handle anything, anytime. After that he hinted the SEC would like to know what I was doing and since I so heavily represented my family, I'd ruin them all if I stopped. Of course I knew it wouldn't last, but I couldn't seem to get control of the situation."

She shook her head. "I know I could have come to you. Obviously, I should have. I was afraid for both of us by then."

"What do you mean afraid?"

"He's unpredictable, Zach. Mean. Cruel, even."

Dread suddenly hammered at him.

Addy was in danger and she was there because of him. "Addy's with him. Do you know where?"

"Who is Addy?"

"A reporter who was going to interview him this morning. Do you know where?"

"He usually does interviews in his office in our home. He says there is no point in having a ten-million-dollar home if you don't show it off."

"Would they be there alone?"

"I don't think so. Mrs. Confrey is usually there all day. He hired the woman. Said she was a good watchdog for the house, a watchdog for me, he meant, but she wouldn't hurt a fly."

"Or be much help in defending a reporter." He pushed up from the chair. "I need to leave."

"What's wrong, Zach?"

The closing door to her office would have to suffice for an answer right now. He whipped out his cell.

Addy, be safe, he thought as he listened to her outgoing message when she didn't pick up.

ADDY HAD BEEN waiting in a coffee shop on Boston Post Road nursing a skim latte and making notes of the questions to ask Carla Blankenstock's husband and in what order. Chief Montcalm had given her a few, as did Hunter Morrison. Zach had silently pleaded with her to be safe. She was well versed by the time she pushed the doorbell of the house big enough to fit her condo inside about fifteen times over.

She could hear the doorbell echoing inside the palatial mansion in Weston near Boston, where the subject of her interview insisted they meet. The approaching footsteps inside told her nothing. There would be help here and Mr. *Blankenstock* would be waiting some place in the house that would put him in the best light, a paneled office or if he wanted to be more casual, a sunroom on such a bright and sunny day.

The door opened to a sixtyish woman in a very formal housekeeper's uniform, à la very old-money Boston. Only this housekeeper had somewhere along the line lost her cool.

"What's the matter?" Addy asked the distraught woman whose uniform was torn and her cheek bruised.

"I don't know what to do." The woman brought her hand to her cheek and pressed the red spot with the back of her fingers.

"I'm Adriana Bonacorda. I'm a reporter and I have an appointment with Mrs. Blanken-stock's husband. May I come in?" Addy knew a source when it was about to break lose. She also knew this woman was in trouble.

The woman nodded and held the door open for her.

They had to step around a very large vase broken on the marble entryway floor. "Is who-ever did this still here?"

"No, no, he left."

"Should I call the police?"

"I don't know. I don't know what to do." The woman led her into an office with wooden pan-els on the walls, of course, and a large, expen-sive desk. The office had been tossed. Pens, paper, books and bookends had been thrown everywhere. The computer monitor must have been hurled against a wall and what was left of a nautical clock lay burst apart on the floor beside the monitor.

"Tell me your name," Addy said to the nervous-looking woman.

"Confrey, I'm Gwendolyn Confrey."

"Can you take me to the kitchen, Gwendolyn?" Addy led the woman out of the office.

Marble, white-stained wood and copper were the theme in the kitchen, beautiful, and best of all the room had not been violently searched. Gwendolyn should feel safer here.

Addy put her arm around the woman to comfort her. "I'll make us some tea for us." *And you can give me a story,* the reporter in Addy thought.

"Did you surprise a thief?"

"I suppose I did. He was searching through everything. I don't know what he was looking for."

"Did you recognize him?"

"Certainly. It was Mrs. Blankenstock's husband. He was pulling things out of the drawers in the office, all the time telling me I was fired and he was leaving this place—he called it a very bad word. He said he was leaving forever."

"He hit you."

She nodded. "He grabbed my uniform to try to throw me out of Mrs. Blankenstock's bedroom when I tried to stop him from searching in there. When I wouldn't go, he hit me with his fist."

Addy winced. She'd felt a fist more than

once while seeking a worthy story. "I'm going to call the police."

Addy dialed 911 while she searched for a plastic bag for a few ice cubes for Gwendolyn's cheek.

The woman sat on a stool at the counter and then leaped to her feet. "I can't leave a mess. Mrs. Blankenstock will be home soon. Do you really think he's gone for good?"

"Sit back down. Put the ice on for a few minutes. We'll go take a look, but you can't clean things up. The police will want to see it as it is."

She nodded.

"Did he take anything?"

She nodded again. "He took some of Mrs. Blankenstock's jewelry. Not the good stuff. That's in her father's lockbox at the bank, except the Palidor Perfection."

Addy must have looked puzzled as the woman explained. "A ruby, very large. It's been in the family since before England's Regency era. It came by way of Italy as a gift."

Addy filled two cups from the instant hot-water dispenser and dropped decaf green-tea bags into the cups.

"I have to go up. I have to go look," the woman said, but stayed perched on the stool.

"All right, but just while our tea steeps. And you won't touch anything."

"I won't touch anything," she repeated, her voice quivering.

In Carla Blankenstock's bedroom chaos reigned. The mattress was off the bed. The bedding had been strewn around the room. The sofa and chairs had been overturned.

"Oh, my." With both hands to her cheeks, the woman ran into the room and snatched up a small photo that had been ripped from its frame. A ruby was at stake and she went for the baby picture. Addy decided right then, she liked Gwendolyn Confrey.

She grabbed the older woman before she could pick up anything else. "The police are coming. Let's allow them to check things before you touch stuff. Mrs. Blankenstock will understand."

"If you think so."

"Addy. Addy, are you here?" a voice came from downstairs.

"He's back. Oh, hide. He's back." Mrs. Confrey grabbed Addy's arm and tugged her toward a closet.

"That's not him. It's not Mr. Blankenstock." The man calling her name unreasonably sounded like Zach, but she knew Chief

Montcalm had him essentially jailed in Bailey's Cove.

"Mr. Spielmann." The housekeeper corrected her use of Mr. Blankenstock. "His name. Nobody used it. Are you really, really sure it's not him?"

"Game man." Appropriate, Addy thought. "It's really, really not him."

"Addy." The call came muffled from a distance.

Jail or not, Zachary Hale was downstairs in Carla Blankenstock's home.

"Mrs. Confrey, I need to leave for a moment."

The woman gave her a sad look of resignation.

"It's not Mr. Spielmann. It's Mr. Hale."

Her face brightened. "I've met him. He's nice."

"Stay here. The police will only be a few minutes."

She ran to the landing. "Zach, I'm here."

In a second he appeared at the bottom of the semicircle of the dark wooden stairs. She ran down as he ran up.

Halfway up or down their kiss was epic.

"You are going to kill me, woman."

"Don't be such a sissy man."

He took her face in his hands and kissed her

lips, her nose and her forehead. "You make me a sissy man. I never was before you came along."

"What are you doing out of the State of Maine?"

"Kissing you."

She tipped her head to the side and then smiled. "Good enough."

Pressing her open mouth to his, she drew him close for the next series of kisses.

"Hello?"

A very small voice came from right behind Addy. She pulled back and turned around. Gwendolyn stood three steps above her with the ice bag to her cheek.

"Zachary Hale, you already know Gwendolyn Confrey."

"Hello, Mrs. Confrey."

"Mrs. Confrey and I are waiting for the police and she's going to tell them how Mr. Spielmann assaulted her, robbed the house and ran away."

Mrs. Confrey nodded her head.

"And we were just about to go down to the kitchen and have tea. Would you like to join us, Zach?"

Mrs. Confrey seemed so relieved at the prospect, Addy could hardly tell the woman she'd rather leave and go be ravaged by the man she loved and maybe even get a declaration of the same.

If the world was fair at all, he loved her in return. If not, she was certain there must be a position for a blogger in Nepal or Bora Bora. She wouldn't need much, just enough for her sorry old self to subsist on.

When they got to the kitchen, Mrs. Confrey insisted on putting milk and honey into their two cups of tea.

Addy reached for another cup, but Zach took her by the arm and that could not mean anything good. She leaned into him.

"I can't stay," he said.

"Why did I already know that? The chief expects you to remain in Bailey's Cove and here you are in Boston. He'll know you've left, you know."

"But chances are the FBI doesn't. If I go back and they don't find out, whatever mysterious credibility our Chief Montcalm has with the Bureau remains intact."

"Mrs. Confrey, I'm going to walk Mr. Hale to the door."

As soon as they were out of sight of the kitchen, she stepped in front of him and reached up to kiss him. His lips were so warm, his embrace so strong. He was so right for her.

Was it possible he didn't know that? Yet it seemed everyone else did.

"Has anything changed?" she asked, hoping against what she already knew.

He shook his head. "Just a few of the details. Hale and Blankenstock is still in deep trouble that may take a long time to sort out."

When he turned and walked down the hall toward the front door she let him go. She knew that in light of the recent spotlight on financial schemes, Zach was implying that he might have to spend some of that time in jail. And that she couldn't tell the story if she were attached to him.

"Mrs. Confrey," she said when she got back to the worst cup of tea she'd ever had. "I want you to tell me everything you know about Mr. Spielmann."

While Mrs. Confrey talked and Addy wrote, her heart tried to keep itself together. By the time the police arrived, she was sure they could not tell by looking at the two of them who had been traumatized by the nefarious scamster, she or Mrs. Confrey.

An hour later when the police were sure they didn't need her anymore, she walked away from the swank home and climbed into her newest tiny rental.

"Hi, Savanna, I hope you get this message

before I arrive. Tell the girls Auntie A. is coming and she's bringing presents."

She tucked her phone away and headed for the nearest mall.

She'd spend some time playing with her nieces and her sister, then she'd polish the already written article on Hale and Blankenstock, mostly Hale, and get it to her editor for tomorrow's Sunday edition.

Tomorrow was another day and another story.

There be treasure in Bailey's Cove. A legend to be told, in a careful way so as not to create a gold rush, of course.

If she filled her life with enough distractions, she might not have to think about how good it had been to have Zach hold her in his arms again to kiss her, even if it had been over in minutes, rather than a lifetime.

At the mall, the store she stopped in front of had fairy-princess dresses and pink and blue ponies. Seemed about right.

CHAPTER TWENTY

ON HER WAY back from her early-morning hike, Addy had picked up a copy of Monday's paper. She had also picked up a copy of Sunday's paper the day before. She never missed a paper copy of those with her personal byline. Call her sentimental, but she liked her first paper to come from the newsstand and not the pile of leftovers at the office.

Smally had put her on the front page of the business section on Sunday with no Jacko Wilson additives to change the flavor. The response had been the best she'd ever gotten from readers, some for and some against her, but a reader was a reader.

Her first impulse had been to pick up her phone and call someone. *Who?* was her next thought. Savanna, if she was up, was most likely making pancakes with the girls. They had invited her to come for Sunday pancakes, but she had said another time.

The person she really wanted to call was

Zach. He was on her mind always. She couldn't close her eyes without seeing his face.

Every day since she had spent the night in his bed with him, no bed was good enough. She slept in the recliner of her living room wrapped in a quilt.

She hurried up to her condo to enjoy a long-standing tradition, coffee and a newspaper. She loved hers in the sunny breakfast nook with a glimpse of the harbor—a glimpse if one stood on the table and the day was crisp clear.

She spread the paper out, flattening the crease with her hands. Then she made coffee, poured in cream and sat down.

The business section was, of course, her first priority.

But even before she looked at the section to find what she wanted to see, she knew there would be no joy no matter what she found.

Jacko Wilson's byline was front and center. Smally had run a counter article with Jacko, as always, skimming along the edge of libel. He almost accused Zach of beating Carla with a legal stick.

Reading the article was like watching a train wreck. She couldn't unglue her eyes until the cars had all derailed, or in this case the last accusation had been made.

By Wednesday morning, it was clear their

editor, Smally, was going to keep pitting them against each other on the internet and in print.

It was a clever idea and had already brought in an unprecedented number of readers to see what Jacko's next veiled accusation would be, and her rebuttal.

She had been unable to get anywhere near Zachary Hale or Carla Blankenstock and neither had Jacko. She did get a follow-up on the record with Gwendolyn. Tomorrow's rebuttal had already been penned using the woman as a character witness against Mr. Spielmann, or Mr. Blank-mann, as Jacko had begun calling him, because he hadn't turned up yet.

Addy called Zach and left yet another message asking him to at least speak with her about what Jacko was writing, give her a hint as to where he thought the other reporter was getting his material so she could more easily counter it.

When he didn't pick up yet again, she took the rental car and pointed it north.

ZACH LISTENED TO Addy's newest voice mail, punishing himself with the sound of her voice. He could call her, but what could he say? "Sorry, just wanted to talk to you. Doesn't mean anything because the wheels of justice move slowly. Go live your life and I'll see you in ten years in the Boston Common like we planned that day in the loft"?

If she remembered at all.

The FBI had questioned him thoroughly. It took longer than Hunter was comfortable with, but Zach had said to let them play the game as long as they wanted. If he had something to hide they could all be surprised by it.

Hunter had let him know that wasn't very funny, but he appreciated that Zach had still found something to make a joke about.

Every day was spent trying to straighten out the mess. Carla had retreated and refused to re-iterate what she had said that day in her office.

It was Hale against Blankenstock now and he had been painted badly. Carla had asked for an across-the-table meeting with him set for this afternoon. Their attorneys would flank them. Hunter would be there with two of the people from the Chicago office.

They would stare at one another across the conference table at Hale and Blankenstock, which had been chosen as neutral ground as the offices were being used for nothing else at this time.

Eight people to discuss something that should never have happened and that should be able to be solved by a discussion between two friends.

Instead of the truth, each side would lay out threats under the guise of offers. The other side would repel the threat with an *offer* of their own.

It had taken three days just to settle on a meeting site. The first offer Carla's side had made was binding arbitration, which Hunter had turned down quickly and succinctly without consulting the rest of the team.

Arbitration could be like flipping a coin. There were no court proceedings and the arbiter could be influenced by anything at all. The decision was final except in rare cases. Carla's team offered it, Hunter had said, because having a fifty-fifty chance of winning was much better than they had without it.

Hunter and his team had uncovered something the FBI refused to confirm or deny. Carla's husband's identity was bogus. According to Hunter the man was a computer genius who dropped out or was kicked out of two prestigious institutes of higher learning, so they were dealing with the aftermath of genius gone wrong.

When Zach wanted to give up, he remembered he'd let down the people who trusted him to invest their money. Even he didn't have the wherewithal to cover the losses incurred by Carla and her husband.

Every day was exactly the same. The proceedings against Blankenstock got nowhere and the day ended with him in his penthouse overlooking Boston. The place he had called home for the last five years, the place where he accepted no visitors, suddenly seemed lonely.

Every night he poured a glass of expensive whiskey and every night he failed to drink it. He'd give up every dollar and every advantage if all this would be resolved so he could go beg Addy's forgiveness and for her to give him another chance.

To tell her how much he loved her.

Sarah O'Brien, a member of the Goldens, slipped her coat off and pushed it into the chair to prop up her back. "You were close to him," she said across the table from Addy.

Was she close to Zach? Addy wondered. She was closer than she had ever been to a man, yet here she was, in his hometown while he was in hers. Life was quirky.

She had spent almost a week in Bailey's Cove coaxing treasure information from the inhabitants. She had come to know the people at Braven's Tavern, where many patrons sat on the same bar stool almost every day. She even got Michael the owner to tell her why it was called a tavern, which traditionally offered food, and not just a bar. "I could tell you we

do offer food and show you a menu of our frozen entrées or I could just say, simple. It's been
Braven's Tavern for two hundred years and it
seemed a bit too soon to change a name that
seemed to work so well."

She laughed and agreed Braven's Tavern
seemed like a great name.

She scanned each of the seven the Goldens
as they all sat at a large table in the corner of
the tavern and already she realized they were
there because they wanted something from her,
not because she had been trying to get them to
meet with her.

"What would you like me to do?"

"Get us in to see the basement." Evelyn
Miller a tall woman, with erect posture and a
head full of steel-gray hair almost demanded.

Yeah, get them into the basement and they'd
see all the collapsed walls and the hole where
the treasure had been. Zach hadn't even let the
contractor back in after their find.

Hunter had been elected by Zach and the
chief as official treasure keeper until it could
best and most safely be revealed to the town.

Addy had sworn her secrecy about the
treasure being found, but she had vowed to
tell the legend of Bailey's Cove. Her secrecy
sworn, she had the privilege to know Hunter
had installed the treasure in the large, usually

empty safe in his office and the only person he told was his fiancé, also sworn to secrecy.

"Will he turn you away if you ask?" she said to the table of people.

Shamus Willis, one of the town's four Shamuses, cackled. "He might."

"We've been pestering him for about a decade about the treasure," Alfred Hammond chimed in. Rotund, fringe of white hair, scalp red, face flushed and unlit cigar stub between his teeth. He was a delightful throwback, the kind of thing that gave small-town charm. "We thought he was wearing a ring from the booty, but it turned out to be something his mother had made for him based on a sketch of hers. It was different, you know. Not like the smooth flashy stuff of today."

"Ask him again," Addy prompted.

"We did, but he said it flooded down there and it might not be safe," Camden Flynn, gnarly looking, the longtime boat captain, said sounding skeptical.

"So he's concerned for your safety."

"But that's why we need to get down there," Mrs. Miller said with some urgency.

"Okay, I didn't know you all were so freaky when I joined. Are you hoping for another body like the one they found in the wall of the Pirate's Roost?" asked Babe Dawson, probably eighty plus and the newest member of the group.

"No. No body," Evelyn said as she elbowed Babe.

"We think the old wall will be exposed—"

Sarah shot Camden a look of dire warning as he spoke.

"Those old walls can tell us how the early settlers carved out basements for storage," Sarah interjected. A clear diversion.

Addy kept a smile to herself. She let them think she too wondered how basements had been constructed by their ancestors. "Can't it wait until things are dried out?"

"We want to see it before too many people try to clean everything up and all the archaeological information is gone," Edwin Beaudin put in. He was another old salt and the man who had said "he's not who you think he is." As stoic as he was, he wasn't much of a liar. Addy wished with all her heart she had known that about him her first day in Bailey's Cove.

All at once it seemed as if everyone at the table started talking.

It was said they should perhaps go through Hunter Morrison, the man's attorney; that Heather Loch from the museum might help them and where was Heather today, she should be here; maybe they should get Cammy who cleaned up on Sea Crest Hill to help.

Time to get to the heart of things before they agreed on a plan to storm the mansion.

Addy stood. "So let me get this straight. We're all talking about treasure."

Beer spewed, there were several gasps, and a fist slammed into the table.

Then there was dead silence.

Sarah O'Brien cleared her throat. She eyed the rest of the tavern, but only Michael, the bar's owner, was there and he was giving his attention to cleaning the beer taps. "We don't want it for ourselves. If we did, we would have come after it years ago."

"You knew." It was Addy's turn to be astonished.

"Course we knew. You think I would'a hung around with these clods if we didn't have something to bind us together?" Camden Flynn, the cloddiest of the bunch said to the laughter of the others.

Babe poked him in the back.

"Thought you knew our secret, didn't ya, Chief?" Edwin Beaudin said as he looked over Babe's shoulder. Chief Montcalm must have entered on his silent cat feet.

The chief stepped up to the table pursed his lips and shook his head, looking duly impressed that there was something about the town that he hadn't known about.

"Why didn't anyone ever say anything?" Addy asked.

"There's no mystery in a treasure found," the chief said, and they all nodded.

She couldn't argue with that.

"And we were kind of saving it in case we needed it," offered Mr. Miller, not related in any way to Mrs. Miller.

"And we need it to fix up Bailey's Cove or the hurricane might be the end of us," said Cam Flynn as he scratched the back of his hand against his whiskers.

"I don't suppose any of you have considered the treasure has an owner and he has to agree to the treasure's distribution," Addy said watching them as she spoke.

"We're not worried about Mr. Hale." Evelyn stopped and looked directly at Addy who had sat back down at the table. "We never were."

"Yeah, I get that now."

Heads nodded.

"I came to tell all of you, you can stop looking for Mr. Marsh. He was found wandering on the road south of town," the chief stated.

"Third time since the storm," Mrs. O'Brien exclaimed.

"Didn't know where he was, did he?" Mr. Beaudin asked.

"Tell Mrs. March not to worry. We'll all look out for him from now on. If he's with one of us, we'll let her know, or we'll just bring him home," Cam growled out, emotion clogging his voice.

All heads nodded.

"Thanks, folks."

"I'll walk out with you, Chief Montcalm." Addy leaped up and followed the law officer outside, sliding on her blue peacoat as she went.

The air was crisp and the wind light, a perfect sunny day.

"Has there been any movement?" She didn't have to finish the question. The chief knew she was asking if there was any movement on where the indictments would fall in the case against Hale and Blankenstock.

These kinds of things can take months, even years to figure out. The chief didn't bother to say so because they both knew.

"Our financial editor said there would have been no way to discern the info without tearing the records apart. If Mr. Hale had spent his time sifting through them to double-check Ms. Blankenstock, there would have been no new investors."

The chief didn't respond at all.

"I believe Zachary Hale is a good man and I'm trying to give my readers a chance to know that."

His features relaxed. "I will tell him what you've said."

"I'd be there at his side if he'd let me."

"He's got a lot of ground to defend, Adriana."

"Still…"

He put a hand on her shoulder. "He knows."

"Thank you, Chief Montcalm." Addy sidestepped him to get to her car.

"Good day, Addy."

She turned back to see him smiling and she nearly leaped with joy and relief. He believed in her.

If she could just see Zach. Tell him how much he mattered to her and how much others' opinions of him did not. Ask him for his forgiveness for her part.

The chief might put in a good word for her, she could only hope.

The shielding she had built up around her heart to get her through every day crumbled and she ran for her rental car.

CHAPTER TWENTY-ONE

SHE WAS BACK at her office at the paper, the early-winter sun was shining and for the first time in a long time, she thought her life might begin to come back together. She had just put the finishing touches on the article about an old town in Maine when her sister called.

"Addy, it's all back. Every cent of what I lost."

The SEC and the FBI had been working hard to recoup whatever moneys they could from every source and to spread it out among the investors who had lost so much. She never thought her sister would come out so well, but she heaved a sigh. With Savanna taken care of, all that left was to report the happy endings and enjoy getting her old office back. She spun in the chair.

A draw had been declared between Adriana Bonacorda and Jacko Wilson when the readers grew tired of financial scandal and had moved on to the newest headlines. All of Boston and the wider world lie outside her window and several story ideas at her fingertips.

The good life.

She opened a file labeled SI's, story ideas she had been collecting over the years. That folder went to wherever her office was. The folder was fat and juicy and ready for picking through.

A man appeared in the doorway of her office, a chauffeur, by the dress of him. Mr. Smally had told her they were sending a car to take her to the two-o'clock awards ceremony, but the guy was early. She looked at her watch. Way early. It wasn't even noon yet.

"Yes."

"I am to deliver this to you personally, ma'am." He handed her an envelope, small, cream colored, not sealed but with the flap tucked neatly inside.

The note was simple and formal looking. Dated with no greetings or salutations.

"I look forward to our day at the Boston Common. Zachary Hale."

So that was it? No second chance for them. He'd given up. They'd meet again in ten years. Addy looked at the uniformed man. Why would Zach send this note today of all days? This was the first day she had begun to think she might survive without him. "Is this all?"

"Yes, ma'am."

The man stood as if waiting for something. Why couldn't he just go away? She needed no reminders of what she had given up, but he didn't budge. Was Zach looking forward to ten years from now when he could bring a wife and kids to meet her with Boston's oldest park spread out around them, filled with a thousand witnesses—to see her epic failure?

She gestured him away, but she couldn't dislodge the man in the doorway.

"Am I supposed to tip you or something?"

"No, ma'am," he answered simply, but apparently had grown roots to the spot where he stood.

"For your sake and mine, please, at least stop calling me *ma'am*."

He nodded. "Yes, Ms. Bonacorda."

"Listen, what can I do for you?"

Indecision painfully flashed across his palace-guard facial expression. "I am not to leave until you figure out the note."

"What is there to figure out?" She looked at the paper. The date was several weeks in the past. That meant Zach had been planning on nothing ever developing between them, even after the scandal had passed, after she had reestablished herself as a journalist by stepping on his back. Could she blame him?

"And then you are to come with me," he offered as if that would explain everything.

"The note doesn't—" Her brain suddenly registered the year connected to the date. Not the past, but the future. Ten years in the future from the date they had parted at Sea Crest Hill.

"Shall we say, noon?" She remembered asking the question as her fingers curled around his, and she remembered wondering if that would be the last time she would touch him.

She looked at her watch again. Ten minutes until noon.

She grabbed the still stoic chauffeur's arm. "Wait here." Then she laughed. "As if you intended to move."

Giddy and suddenly filled with hope she raced to the closet and grabbed her coat. In as fast a time as the driver could get her to the Common in the heart of Boston, she was going to see Zach again, touch him, kiss him, hear him say her name.

The Boston Common would be covered by last night's blanket of snow and the Christmas tree, donated by the grateful people of Nova Scotia, would be in full regalia.

But the park was so big. Fifty acres. Where would they meet? She sure hoped this guy knew where he needed to take her.

Struggling to get an arm in her jacket, she shot past the chauffeur. "S'go, man."

He sprinted ahead to the elevator and punched the down button, and sprinted again to hold open the door to the street.

A sleek black and very expensive car stood at the curb. Zach leaned against the hood, his long legs stretched out, his feet planted, a long black cashmere overcoat open and framing his luscious body, hands in the pockets of his expensive suit.

His tie knotted up against the collar of his white shirt. Sun glinted in his sandy hair and his face held the casual lopsided grin she had seen only on Sea Crest Hill.

She stopped short of hurling herself in his arms and held out a hand. "Mr. Hale, it's so good to see you again after these ten years. I'm happy to see your hair hasn't turned completely gray."

He took her hand in his, gripped firmly and shook. "Ms. Adriana Bonacorda, how good to see you again also."

"You are looking—"

She meant to say well preserved, but his thumb stroked the palm of her hand and all she got out was a croak.

His grin widened. "Did you bring the husband and kids?"

"I'm still looking for them." She would like only one particular extraordinary man as her husband and that man had declared himself off-limits to her. Now he was here and she didn't dare let herself hope.

He reached in his pocket and pulled out a small box, a ring box.

Speechless, Addy stared at the black velvet and cringed.

"Zach, you are killing me here. Is that your intent? That I expire on the spot and be gone forever?"

He opened the box and in it was the ring from the rose covered wooden box that had fallen from the attic that day. The gold gleamed brighter and the rubies seemed much larger than she remembered.

"I can't accept that ring. I can't. It's historical and I could never wear it."

"That's why it's not that ring."

"A duplicate?"

"Nearly, but I thought you deserved better."

He got down on one knee of his expensive suit and looked up at her. "Adriana Bonacorda, I love you. Will you marry me?"

"Are you sure? Nothing has changed."

"This morning Hale and Blankenstock was officially dissolved. For her freedom, Carla confessed to the wrongdoing and has volunteered to surrender all the assets she has left, as well as all her share of her family's money. The FBI has collected the gains from those who made big money and helped to get everyone an equal share of what is left."

"You, of course, surrendered everything you made with generous interest."

"I did."

"I can't fry you for that. And you repaid every cent my sister lost with that same interest, most likely making up the difference from your own pocket."

"Guilty."

"I'm sure I don't know what to do with you."

"You can do whatever you want with me if you say yes and let me get up."

"Big-shot journalist brings financial wizard to his knees."

He lowered his other knee to the pavement.

"Yes. Yes. Yes," she cried and held out her hand. "I love you, too."

He slid the most perfect ring onto her finger, and she reached for his free hand to tug him to his feet. His strong arms pulled her to him, and when his mouth covered hers, she leaned into him, pressing close. Finally and at last, she was in the place she most wanted to be, in the arms of the man she loved.

She pulled back. "What happened? Why did she cave? Can I have the exclusive?"

"You're such a journalist. Carla says she'll talk to the press if you do the interview."

She clapped her arms around his neck, "I love you so much, and I have to get started."

He laughed. "Of course you do. That's why I brought Charles and the limo. He'll take you anywhere you need to go and Jerry will take me back to my office."

She looked from Zach to Charles who stood a respectable distance away with his hands behind his back and then she looked at Zach.

"Did I tell you I love you?"

"You did." He covered her mouth briefly with his. "I have something special planned for whenever you are finished. Charles will bring you to my place, if that's all right with you."

"It will always be all right with me." She guaranteed that promise with a kiss.

As TWILIGHT BEGAN to fall, Addy stood in the elevator of Zach's high-rise building in the heart of Boston's glitz and glory. Charles had keyed the elevator to go to the top floor. Of course, Zach lived in the penthouse.

She had prayed for coherent thoughts as she wrote the article about how the mighty still stood and how he showed mercy toward Carla

Blankenstock. Addy had sent her article to her editor along with a prayer he would still pay her for her work after he read a story she was sure was fraught with typos and oversight errors.

As the elevator slid upward she began to feel nervous. Adriana Bonacorda nervous. She had known Zach was rich, richer than she could ever imagine, but it never even occurred to her that she would have to interact with that part of his life until this moment.

She plucked at the blouse she had put on this morning and wondered if she should have gone home to take a shower before coming. Who was she fooling? She just hadn't thought about it. Zach had seen her at her worst and he still wanted to marry her. All she needed was a little water to dance around in and she'd be good to go.

He would be impeccably dressed. She hoped he had at least loosened his tie.

What if there was a butler there to frown at her for looking so, so blue collar.

The elevator stopped.

Too late for any worries.

The sight she saw when the doors opened made her grab her stomach and laugh out loud.

"I love you," she shouted from the elevator and ran to him.

Zach was dressed in his flannel shirt and jeans. Over the back of the couch he had laid two robes like the ones at the mansion on Sea Crest Hill.

She flung herself into his arms and he caught her up against him. He smelled of wood smoke and lavender and her mouth found his.

Two hours and two showers later she and Zach emerged from the bedroom to prowl the kitchen.

"Turn around." He made a circle gesture with his finger.

Without question, Addy twirled for him.

"It's a fact, Ms. Bonacorda. If you want to report it? I cannot get enough of you wearing one of those robes cinched at the waist, the gentle sway of your hips when you walk, the sleek line of your calves."

"Gentle sway, sleek lines, you say?" She obliged him by walking away.

"Luscious and lovely."

"Oh, Mr. Hale, you are a charmer."

"I know."

"And I love you."

"Yes, you do."

EPILOGUE

ADDY WROTE A set of historical novels based on the legend of Bailey's Cove. She has just sent book three to her editor and she expects a third bestseller.

To celebrate, Addy and Zach have driven up to Bailey's Cove to spend time with the fine people in the refurbished town and to celebrate the opening of the new museum.

Addy Bonacorda and Zach Hale, Mia and Daniel MacCarey with their newborn twins, Delainey and Hunter Morrison with Brianna, Heather Loch, Chief Montcalm, Monique and Lenny Gardner with their three year old, Christina and Gregory Miller, Edwin Beaudin with the rest of the Goldens (all still alive as there is not one of them that would miss this moment), Shamus and Connie Murphy (Connie looking the picture of health) stand on the museum's front steps. They proudly look down on the town they brought back to life with their hands, their money, their love and lots of help from the hardy and hearty townsfolk—and the proceeds from a pirate's booty, as well as a little infusion from their local billionaire.

The treasure of the pirate Liam Bailey has been disbursed to museums up and down the eastern seaboard and across the ocean, for a fair sale price. Before rendering the items for sale, replicas were made for display at the town's museum.

Champagne is raised, the staff from Pirate's Roost serves hors d'oeuvres followed by dinner and plans are discussed that very night for the minigolf, the theater and the new mall to be built.

Perhaps the spirits of Liam Bailey and his Colleen Rose look on, smiling at the town established by him and then two centuries later saved from oblivion by his seafaring adventures.

Zachary Hale slips a necklace with a very large emerald on a long gold chain into the pocket of his wife's jeans, making sure she knows he is doing it. She remembers his words from her first stay in Bailey's Cove, *I would always see you in emeralds if it were up to me. And then I would see you out of them,* and as soon as is socially possible she will whisk him away to the loft above the garage.

* * * * *

LARGER-PRINT BOOKS!

HARLEQUIN *Presents*

PASSION
GUARANTEED
SEDUCTION

GET 2 FREE LARGER-PRINT
NOVELS PLUS 2 FREE GIFTS!

YES! Please send me 2 FREE LARGER-PRINT Harlequin Presents® novels and my 2 FREE gifts (gifts are worth about $10). After receiving them, if I don't wish to receive any more books, I can return the shipping statement marked "cancel." If I don't cancel, I will receive 6 brand-new novels every month and be billed just $5.05 per book in the U.S. or $5.49 per book in Canada. That's a saving of at least 16% off the cover price! It's quite a bargain! Shipping and handling is just 50¢ per book in the U.S. and 75¢ per book in Canada.* I understand that accepting the 2 free books and gifts places me under no obligation to buy anything. I can always return a shipment and cancel at any time. Even if I never buy another book, the two free books and gifts are mine to keep forever.

176/376 HDN F43N

Name	(PLEASE PRINT)	
Address		Apt. #
City	State/Prov.	Zip/Postal Code

Signature (if under 18, a parent or guardian must sign)

Mail to the **Harlequin® Reader Service:**
IN U.S.A.: P.O. Box 1867, Buffalo, NY 14240-1867
IN CANADA: P.O. Box 609, Fort Erie, Ontario L2A 5X3

**Are you a subscriber to Harlequin Presents books
and want to receive the larger-print edition?
Call 1-800-873-8635 today or visit us at www.ReaderService.com.**

HPLP13R